'Gripping, beautifully written, surprising and devastating.
Thomas H. Cook has long been one of my favourite
writers'   *Harlan Coben*

'A good thriller doesn't necessarily require flying fists,
bombs and bullets; a sure and measured build-up of
tension does just as well, and few are better at the fine art
of sure and measured than Thomas H. Cook' *Guardian*

'In Cook's hands, the crime novel moves firmly into
literature'   *Peter Straub*

'Cook, writing in a wonderfully understated prose, calmly
and methodically builds everything up to climax of
multiple tragedies ... bravura suspense writing'
                                                  Crime Time

'Terrific'   *Observer*

'Thomas Cook's night visions, seen through a lens darkly,
are haunting ... *The Chatham School Affair* will cement
this superb writer's position as one of crime fiction's most
prodigious talents, a master of the unexpected ending'
                                    New York Times Book Review

'Powerful and trenchant storytelling'   *Good Book Guide*

Also by Thomas H. Cook

FICTION

Blood Innocents
The Orchids
Tabernacle
Elena
Sacrificial Ground
Flesh and Blood
Streets of Fire
Night Secrets
The City When It Rains
Evidence of Blood
Mortal Memory
Breakheart Hill
Instruments of Night
Places in the Dark
The Interrogation
Taken (based on the teleplay by Leslie Boehm)
Moon over Manhattan (with Larry King)
Peril
Into the Web
Red Leaves
The Murmur of Stones

NON-FICTION

Early Graves
Blood Echoes
Best American Crime Writing: 2002 edition
(ed. with Otto Penzler)
Best American Crime Writing: 2003 edition
(ed. with Otto Penzler)
Best American Crime Writing: 2004 edition
(ed. with Otto Penzler)

THE CHATHAM SCHOOL AFFAIR

Thomas H. Cook

AN OTTO PENZLER BOOK

Quercus

First published in Great Britain in 2008 by Quercus
This paperback edition published in 2008 by

Quercus
21 Bloomsbury Square
London
WC1A 2NS

A CIP catalogue record for this book is available
from the British Library

ISBN 978 1 84724 551 9

10 9 8 7 6 5 4 3 2 1

Typeset by Deltatype Ltd, Birkenhead, Merseyside
Printed and bound in Great Britain by Clays Ltd, St Ives plc

For Kate Miciak
Sine qua non

He sees enough who doth his darkness see
LORD HERBERT OF CHERBURY

PART I

ONE

My father had a favorite line. He'd taken it from Milton, and he loved to quote it to the boys of Chatham School. Standing before them on opening day, his hands thrust deep into his trouser pockets, he'd pause a moment, facing them sternly. 'Be careful what you do,' he'd say, 'for evil on itself doth back recoil.' In later years he could not have imagined how wrong he was, nor how profoundly I knew him to be so.

Sometimes, particularly on one of those bleak winter days so common to New England, wind tearing at the trees and shrubbery, rain battering the roofs and windows, I feel myself drift back to my father's world, my own youth, the village he loved and in which I still live. I glance outside my office window and see the main street of Chatham as it once was – a scattering of small shops, a ghostly parade of antique cars with their lights mounted on sloping fenders. In my mind, the dead return to life, assume their earthly shapes. I see Mrs Albertson delivering a basket of quahogs to Kessler's Market; Mr Lawrence lurching forward in his homemade snowmobile, skis on the front, a set of World War I tank tracks on the back, all hooked to the battered chassis of an old roadster pickup. He waves as he goes by, a gloved hand in the timeless air.

Standing once again at the threshold of my past, I feel fifteen again, with a full head of hair and not a single liver spot, heaven far away, no thought of hell. I even sense a certain goodness at the core of life.

Then, from out of nowhere, I think of her again. Not as the young woman I'd known so long ago, but as a little girl, peering out over a glittering blue sea, her father standing beside her in a white linen suit, telling her what fathers have always told their children: that the future is open to them, a field of grass, harboring no dark wood. In my mind I see her as she stood in her cottage that day, hear her voice again, her words like distant bells, sounding the faith she briefly held in life. *Take as much as you want, Henry. There is plenty.*

In those days, the Congregationalist Church stood at the eastern entrance of Chatham, immaculately white save for its tall, dark spire. There was a bus stop at the southern corner of the church, marked by a stubby white pillar, the site where Boston buses picked up and deposited passengers who, for whatever reason, had no liking for the train.

On that August afternoon in 1926, I'd been sitting on the church steps, reading some work of military history, my addiction at the time, when the bus pulled to a stop yards away. From that distance I'd watched its doors open, the metal hinges creaking in the warm late-summer air. A large woman with two children emerged first, followed by an elderly man who smoked a pipe and wore a navy blue captain's cap, the sort of 'old salt' often seen on Cape Cod in those days. Then there'd been a moment of suspension, when no one emerged from the shadowy interior of the bus, so that I'd expected it to pull away, swing left and head toward the neighboring town of Orleans, a trail of dust following behind it like an old feather boa.

4

But the bus had stayed in place, its engine rumbling softly as it idled by the road. I could not imagine why it remained so until I saw another figure rise from a seat near the back. It was a woman, and she moved forward slowly, smoothly, a dark silhouette. Near the door she paused, her arm raised slightly, her hand suspended in midair even as it reached for the metal rail that would have guided her down the stairs.

At the time I couldn't have guessed the cause for her sudden hesitation. But in the years since then, I've come to believe that it was precisely at that moment she must have realized just how fully separate our world was from the one she'd lived in with her father during the many years they'd traveled together, the things she'd seen with him, Florence in its summer splendor, the canals of Venice, Paris from the steps of Sacre-Coeur. How could anything in Chatham ever have compared with that?

Something at last urged her forward. Perhaps necessity, the fact that with her father's recent death she had no other option. Perhaps a hope that she could, in the end, make her life with us. I will never know. Whatever the reason, she drew in a deep breath, grasped the iron rail, and made her way down the stairs and into the afternoon stillness of a tiny seacoast village where no great artist had ever lived, no great event ever happened, save for those meted out by sudden storms or the torturous movement of geologic time.

It was my father who greeted her when she stepped from the bus that afternoon. He was headmaster of Chatham School, a man of medium height, but whose manner, so expansive and full of authority, made him seem larger than he was. In one of the many pictures I have of him from that time, this one printed in the Chatham School

Annual for 1926, he is seated in his office, behind a massive oak desk, his hands resting on its polished surface, his eyes staring directly into the camera. It was the usual pose of a respectable and accomplished man in those days, one that made him appear quite stern, perhaps even a bit hard, though he was nothing of the kind. Indeed, when I remember him as he was in those days, it is usually as a cheerful, ebullient man with an energetic and kindly manner, slow to anger, quick to forgive, his feelings always visible in his eyes. 'The heart is what matters, Henry,' he said to me not long before his death, a principle he'd often voiced through the years, but never for one moment truly lived by. For surely, of all the men I've ever known, he was the least enslaved by passion. Now an old man too, it is hard for me to imagine how in my youth I could have despised him so.

But I did despise him. Silently. Sullenly. Giving him no hint of my low regard, so that I must have seemed a perfectly obedient son, given to moodiness, perhaps, but otherwise quite normal, rocked by nothing darker than the usual winds of adolescence. Remembering him, as I often do, I marvel at how much he knew of Cicero and Thucydides, and how little of the boy who lived in the room upstairs.

Earlier that morning he'd found me lounging in the swing on the front porch, given me a disapproving look, and said, 'What, nothing to do, Henry?'

I shrugged.

'Well, come with me, then,' he said, then bounded down the front steps and out to our car, a bulky old Ford whose headlights stuck out like stubby horns.

I rose, followed my father down the stairs, got into the car, and sat silently as he pulled out of the driveway, my face showing a faint sourness, the only form of rebellion I was allowed.

On the road my father drove at a leisurely pace through the village, careful to slow even further at the approach of pedestrians or horses. He nodded to Mrs Cavenaugh as she came out of Warren's Sundries, and gave a short cautionary beep on the horn when he saw Davey Bryant chasing Hattie Shaw a little too aggressively across the lighthouse grounds.

In those days, Chatham was little more than a single street of shops. There was Mayflower's, a sort of general store, and Thompson's Haberdashery, along with a pharmacy run by Mr Benchley, in which the gentlemen of the town could go to a back room and enjoy a glass of illegal spirits, though never to the point of drunkenness. Mrs Jessup had a boardinghouse at the far end of Main Street, and Miss Hilliard a little school for 'dance, drama, and piano,' which practically no one ever attended, so that her main source of income came from selling cakes and pies, along with keeping house for several of the rich families that summered in spacious, sun-drenched homes on the bay. From a great height Chatham had to have looked idyllic, and yet to me it was a prison, its buildings like high, looming walls, its yards and gardens strewn around me like fields of concertina wire.

My father felt nothing of the kind, of course. No man was ever more suited to small-town life than he was. Sometimes, for no reason whatever, he would set out from our house and walk down to the center of the village, chatting with whoever crossed his path, usually about the weather or his garden, anything to keep the flow of words going, as if these inconsequential conversations were the very lubricant of life, the *numen*, as the Romans

7

called it, that divine substance which unites and sustains us.

That August afternoon my father seemed almost jaunty as he drove through the village, then up the road that led to the white facade of the Congregationalist Church. Because of that, I knew that something was up. For he always appeared most happy when he was in the midst of doing some good deed.

'Do you remember that teacher I mentioned?' he asked as we swept past Warren's Sundries. 'The one who's coming from Africa.'

I nodded dully, faintly recalling the brief mention of such a person at dinner one night.

'Well, she's arriving this afternoon. Coming in on the Boston bus. I want you to give her a nice welcome.'

We got to the bus stop a few minutes later. My father took up his place by the white pillar while I wandered over to the steps of the church, slumped down on its bottom stair, and pulled the book I'd been reading from the back pocket of my trousers.

I was reading it a half hour later, by then lost in the swirling dusts of Thermopylae, when the bus at last arrived. I remained in place, grudgingly aware that my father would have preferred that I rush down to greet the new teacher. Of course, I was determined to do nothing of the kind.

And so I don't know how he reacted when he first saw Miss Channing emerge from the bus that afternoon, for I couldn't see his face. I do know how beautiful she was, however, how immaculately white her throat looked against the wine-red collar of her dress. I have always believed that as she stepped from the gray interior of the bus, her face suddenly captured in a bright summer light, her eyes settling upon my father with the mysterious richness I was to see in them as well, that at that moment, in that silence, he surely caught his breath.

TWO

Inevitably, when I recall that first meeting, the way Miss Channing looked as she arrived in Chatham, so young and full of hope, I want to put up my hand and do what all our reading and experience tells us we can never do. I want to say 'Stop, please. Stop, Time.'

It's not that I want to freeze her there for all eternity, of course, a young woman arriving in a quaint New England town, but that I merely wish to break the pace long enough to point out the simple truth life unquestionably teaches anyone who lives into old age: since our passions do not last forever, our true task is to survive them. And one thing more, perhaps: I want to remind her how thin it is, and weaving, the tightrope we walk through life, how the smallest misstep can become a fatal plunge.

Then I think, *No, things must be as they became.* And with that thought, time rolls onward again, and I see her take my father's hand, shake it briefly, then let it go, her face turning slightly to the left so that she must have seen me as I finally roused myself from the church steps and headed toward her from across its carefully tended lawn.

'This is my son, Henry,' my father said when I reached them.

'Hi,' I said, offering my hand.

Miss Channing took it. 'Hello, Henry,' she said.

I can clearly recall how she looked at that first meeting,

her hair gathered primly beneath her hat, her skin a perfect white, her features beautiful in the way certain female portraits are beautiful, not so much sensuous as very finely wrought. But more than anything, I remember her eyes, pale blue and slightly oval, with a striking sense of alertness.

'Henry's going to be a sophomore this year,' my father added. 'He'll be one of your students.'

Before Miss Channing could respond to that, the bus driver came bustling around the back of the bus with two leather valises. He dropped them to the ground, then scurried back into the bus.

My father nodded for me to pick up Miss Channing's luggage. Which I did, then stood, a third wheel, as he immediately returned the full force of his attention to Miss Channing.

'You'll have an early dinner with us,' he told her. 'After that we'll take you to your new home.' With that, he stepped back slightly, turned, and headed for the car, Miss Channing walking along beside him, I trudging behind, the two leather valises hanging heavily from my hands.

We lived on Myrtle Street in those days, just down from Chatham School, in a white house with a small porch, like almost all the others in the village. As we drove toward it, passing through the center of town on the way, my father pointed out various stores and shops where Miss Channing would be able to buy her supplies. She seemed quite attentive to whatever my father told her, her attention drawn to this building or that one with an unmistakable appreciativeness, like someone touring a gallery or a museum, her eyes intently focused on the smallest things, the striped awning of Mayflower's, the hexagonal bandstand on the grounds of the town hall, the knot of young men who lounged in front of the bowling alley, smoking cigarettes, and in whose desultory habits and loose morals my father claimed to glimpse the grim approach of the coming age.

A hill rose steadily from the center of town, curving to the right as it ascended toward the coastal bluff. The old lighthouse stood at the far end of it, its grounds decorated with two huge whitewashed anchors.

'We once had three lighthouses here in Chatham,' my father said. 'One was moved to Eastham. The second was lost in the storm of 'twenty-three.'

Miss Channing gazed at our remaining lighthouse as we drifted by it. 'It's more striking to have only one,' she said. She turned toward the backseat, her eyes falling upon me. 'Don't you think so, Henry?'

I had no answer for her, surprised as I was that she'd bothered to ask, but my father appeared quite taken by her observation.

'Yes, I think that's true,' he said. 'A second makes the first less impressive.'

Miss Channing's eyes lingered on me a moment, a quiet smile offered silently before she turned away.

Our house was situated at the end of Myrtle Street, and on the way to it we passed Chatham School. It was a large brick building with cement stairs and double front doors. The first floor was made up of classrooms, the second taken up by the dormitory, dining hall, and common room.

'That's where you'll be teaching,' my father told her, slowing down a bit as we drove by. 'We've made a special room for you. In the courtyard.'

Miss Channing glanced over to the school, and from her reflection in the glass, I could see that her eyes were very still, like someone staring into a crystal ball, searching for her future there.

We pulled up in front of our house a few seconds later. My father opened the door for Miss Channing and escorted her up the front stairs to the porch, where my mother waited to be introduced.

'Welcome to Chatham,' my mother said, offering her hand.

She was only a few years younger than my father, but considerably less agile, and certainly less spirited, her face rather plain and round, but with small, nervous eyes. To the people of Chatham, she'd been known simply as the 'music teacher' and more or less given up for a spinster. Then my father had arrived, thirty-one years old but still a bachelor, eager to establish a household in which he could entertain the teachers he'd already hired for his new school, as well as potential benefactors. My mother had met whatever his criteria had been for a wife, and after a courtship of only six weeks, he'd asked her to marry him. My mother had accepted without hesitation, my father's proposal catching her so completely by surprise, as she loved to tell the women in her sewing circle, that at first she had taken it for a joke.

But on that afternoon nearly twenty years later, my mother no longer appeared capable of taking anything lightly. She'd grown wide in the hips by then, her figure large and matronly, her pace so slow and ponderous that I often grew impatient with it and bolted ahead of her to wherever we were going. Later in life she sometimes lost her breath at the top of the porch stairs, coming to a full stop in order to regain it, one hand grasping a wooden supporting post, the other fluttering at her chest, her head arched back as she sucked in a long, difficult breath. In old age her hair grew white and her eyes dimmed, and she often sat alone in the front room, or lay curled on her bed, no longer able to read and barely able to attend to the radio. Even so, something fiery remained in her to the very end, fueled by a rage engendered by the Chatham School Affair, one that smoldered forever after that.

She died many years after the affair had run its frightful course, and by then much had changed in all our lives: the large house on Myrtle Street no more than a memory, my father living on a modest pension, Chatham School long closed, its doors locked, its windows boarded, the playing fields gone to weed, all its former reputation by then reduced to a dark and woeful legacy.

My mother had prepared a chowder for us that afternoon, buttery and thick with clams and potatoes, the sort typical of Cape Cod. We ate at the dining table, Sarah Doyle, the teenage servant girl my father had brought from Boston only two years before, ladling the fragrant chowder into large china bowls.

Sitting at the table, Miss Channing asked few questions as my father went through his usual remarks about Chatham School, what its philosophy was, how it had come to be, a lecture my mother had heard countless times, but which clearly engaged Miss Channing's interest.

'Why only boys?' she asked at one point.

'Because girls would change the atmosphere of the school,' my father answered.

'In what way?'

'The boys would feel their presence,' my father told her. 'It would cause them to show off, to act foolishly.'

Miss Channing thought a moment. 'But is that the fault of the girls or the boys, Mr Griswald?'

'It's the fault of the mixture, Miss Channing,' my father told her, obviously surprised by the boldness he detected in her question. 'It makes the atmosphere more ... volatile.'

My father fully expected to have brought the subject to a close with that. An expectation I shared so completely that when Miss Channing suddenly spoke again, offering what amounted to a challenge, I felt something like a call to arms.

'And without the girls, what's the atmosphere?' she asked.

'Studious and serious,' my father answered. 'Disciplined.'

'And that's the atmosphere you want at Chatham School?'

'Yes,' my father replied firmly. 'It is.'

Miss Channing said nothing more on the subject, but sitting across from her, I sensed that there was more she might have said, thoughts that were in her head, bristling there, or firing continually, like small explosions.

At the end of the meal my father led Miss Channing and my mother into the little parlor at the front of the house for a cup of tea. I lingered at the table, watching Sarah clear away the dishes after she'd served them. Though my father had closed the French doors that separated the parlor from the dining room, it was still possible for me to see Miss Channing as she sat listening quietly to my father.

'So, what do you think of the new teacher?' I asked Sarah as she leaned over my shoulder and plucked a bowl from the table.

Sarah didn't answer, so I glanced up at her. She was not looking at me, but toward the parlor, where Miss Channing sat by the window, her hands held primly in her lap, the Joan Crawford hat sitting firmly on her head.

'Such a fine lady,' Sarah said in an almost reverential tone. 'The kind folks read about in books.'

I looked back toward Miss Channing. She was taking a sip from her cup as my father went on, her blue eyes peering just over the rim, sharp and evaluating, as if her mind ceaselessly sifted the material that passed through it, allowing this, dismissing that, her sense of judgment oddly final, a court, as it would prove to be, from which there could be no appeal.

I was in my room an hour later, perusing the latest issue of *Grady's Illustrated Magazine for Boys*, when my father summoned me downstairs.

'It's time to take Miss Channing home,' he told me.

I followed him out the door, then down the front stairs to where Miss Channing was already waiting in the car.

'It's only a short drive,' my father said to her as he pulled himself in behind the wheel. 'Perhaps I can get you there ahead of the rain.'

But he could not, for as we drove toward the cottage, the overhanging clouds suddenly disgorged their burden, thunderously and without warning, as if abruptly being called to account.

Once outside the village center, my father turned right, onto the coastal road, past the great summer houses that rose along the shore, then on toward the marsh, with its shanties and fishermen's houses, their unkempt yards scattered with stacks of lobster traps and tangled piles of gray netting.

Given the torrent, the drive was slow, the old Ford sputtering along, battered from all directions by sudden whipping gusts, the windshield wipers squeaking rhythmically as they swept ineffectually across the glass.

My father kept his eyes on the road, of course, but I noticed that Miss Channing's attention had turned toward the landscape of Cape Cod, its short, rounded hills sparsely clothed in tangles of brush and scrub oak, wind ripping through the sea grass that sprouted from the dunes.

'The Cape's pretty, don't you think, Miss Channing?' my father said cheerfully.

Her reply must have startled him.

'It looks tormented,' she said, staring out the window on the passenger side, her voice suddenly quite somber, as if it came from some darker part of her mind.

My father glanced toward her. 'Tormented? What do you mean?'

'It reminds me of the islands of the Florida Keys,' she answered, her eyes still concentrated on the landscape. 'The name the Spanish gave them.'

'What name was that?'

'Los Martires,' Miss Channing answered. 'Because they looked so tormented by the wind and the sea.'

'Forgive my ignorance,' my father said. 'But what does "Los Martires" mean?'

Miss Channing continued to gaze out the window. 'It means "the martyrs",' she said, her eyes narrowing somewhat, as if she were no longer looking at the dunes and the sea grass beyond her window, but at the racked and bleeding body of some ancient tortured saint.

My father drew his attention back to the road. 'Well, I've never thought of the Cape as looking like that,' he said. Then, to my surprise, I saw his eyes lift toward the rearview mirror, fix on mine. 'Have you ever thought of the Cape like that, Henry?'

I glanced out the window at my right, toward a

landscape that no longer seemed featureless and inert, but beaten and bedeviled, lashed by gusts of wind and surging waters. 'Not until just now,' I said.

At about a mile beyond town we swung onto a stretch of road bordered on all sides by dense forest and covered with what had once been a layer of oyster shells, but which past generations of hooves and feet and wagon wheels had since ground into little more than a fine powder.

The woods had encroached so far into the road that I could hear the surrounding vegetation slap and scrape against the side of the car as we bumped along the road.

'It gets pretty deserted out this way,' my father said. He added nothing else as we continued in silence until the road forked, my father taking the one to the right, moving down it for perhaps a quarter mile, until it widened suddenly, then came to an abrupt dead end before a small white cottage.

'There it is,' my father said. 'Milford Cottage.'

It was tiny compared to our house on Myrtle Street, so dwarfed by the surrounding forest that it appeared to crouch fearfully within a fist of green, a dark stretch of water sweeping out behind it, still and lightless, its opaque depths unplumbed, like a great hole in the heart of things.

'That's Black Pond,' my father said.

Miss Channing leaned forward slightly, peering at the cottage very intently through the downpour, like a painter considering a composition, calculating the light, deciding where to put the easel. It was an expression I would see many times during the coming year, intense and curious, a face that seemed to draw everything into it by its own strange gravity.

'It's a simple place,' my father told her. 'But quite nice. I hope you'll at least find it cozy.'

'I'm sure I will,' she said. 'Who lived here?'

'It was never actually lived in,' my father answered. 'It was built as a honeymoon cottage by Mr Milford for his bride.'

'But they never lived there?'

My father appeared reluctant to answer her but obligated to do so. 'They were both killed on the way to it,' he said. 'An automobile accident as they were coming back from Boston.'

Miss Channing's face suddenly grew strangely animated, as if she were imagining an alternative story in her mind, the arrival of a young couple who never arrived, the joys of a night they never spent together, a morning after that was never theirs.

'It's not luxurious, of course,' my father added quickly, determined, as he always was, to avoid disagreeable things, 'but it's certainly adequate.' His eyes rested upon Miss Channing for a moment before he drew them away abruptly, and almost guiltily, so that for a brief instant he looked rather like a man who'd been caught reading a forbidden book. 'Well, let's go inside,' he said.

With that, my father opened the door and stepped out into the rain. 'Quickly now, Henry.' He motioned for me to get Miss Channing's valises and follow him into the cottage.

He was already at the front door, struggling with the key, his hair wet and stringy by the time I reached them. Miss Channing stood just behind him, waiting for him to open the door. As he worked the key, twisting it right and left, he appeared somewhat embarrassed that it wouldn't turn, as if some element of his authority had been called into question. 'Everything rusts in this sea air,' I heard him murmur. He jerked at the key again. It gave, and the cottage door swung open.

'There's no electricity out this way,' my father explained as he stepped into the darkened cottage. 'But the fireplace has been readied for winter, and there are quite a few kerosene lamps, so you'll have plenty of light.' He walked to the window, parted the curtains, and looked out into the darkening air. 'Just as I explained in my letter.' He released the curtain and turned back to her. 'I take it that you're accustomed to things being a little ... primitive.'

'Yes, I am,' Miss Channing replied.

'Well, before we go, you should have a look around. I hope we didn't forget anything.'

He walked over to one of the lamps and lit it. A yellow glow spread through the room, illuminating the newly scrubbed walls, the recently hung lace curtains, the plain wooden floor that had been so carefully swept, a stone fireplace cleared of ash.

'The kitchen's been stocked already,' he told her. 'So you've got plenty of lard, flour, sugar. All of the essentials.' He nodded toward the bedroom. 'And the linens are in the wardrobe there.'

Miss Channing glanced toward the bedroom, her eyes settling upon the iron bedstead, the sheets stretched neatly over the narrow mattress, two quilts folded at the foot of the bed, a single pillow at its head.

'I know that things take getting used to, Miss Channing,' my father said, 'but I'm sure that in time you'll be happy here.'

I knew well what my father meant by the word 'happy', the contentment it signified for him, a life of predictable events and limited range, pinched and uninspired, a pale offering to those deeper and more insistent longings that I know must have called to him from time to time.

But as to what Miss Channing considered happiness, that I could not have said. I knew only that a strange energy surrounded her, a vibrancy and engagement that was almost physical, and that whatever happiness she might later find in life would have to answer to it.

'I hope you'll like Chatham as well,' my father said after a moment. 'It's quite a lovely little town.'

'I'm sure I will,' Miss Channing told him, though even as she said it, she might well have been comparing it to Rome or Vienna, the great cities she'd visited, the boulevards and spacious squares she'd strolled along, a wider world she'd long known but that I had only dreamed of.

'Well, we should be going now,' my father said. He nodded toward the two leather valises in my hands. 'Put those down, Henry.'

I did as I was told, and joined my father at the door.

'Well, good night, then, Miss Channing,' he said as he opened it.

'Good night, Mr Griswald,' she said. 'And thank you for everything.'

Seconds later we were in the car again, backing onto Plymouth Road. Through the cords of rain that ran down the windshield as we pulled away, I could see Miss Channing standing at the threshold of the cottage, her face so quiet and luminous as she waved good-bye that I have often chosen to recall her as she was that first night rather than as she appeared at our last meeting, her hair clipped and matted, her skin lusterless, the air around her thick with a dank and deathly smell.

THREE

My father's portrait hangs on the large wood-paneled wall opposite my desk and over the now-unused marble hearth, shelves of law books arrayed on either side. He is dressed in a black three-piece suit, the vest neatly buttoned, a formal style of dress common to portraiture at that time. But there is something unusual about the composition nonetheless. For although my father is dressed appropriately enough, he is not posed behind his desk or standing before a wall of books, but at a large window with dark red curtains held in place by gold sashes. Outside the window, it is clearly summer, but nothing in the landscape beyond the glass in the least resembles either Chatham or Cape Cod.

Instead, my father gazes out into a strange, limitless plain, covered in elephant grass and dotted with fire trees, a vast expanse that sweeps out in all directions until it finally dissolves into the watery reaches of a distant blue lake, his attention focused on something in the exotic distance, perhaps the farther shore of that same lake, an effect that gives his face a look of melancholy longing.

It is the tragic fate of goodness to lack the vast attraction of romance. Because of that, I have never been able to see my father as a man capable of the slightest allure. And yet, for all that, he was a man in love, I think. Though with a school, rather than a woman. Chatham School was his great passion, and the years during which he served as its founder and headmaster, a guiding spirit to its boys, a counselor to its teachers, he'd felt more deeply than he ever would again that his life was truly whole.

I have looked at this portrait countless times, studying it as a way of studying my father, concentrating upon what lies mysteriously within it. Inevitably, I turn from it in a mood of vague frustration and uneasiness, my eyes drawn to the artist's signature, her name written out in tiny broken letters: *Elizabeth Rockbridge Channing*.

The portrait was painted during the last days of that school year, my father standing at the window of his office, peering out, while Miss Channing remained stationed at her easel a few yards away, her body draped in a gray, paint-dabbled smock, her hair falling to her shoulders in a great unruly mass. By that April, she no longer looked as she had upon her arrival the previous August. The blush of youth was gone, a haggardness in its place, and glimpsing her alone in her classroom during those last days, or as she made her solitary way down the coastal road, I could see nothing left of the young woman who'd stood in the doorway of Milford Cottage only a few months before, waving good-bye as my father backed our car onto Plymouth Road.

I never knew precisely what Miss Channing did after my father and I drove away that evening, leaving her alone in the cottage. I have always imagined her opening the two valises and unpacking her things, putting her new hat on the narrow shelf at the top of the wardrobe, hanging her dresses on the wooden bar that ran nearly its entire length, tucking her undergarments in the drawers that rested at its base.

From the look of the cottage when I saw it again the next day, I know that she had found a nail already in place and hung a portrait of her father, one taken years before in the courtyard of the Uffizi, the Florentine sun pouring over him, dressed stylishly in white trousers, a navy blue jacket, and a straw bowler, his fingers around the silver head of a polished wooden cane.

I also know that the randomly placed kerosene lamps must have cast heavy shadows throughout her new home, because I could tell from the positions I later saw them in that at some point during her first night in the cottage she arranged them in different places throughout the rooms, moving them here and there until, at last, a steady, even glow pervaded its shadowy interior, its darkened corners now brushed with light.

But more than anything, and with a certainty I cannot claim for other things, I know that toward midnight, when the rain finally stopped, she strolled out to the very edge of the pond, glanced over the water, and noticed a faint movement on its otherwise unmoving surface. It was then that a bank of clouds parted, a shaft of moonlight falling upon the water so that she could see the white prow of a rowboat as it skirted briefly along the far rim of light, then disappeared into the covering darkness. There was a figure in the boat, almost completely draped in a black poncho, as she later described it, so that she could make out only one small square of flesh, a hand, large and masculine, gripping a single moving oar.

I know all this absolutely, because she said as much on a sweltering summer day nearly a year later, the crowd shifting frantically to get a better view of her, craning their necks and lifting their heads, muttering grimly as they did so, talking of death and suicide and murder, their eyes following with a macabre fascination as she moved across the room and took her seat upon the witness stand.

*

In later life, after I'd returned to Chatham and begun my legal practice, I had only to glance out my office window to see the name of the man who'd cross-examined Miss Channing on that August afternoon in 1927. For in those days, Mr Parsons' office had been located just across the street from where I now have mine, and which his son, Albert Parsons, Jr., still occupies, a lawyer who specializes in personal injury litigation and contract disputes, rather than the prosecution of criminal cases for which his father was renowned throughout the state.

The younger Parsons' shingle swings above the same little rectangle of grass where his father's once swung, and which I must have seen quite clearly on the very day my father picked up Miss Channing at the bus stop, our old Ford sweeping past it as we drove to our house on Myrtle Street, my father at the wheel, Miss Channing in the passenger seat, I crowded in the backseat with her luggage, so young and inexperienced, so lost to the iron laws of life that even had they been presented to me, I would have denied their right to hold me down. Certainly, I could not have known how often I would glance at Mr Parsons' shingle in the coming years, hear his voice thunder out of the past: *It was you, Miss Channing, you and you alone who brought about this death.*

In those days Albert Parsons held the office of commonwealth attorney. A short, stocky man with wire-rimmed glasses, I often saw him making his way along the wooden sidewalk to his office, puffing his briar pipe and doffing his gray homburg to passersby. He'd appeared perfectly self-assured back then, confident in his own abilities, a man who expected to live out his life in a world whose rules were clear to him, a paradise, as he must have considered

Chatham, poised on the rim of heaven.

I remember seeing Mr Parsons in old age, when he would sit on the wooden bench in front of the town hall, tossing broken pieces of soda cracker to the pigeons gathered at his feet, his eyes watching them with a curious lack of focus. But before that, in the first years of his retirement, he'd built a workroom in his backyard, furnished it with metal bookshelves, a wooden desk, a brass reading lamp, and an old black typewriter. It was there that he'd written his account of the Chatham School Affair, utterly convinced that he had unearthed the darkest of its secrets.

Down through the years I've often thought of him, the pride he took in having discovered the cause of so much death, then the way he later strode the streets of Chatham, boldly, proudly, as if he were now the exclusive guardian of its health, Miss Channing no more than a dark malignancy he'd successfully cut out.

It was a Saturday, clear and sunny, the last one before school was scheduled to begin, when I next saw Miss Channing.

My father had already left for Osterville, as my mother told me that morning, but he'd left instructions for me to look in on Milford Cottage, see if Miss Channing needed anything, then run whatever errands she required.

Milford Cottage was almost two miles from the center of Chatham, so it took me quite some time to walk there. I arrived at around ten, knocked lightly at the door, and waited for Miss Channing to open it. When there was no answer, I knocked again, this time more loudly. There was still no answer, so I rapped against the door a third time.

That's when I saw her. Not as I'd expected, a figure inside the cottage, or poised beside its open door, but strolling toward me from the edge of the woods, no longer dressed formally as she'd been before, but in a pale blue summer dress, billowy and loose-fitting, her black hair falling in a wild tangle to her shoulders.

She didn't see me at first, and so continued to walk in the woods, edging around trees and shrubs, her eyes trained on the ground, as if following the trail of something or someone who'd approached the cottage from the surrounding forest, lingered a moment, then retreated back into its concealing depths. At the very edge of the forest she stopped, plucked a leaf from a shrub, lifted it to the sun, and turned it slowly in a narrow shaft of light, staring at it with a kind of childlike awe.

When she finally glanced away from the leaf and saw me, I could tell she was surprised to find me at her door.

'Good morning, Miss Channing,' I called.

She smiled and began to walk toward me, the hem of her skirt trailing lightly over the still-moist ground.

'I didn't mean to scare you,' I said.

She appeared amused by such a notion. 'Scare me? You didn't scare me, Henry. Why would you think that?'

I shrugged, finding her gaze so penetrating that I began to sputter. 'Anyway, my father sent me to make sure that everything is all right. Particularly with the cottage. He wanted to know if anything else needed fixing. The roof, I mean. How it held up. Against the rain, that is. Leaks.'

'No, everything's fine,' Miss Channing said, watching me intently, as if memorizing my features, carefully noting their smallest dips and curves, the set of my jaw, the shape of my eyes.

It gave me an uncomfortable feeling of being exposed, my skin peeled away layer by layer, revealing what lay beneath, the bony tower, the circuitry of arteries and veins, the resentment I so carefully suppressed. I felt my hand toy with the button at my throat.

'Well, is there anything else you need?' I asked, still mindful of my father's instructions, but eager now to get away. 'I mean, between now and Monday, when school starts?'

'No, I don't think so.'

'All right, then,' I said. 'I guess I'll see you at school on Monday.'

With that, I nodded good-bye and started back toward the road, ambling slowly, not wanting to give an impression of flight.

I was halfway down the path that led from her door to the road when I heard her call to me.

'Are you walking back to the village, Henry?'

I stopped and turned toward her. 'Yes,' I said.

'Would you mind if I came along with you? I haven't really seen it yet.'

I didn't relish the idea of being seen with a teacher outside a classroom setting. 'It's a long way into town, Miss Channing,' I said, hoping to dissuade her.

She was undeterred. 'I'm used to long walks.'

Clearly, there was no way out. 'All right,' I said with an unenthusiastic shrug.

She came forward, quickening her pace slightly until she reached my side.

Sometime later, after I'd read her father's book and realized all the exotic places he'd taken her during the years they'd traveled together, it would strike me as very strange that she'd wanted to go into the village at all that morning. Certainly, given the breadth of her experience, Chatham could only have seemed quaint. And yet her curiosity seemed real, her need to explore our small streets and shops not in the least diminished by the fact that she'd strolled the narrow alleyways of Naples and the plazas of Madrid, her father at her side relating gruesome stories of Torquemada's Inquisition and the visions of Juana the Mad in that same tone of ominousness and impending death that later fathers would use as they led their children along the banks of Black Pond, grimly spinning out a tale whose dreadful course they thought had ended there.

FOUR

I have always wondered if, during that first walk down Plymouth Road with Miss Channing, I should have noticed some hint of that interior darkness Mr Parsons later claimed to have unearthed in her. Often, I've tried to see what he saw in his first interrogation of her, the 'eeriness' he described in his memoir, the sense that she had 'delved in black arts'.

She carefully kept pace with me that morning, a breeze playing lightly in her hair, her conversation generally related to the plant life we saw around us. She asked the names of the trees and flowers that bordered the road, often very common ones like beach plum or Queen Anne's lace.

'I guess you had different plants in Africa,' I said.

'Yes, very different,' she said. 'Of course, it wasn't at all the sort of place people think of when they think of Africa. It wasn't a jungle, or anything like that. It was a plain, mostly grasslands. With a river running through it, and animals everywhere.' She smiled. 'It was like living in the middle of an enormous zoo.'

'Did you like living there?'

'I suppose,' she answered. 'But I really didn't live there long. Only a few months after my father died. With my uncle and his family.' She stopped and peered out into the surrounding forest. 'It must have looked like this when the first explorers came.'

I could hardly have cared less about anything so distant. 'Why did you leave Africa?' I asked.

She drew her attention back to me. 'I needed a job. My uncle went to school with your father. He wrote to him, hoping he might know of a position. Your father offered me one at Chatham School.'

'What do you teach?'

'Art.'

'We've never had an art teacher,' I told her. 'You'll be the first one.'

She started to speak, then glanced toward the ground at the white dust that had begun to settle on her feet and shoes.

'It comes from the oyster shells,' I told her, merely as a point of information. 'That white dust, I mean.'

She turned toward me sharply. 'Oyster shells?'

'Yes. That's what they used to put on the roads around here.'

She nodded silently, then walked on, suddenly preoccupied, my first hint of the strange life she'd lived before coming to Chatham, how deeply it had formed her. 'That's what they killed Hypatia with,' she said.

She saw the question in my eyes, and immediately answered it. 'She was the last of the pagan astronomers. A Christian mob murdered her.' Her eyes drifted toward the road. 'They scraped her to death with oyster shells.'

I could tell by the look on her face that she was seeing the slaughter of Hypatia at the instant she described it, the mocking crowd in its frenzy, Hypatia sinking to the ground, bits of her flesh scooped from her body and tossed into the air.

'There was nothing left of her when it was over,' she said. 'No face. No body. Torn to bits.'

It was then I should have glimpsed it, I suppose, the fact that she had lived in many worlds, that they now lived in her, strange and kaleidoscopic, her mind a play of scenes. Some quite beautiful – Mont Saint Michel like a great ship run aground in dense fog. Others hung in death and betrayal – the harbor in which the last weary remnants of the Children's Crusade had trudged onto waiting ships, then disappeared into the desert wastes of Arab slavery.

But at the time I could only react to what Miss Channing had just told me. And so I grimaced, pretending a delicacy I didn't actually feel, knowing all the while that some part of her story had intrigued me.

'How do you know about Hypatia?' I asked.

'My father told me about her,' Miss Channing answered.

She said nothing more about her father, but merely began to move forward again, so that we walked on in silence for a time, the sound of our feet padding softly over the powdered shells as the wind rustled through the forest that bore in upon us from both sides.

When we reached the outskirts of Chatham, Miss Channing stopped for a moment and peered down the gently curving road that led from the center of the village to the lighthouse on the bluff. 'It looks very ... American,' she said.

I'd never heard anyone say anything quite so odd, and I suppose that it was at that moment I knew that something truly different had entered my life.

Of course, I kept that early intimation to myself, and so merely watched silently as she stood at the threshold of our village. From there she would have been able to see all the way down Main Street, from the Congregationalist

Church, where the bus had let her off the day of her arrival, to the courthouse, where she would later come to trial, hear the shouts of the crowd outside: *Murderess. Murderess.* If she'd looked closely enough, concentrating on the small details, she might even have seen the wooden bench where, years later, Mr Parsons would sit alone in the afternoon, thinking of his memoir, convinced that he had plumbed the black depths of her heart.

I left Miss Channing on the outskirts of town, then walked up the hill that ran along the edge of the coastal bluff. At the top, I turned onto Myrtle Street, passing Chatham School as I made my way home.

By then some of the boys had begun to arrive. I could see them lugging their trunks and traveling cases down the long concrete walkway that led to the front of the building. From there I knew they would drag them up the stairs to the dormitory, then empty their contents into the old footlockers that rested at the end of each bed.

Many of the boys have blurred with time, but I can remember Ben Calder, who would later run a large manu-facturing enterprise, and Ted Spencer, destined for the New York Stock Exchange, and Larry Bishop, who would go on to West Point and the leading of his men toward the shores of Okinawa.

In general, they were from good families, and most of them were good boys who'd merely exhibited a bit of rude behavior their parents sought to correct by placing them at Chatham School. They were reasonably bright, at least adequately studious, and for the most part they later followed the route that had been prepared for them all along, taking up acceptable professions or running either their own businesses or those first established by their fathers or grandfathers. They did not seek a grandly romantic life, nor anticipate one. They had no particular talents, except, perhaps, for that peculiar one that enables us to persevere – often for a lifetime – in things that do not particularly interest us and for which we feel little genuine passion. In later life, after leaving Chatham School, they would do what had always been expected of them, marry, support themselves, have children of their own. I thought them dull and uninspired, while my father saw them as inestimably dutiful and fine.

I was sitting in the swing on our front porch when my father returned from Osterville at around five that afternoon. Coming up the stairs, he spotted me slouched languidly before him, my legs flung over the wooden arm of the swing, a posture he clearly didn't care for.

'So there wasn't much to do at Milford Cottage, I take it?' he asked doubtfully.

'No, there wasn't,' I told him.

'The roof didn't leak?'

'No.'

'You asked Miss Channing that directly?'

'Yes, sir. I told her you were concerned about it. She said it was fine.'

He nodded, still looking at me in that questioning way of his. 'Well, did you do anything at all for Miss Channing?'

'I walked her into town. That's all she wanted me to do.'

He thought a moment, then said, 'Well, get in the car, Henry. I want to make sure she's got everything she needs.'

Had I not gone with my father to Milford Cottage that afternoon, I might never have seen what Miss Channing later captured in her portrait of him, the look on his face as he peered through the red curtains, his eyes fixed on the exotic blue lake that so clearly beckoned to him with an unmistakable sensuousness, but toward which he would not go.

The cottage looked deserted when my father brought the car to a halt in front of it. The front door was securely closed, no lamp yet lighted, despite the fact that it was late afternoon by then, the sun already setting.

'Maybe she's still in the village,' I said as my father and I lingered in the car.

'Could be,' my father said. He stared at the cottage a moment longer, perhaps trying to decide whether to knock at the door or simply return to Chatham, content that he had at least done his duty in dropping by.

Then the door of the cottage opened, and Miss Channing walked out onto the cool grass of the front lawn. She was barefoot, and as she came toward us, I noticed that my father's eyes dropped toward her feet, his lips parting. Then, just as suddenly, he returned to himself, opened the door of the car, and stepped out.

'I have only a moment,' he said a little stiffly and hurriedly, like a man who had more important things to do.

Miss Channing continued to move toward him, her feet padding softly across the grass.

'But I wanted to make sure that everything was in order,' my father added in the same vaguely harried tone. I remained inside the car, but despite its dusty windshield, I could see that she had washed her hair so that it now hung wet and glistening in the darkening air, giving her that appearance of female dishabille that has forever after seemed so beautiful to me.

'I didn't mean to disturb you,' my father continued.

She came to a halt perhaps no more than three feet from where he stood. 'Thank you for sending Henry to me this morning,' she said. 'There was really nothing more for him to do.'

'Yes, he told me that.' My father paused for a moment, lifting his eyes upward slightly as he reached into the pocket of his jacket. 'I wanted to bring you this,' he said, drawing out a large envelope. 'It's the schedule for the school. It tells you when your classes are held, when you take lunch, that sort of thing. You should bring it with you Monday morning. I would have mailed it to you, of course,' my father added quickly as she took the envelope from him, 'as I generally do with the other teachers. But then, you were in Africa, and so ... well ...'

A silence fell over him and I expected him to break it with a quick good-bye, then get back into the car. Instead, he uttered a question that seemed very odd to me. 'Do you ever plan to have a family of your own, Miss Channing?'

I could tell that she'd never been asked such a question, so ordinary and domestic, nor once considered the way of life it suggested. 'I don't know,' she answered quietly.

'It has its compensations,' my father said, though more to himself, it seemed, than to her. 'Family life.'

She stared at him, puzzled, as I was, by his remark.

He looked suddenly embarrassed by what he'd said, like a man who'd inadvertently revealed some small, sad aspect of himself. Then he spoke hurriedly again, resuming his schoolmaster pose. 'Well, Henry and I had best be getting home. Good night, Miss Channing.'

'Good night,' she answered, the same quizzical look in her eyes as she watched my father stride back to his car, get in, and pull away.

We arrived back home a few minutes later. My mother

had prepared one of her pot roasts and throughout the meal my father appeared no different than usual, eating with the same careful attention to manners, dabbing the white cloth napkin at the corners of his mouth after almost every bite.

But when it was over, rather than retiring to the parlor as was his custom, he walked down Myrtle Street to the school, saying only that he had 'a few last minute details' he wanted to look over before classes started the following Monday morning.

My mother didn't question him. Nor did I. But toward sunset, while I was sitting on the front steps of our house, I glanced up and saw my father standing in the school's bell tower, alone, facing out over the village. It was only minutes before nightfall, and a great stillness had settled over everything. I knew that from his place in the bell tower my father could stare out over all the roofs of Chatham and watch the low, unhurried beam of the lighthouse as it swept smoothly across the darkening sea, then over the village and finally beyond it, to the ebony waters of Black Pond.

I have always believed that at that moment he was thinking of Miss Channing, of her oval eyes and wet, glistening hair, seeing her again as he had earlier that afternoon, her bare feet nestled in a cool bed of dark green grass, his eyes closing for a moment as he reveled in that vision, then opening again, focused now upon the village, the school he'd labored all his life to build, the house on Myrtle Street, its small lights, his mind accepting without bitterness or rancor the path that he had taken, along with all the obligations it required, yet recognizing, too, as I believe he must have, that there was a certain shuddering ecstasy he would never know.

FIVE

I've kept only a single photograph to remind me of what I was, what I did, all that followed after that. It is a grainy photograph, artlessly taken from the roof of one of the buildings across from the courthouse, its vista cross-hatched with wooden poles and power lines, but clear enough to show the swarm of men and women who'd gathered around the building that day, their numbers pouring down its wide cement steps. And yet, it wasn't the crowd of people that had caught my attention when I'd first seen it, but a single, crudely written sign thrust up from among them, its message scrawled in huge black letters: *Hang her*.

It is a phrase that has returned to me often over the years, and which can still prompt my deepest speculations. Especially given the fact that on her arrival at Chatham School, no one would have been able to suggest that Miss Channing might ever stir up such violent emotions, or even that her time among us would be any different from that of the many other teachers who'd come and gone over the years.

On that first day, as I stood with the other boys, all of us gathered in front of the school to hear my father's customary opening remarks, I saw her turn onto Myrtle Street, her arms at her sides, no books or papers in them, no overstuffed briefcase dangling from her bare hand.

In all other ways, however, she'd done her best to blend in, wearing a plain white dress with a pleated skirt, and a pair of square-heeled black shoes with large silver buttons. She'd changed her hair as well, so that it was now wound in a tight bun at the back of her neck and secured with an ornate silver clasp. I could almost imagine her standing before the mirror in her bedroom a moment before leaving the cottage, looking herself over, her mind pronouncing an identity that – given the exalted vision of life her father had presented to her – she may well have found rather uninspired: *School marm* ...

'Good morning, Miss Channing,' I said as she passed by.

She glanced toward me, smiled, then continued on across the lawn, over to where the other teachers were assembled. I saw a few of them turn and greet her, Mr Corbett, the math teacher, even going so far as to remove his old felt hat. Later, some of them would tell their fellow villagers that she'd never really fit in, that from the very beginning she'd set herself apart, telling the boys grim and savage tales from her travels with her father, creating dark and bloody landscapes in their young minds. Some went even further, claiming powers of clairvoyance, as if they'd known all along that Miss Channing was destined to be the prime mover in what Professor Peyton would later call with typical hyperbole 'a grim Shakespearean orgy of violence and death'. 'I saw trouble the minute I laid eyes on her,' I heard my history teacher Mrs Cooper say one afternoon in Warren's Sundries, though I'm sure she'd seen nothing of the kind.

Of course, the one thing that did unquestionably separate Miss Channing from the other teachers at Chatham School was her youth and beauty, and from the way my fellow students watched her as she approached that morning, it was clear that their interest in her went far deeper than the usual curiosity inspired by a new teacher.

'Who's that?' I heard Jamie Phelps ask Winston Bates, poking him with his elbow.

I took the opportunity to demonstrate the insider's knowledge I possessed as the headmaster's son. 'That's the new teacher,' I told them authoritatively. 'She came all the way from Africa.'

'That's where she got that bracelet, I guess,' Jamie said, pointing to the string of brightly colored wooden beads that circled Miss Channing's wrist, the very one Mr Parsons would later find at the edge of Black Pond, broken by then, the beads scattered across the muddy ground.

As usual on the first day of classes, my father stood at the entrance of the school, the teachers and administrative staff to his left, the boys to his right, all of them dressed in what amounted to the uniform of Chatham School, white shirts, black trousers, gray ties, and black suspenders. Dark gray jackets would be added later in the fall.

'All right, let me have your attention, please,' my father began. 'I want to welcome all of you back to Chatham School. Most of us are very familiar with the routine, as well as each other, but we have a new teacher this year, and I want to introduce her to you.'

He motioned for Miss Channing to join him on the stairs, which she did, moving gracefully beside him, glancing first at her fellow teachers, then at the boys.

'This is Miss Channing,' my father said. 'She has come all the way from Africa to join us here at Chatham School, and she'll be teaching art.'

There was polite applause, then Miss Channing stepped back into the cluster of teachers and listened quietly while my father continued his introductory remarks, going over the necessary administrative details, reminding the boys of various school rules, that there was to be no cheating, no plagiarism, no profanity, no smoking, nor any drinking of alcoholic beverages, as he put it, 'anywhere, anytime, for any reason, ever'.

I have often wondered what came into Miss Channing's mind as she listened to my father recite the rules by which we were all to conduct ourselves at Chatham School, rules that stressed humility, simple honesty, and mutual faith, and which stood four-square against every form of recklessness and betrayal and self-indulgence. How different they must have seemed to the visionary teachings her father had laid down, how deeply rooted in the very kind of humble, uninspired, and profoundly predictable village life he had taught her to revile.

Once my father had finished, the boys already shifting restlessly and muttering impatiently to each other, he clapped his hands together once, then uttered a final remark whose tragic irony he could not have guessed. 'Welcome to another splendid year in the history of Chatham School,' he said.

I entered Miss Channing's class about an hour later.

It was a small room, formerly used to store school furniture and various supplies, but now converted to other purposes. It was not physically connected to the school, but stood apart from it in a little courtyard to the rear. Still, it seemed adequate enough, with three long tables lined up one behind the other in front of the much smaller one that served as Miss Channing's desk. On the far wall, half a dozen gray aprons hung from wooden pegs beside a metal cabinet upon which someone had painted the words

ART SUPPLIES in large white letters. In the far corner a few wooden sculpting pedestals had been stacked base to base, the legs of the upper pedestals stretching almost to the room's tin ceiling.

As for art, there were portraits of George Washington and Abraham Lincoln, along with a framed photograph of the current president, Calvin Coolidge.

There were only five of us in the class, but we scattered ourselves widely throughout the room. Ralph Sherman and Miles Clayton took possession of the rear table, Biff Conners and Jack Slaughter the middle one, leaving the front table to me.

Miss Channing didn't smile at us or say a word of welcome as we entered the room. She'd already placed one of the sculpting pedestals in front of her, and as we filed in, she began to knead the clay gently, hardly glancing up from it as we took our seats. Then, once we'd taken our places, she drew her hands from the clay and looked at us, her eyes moving from one boy to another. She did not acknowledge me in any way.

'I've never taught art,' she said. 'Or been taught it by anyone else.'

Her fingers moved over the clay's wet surface, shaping it with slow, graceful strokes as she searched for her next remark.

'When my father died, I went to live with my uncle and his family in Africa,' she said finally. 'He had a mission near a village where the natives lived in wooden huts. It was just a clearing in the plain. The people who lived in the village did all their cooking in their huts, and there was no way for the smoke to get out except through a small hole in the roof. When they came out of their huts in the morning, a sheet of smoke trailed behind them.' Her eyes lifted toward us, and I saw them take on a certain wonder and delight. It was as if in telling stories, she could find a voice to teach in, a way of reaching us. 'Like wings that dissolved in the light,' she said.

'That's where I learned to paint.' She was kneading the clay more quickly now, in short, quick thrusts. 'In Africa.' She stopped suddenly and settled her eyes upon us. I could tell that a thought had just occurred to her, that in the very course of talking to us she'd discovered something. 'That's where I learned that to be a painter or a sculptor, you have to change your senses,' she said. 'Switch them around, so that you *see* with your fingertips and *feel* with your eyes.'

I didn't see Miss Channing again until much later that same day. The last class had been dismissed for nearly an hour, and I was busily doing my assigned tasks around the school.

Under my father's leadership, it was the policy of Chatham School to combine academics with physical labor, and so from the time of his arrival, each boy was assigned various chores. Some of the boys swept the classrooms and the dormitory, some washed the sheets and blankets, some worked on the grounds, pruning shrubbery or mowing grass or maintaining the playing fields. In the winter everyone shoveled snow or took turns unloading coal.

On that particular afternoon it was my job to return any books that lay on the library tables to their proper shelves, carefully keeping them in order according to the Dewey decimal system Mrs Cartwright, the school librarian, had established. After that I was to dust the bookshelves with the old feather duster my mother had donated to the school after buying a new one at Mayflower's a month before.

It was nearly four by the time I'd finished. Mrs Cartwright surveyed the now-empty tables and ran a finger over the top of one of the bookshelves. 'Very good, Henry,' she said when she found it clear of dust. With that statement of satisfaction I was released for the remainder of the afternoon.

I remember the feeling of relief that swept over me each time I ran down the stairs, bolted through the broad double doors of Chatham School, and raced out into the open air. I don't know why I felt the weight of Chatham School so heavily, or so yearned to be rid of it, for it was by no means a prison, my father by no means a tyrant. And yet, in my raw youth, the days seemed to drag along behind me like a ball and chain. Every stricture burned like a lash, and sometimes, at night, I would feel as if my whole life lay smothered beneath a thick blanket of petty obligations and worn-out rules.

Miss Channing's class had offered a certain relief from that musty atmosphere, so that even on that first afternoon I found that I looked forward to the next one in a way that I'd never looked forward to Mr Crawford's Latin lectures or the interminable recitations of Mrs Dillard's history class. There'd been a freshness to her approach, a sense of something less hindered by the ancient forms of instruction, something young, as I was young, already free in a way I one day hoped to be.

As I came out of the school, already vaguely considering a quick stroll into the village, perhaps even a secret cigarette behind the bowling alley, I saw Miss Channing sitting on one of the wooden benches that rested near the edge of the coastal bluff. Normally it would not have occurred to me to approach a teacher outside of class, but she already seemed less a teacher to me than a comrade of some sort, both of us momentarily stranded at Chatham School, but equally destined to go beyond it someday.

She didn't appear surprised when I drifted past her, took hold of the rail that stretched along the edge of the bluff, and stared out to sea, my back to her, pretending that I hadn't noticed her sitting directly behind me.

'Hello, Henry,' she said.

I turned toward her. 'Oh, Miss Channing,' I said. 'I didn't see—'

'It's a marvelous view, isn't it?'

'Yes, it is.'

I glanced back over the bluff. Below, the sea was empty, but a few people strolled along the beach or lounged beneath striped umbrellas. I tried to see the view through her eyes. From behind me, I heard her say, 'It reminds me of the Lido.'

'The Lido?'

'A beach near Venice,' she said. 'It was always filled with striped umbrellas. The changing rooms were painted with the same stripes. Yellow. Bright yellow.' She shook her head. 'Actually, it doesn't remind me of the Lido at all,' she said, her voice a shade lower, as if now talking to me in confidence. 'It's just that I was thinking of it when you came up.'

'Why?' I asked, no other question occurring to me.

'Because my father died on the Lido,' Miss Channing said. 'That's what I was really thinking of just now.'

In later life we forget what it was like, the sweetness and exhilaration of being spoken to for the first time as something other than a child. And yet that was what I felt at that moment, sweetness and exhilaration, a sense that some part of my boyhood had been peeled away and cast aside, the man beneath allowed to take his first uneasy breaths.

'I'm sorry,' I said, immediately using a phrase I'd heard so many times on similar occasions.

Her expression did not change. 'There's nothing to be sorry for, really. He lived a good life.'

I could see the love she'd had for him and wondered what it was like to have had a father you admired.

'What did he do?' I asked.

'He was a writer. A travel writer.'

'And you traveled with him?'

'From the time I was four years old. That was when my mother died. After that we traveled all the time.'

As if my father had suddenly assumed my shape, I asked a question that seemed more his than mine. 'What about school?'

'My father was my school,' Miss Channing answered. 'He taught me everything.' She rose and joined me at the rail, the two of us now looking out over the beach below. 'He believed in going his own way.' She paused a moment, a line coming to her, one I later read in her father's book, and which she now repeated to me.

'An artist should follow only his passions,' she said. 'All else is a noose around his neck.'

Now, when I recall that line, the calm with which she said it, I feel its dreadful premonition, and in my mind see an old car hurling down a weedy, overgrown embankment, a figure turning at the water's edge, eyes wide, aghast, uncomprehending. And after that, forever after that, the long, unfading echo of her scream.

SIX

In the years following Miss Channing's trial, my father assembled a small collection of materials concerning the Chatham School Affair, one he bequeathed to me at his death, and which I've been unable to discard. I've given other things away – my mother's knitting needles, my father's quill pen, stacks of books to the village library. But my father's collection has remained intact, tucked into the bottom corner of the bookshelf in my office, all but hidden by the floor lamp that stands in front of it. It is a slender archive, especially given the events it summons up. Madness and suicide and murder, the forlorn world left in their wake. And yet there are times when my attention lingers on it with a curious nostalgia. For I know that it holds the defining moment of my youth.

It consists of nothing more than a folder containing a single copy of the Chatham School Annual for 1927, a few newspaper clippings and photographs. There is even one of Sarah Doyle, though it was unintended. In the picture she is rushing down the little walkway beside the school. Her back is to the camera, and snow is falling all around her, gathering on her long, dark cape, while the boys in the yard – the real focus of the picture – playfully heave packed snowballs at each other, my father on the front steps of the school, arms folded over his chest, looking on with mock disapproval.

47

To these few things my father added three books, two of them directly related to what happened on Black Pond, one considerably less so.

The first is Mr Parsons' memoir, the work he quickly put together and had privately published just after the trial. As a book, it leaves a great deal to be desired. In fact, it is little more than an assortment of quotations from the trial transcript awkwardly strung together by Mr Parsons' own rather tedious narrative.

The second volume is more detailed. Titled *A Mortal Flaw*, it was written by one Wilfred M. Peyton, a professor of moral philosophy at Oberlin College. Scarcely a hundred pages long, it is essentially an extended essay published in 1929 by a small religious press, and hampered not only by Professor Peyton's harsh, sermonizing tone, but by the way he singled out Miss Channing as the true villain in what he insists on calling – over and over again, like words from a warlock's chant – 'The Black Pond Murders'. Such was his rage against Miss Channing that whenever he spoke of her, it was with an Old Testament prophet's infuriated rebuke. 'To her father, she was "Libby",' he wrote in a typical passage, 'for by such endearment did he call her in her youth. But to the ages she should be more rightly known as Elizabeth, a cold and formal name that must be included among those of other women like herself: Delilah, Salome, and Jezebel.'

Of the three volumes of my father's archive, Professor Peyton's was the only one he clearly hated. So much so that he scribbled angry notes throughout its text, sometimes disputing a small, inconsequential fact (noting, for example, that the school library had three thousand books, not the mere two thousand attributed by Peyton), sometimes quarreling with an interpretation, but always seeking to undermine the book's authority to those who might later read it.

The reason my father so detested Professor Peyton's book is obvious. For it was not only an attack upon Miss Channing, but upon Chatham School itself, as an 'indulgent, coddling retreat for wealthy, dissolute boys.' Indeed, at the end of the book Professor Peyton flatly concluded that 'the unspeakable outrage which occurred on the otherwise tranquil surface of Black Pond on 29 May 1927 was emblematic of the moral relativism and contempt for established authority that has emerged in educational theory during the last two decades, and of which Chatham School is only the most odious example.' It never surprised me, of course, that this was a passage my father had underlined in black ink, then appended his own heartrending cry of 'NO! NO! NO!'

But for all its bluster and moral posturing, for all the pain it caused my father, *A Mortal Flaw* was, at last, a completely dismissible book, one which, after I read it, I never found the slightest need to pick up again.

I can't say the same for the final volume in my father's collection, however. For it was a book I have returned to many times, as if looking for some answer to what happened on Black Pond that day, perhaps even for what might have prevented it, some way to sedate our hearts, make them satisfied with less.

The third book is entitled *A View from the Window*, and on the back of the book's cover there is a photograph of its author, Jonathan Channing, a tall, somber man in his late forties, staring at the camera from the courtyard of the Louvre.

'You can take it if you want,' Miss Channing said the day she lent it to me.

It was late on a Friday afternoon, the first week of class now ended. My father had sent me to Miss Channing's classroom with a box of art books he'd picked up at a Boston bookstore the day before. Always somewhat impulsive, he'd been eager to get Miss Channing's opinion of them before turning them over to Mrs Cartwright in the library on Monday morning.

She'd been standing at the cabinet, putting away her supplies, when I came through the door.

'My father wanted you to take a look at these.' I lifted the box slightly. 'Art books.'

She closed the door of the cabinet and walked to her desk. 'Let's see them,' she said.

I brought them to her, then watched while she looked through each book in turn, slowly turning the pages, pausing to gaze at the paintings she found reproduced there, sometimes mentioning the name of the gallery in which a painting now hung. 'This is in Florence,' she'd say, or 'I saw this at the Prado.' She turned the book toward me. 'This one always frightened me. What do you think, Henry?'

I looked at the painting. It showed a little girl with stringy blond hair, crouched before an enormous tree, its jagged limbs stretching to both sides of the canvas, the gnarled limbs hung with surreal images of floating heads and body parts, the colors livid, greens the color of bile, reds the color of fresh blood. Staring at the tree, the child appeared frozen by the terror and immensity of what she faced.

'Have you ever felt like her?' Miss Channing asked me quietly, her gaze fixed on the illustration, rife with its malicious and chaotic gore.

I shook my head. 'I don't think so, Miss Channing.' Which was true then, though it is no longer so.

She turned the book back around, leafing through it once again, until she came upon a photograph of the courtyard at the Louvre. 'There's a picture of my father standing here,' she told me. 'They used it for his book.'

'His book?'

'Yes,' Miss Channing said. 'He was a travel writer. He wrote a great many articles, but only one book.'

Out of mere politeness I said, 'I'd like to read it sometime.'

She took this as a genuine expression of interest, opened the drawer of her desk, and drew out a single volume. 'This is it,' she said as she handed it to me. 'The picture I mentioned is on the back.'

I turned the book over and looked at the photograph. It showed a tall, slender man, handsome in a roguish sort of way, dressed in dark trousers and a white dinner jacket, his hair slicked back in the fashion of the time, but with a wilder touch added in the form of a single black curl that fell just over the corner of his right eye.

'I was ten years old when that picture was taken,' Miss Channing said. 'We'd just gotten back from a visit to Rouen. My father was interested in the cathedral there.'

'Was he religious?'

'Not at all,' she said with a smile I found intriguing.

I lifted the book toward her, but she made no move to reclaim it.

'You can take it if you want,' she said.

I had not really wanted to read her father's book, but I took it with me anyway, reluctantly, unable to find an acceptable way to refuse it.

As it turned out, I read it that same afternoon, sitting alone on the coastal bluff, the other boys of Chatham School either engaged in a game of football on the playing field or gathered outside Quilty's Ice Cream Parlor in the village.

In earlier years I'd tried to be one of them. I'd joined them in their games, even participated in the general mischief, playing pranks on teachers or making up nicknames for them. But in the end it hadn't worked. For I was still the headmaster's son, a position that made it impossible for them to accept me as just another boy at Chatham School, one with whom they could be as vulgar and irreverent as they pleased, calling my father 'Old Grizzlewald', as I knew they often did.

Though never exactly ostracized, I'd finally turned bookish and aloof, a boy who could often be found reading in the porch swing or at the edge of the playing field, a 'scholarly lad' as my father sometimes called me, though in a tone that never struck me as entirely complimentary.

Recalling the boy I was in those days, so solitary and isolated, I've sometimes thought myself one of the victims of the Chatham School Affair, my life no less deeply wounded by the crime that rocked Black Pond. Then, as if to bring me back to what really happened there, my mind returns me to a little girl on a windy beach. She is running against the wind, an old kite whipping left and right behind her. Finally it lifts and she watches it joylessly, her eyes wreathed in that forsakenness that would never leave them after that. Remembering how she looked at that moment in her life, I instantly recognize who Black Pond's victims truly were, and in that captured moment perceive the terror I escaped, the full depth of a loss that was never mine.

I learned a great deal about Miss Channing the afternoon I read her father's book. I learned about her father too: the fact that he'd been born into a privileged Massachusetts family, educated at Harvard College, and worked as a journalist in Boston during the years following his graduation. At twenty-three he'd married the former Julia Mason Rockbridge, also from a distinguished New England family. The two had taken up residence on Marlborough Street, near Boston Common, and in 1904 had a daughter, Elizabeth Rockbridge Channing. After that Mr Channing continued to work for the *Boston Globe*, while his wife performed the usual functions of an upper-class woman of that time. Then, in the fall of 1908, Julia Channing fell ill. She lingered for some weeks, but finally died in January 1909, leaving four-year-old Elizabeth entirely to her father's care.

More than anything, *A View from the Window* is a day-to-day record of the years Miss Channing lived and traveled with her father, a period during which they'd never actually had a fixed abode of any kind, nor any permanent attachments, save for each other. The purpose of such a rootless life, Mr Channing's purpose in insisting upon it, is revealed in the opening paragraphs of his narrative:

After my wife's death, to stay in Boston seemed doom to me. I walked about our house on Marlborough Street, gazing at the many luxuries she had acquired over the years, the velvet curtains, the Tiffany lamp, and a host of other appendages that, like Julia, were elegant in their way, but for which I could no longer feel any enduring affection. And so I decided to move on, to live in the world at large, to acquaint my daughter Libby with its most spacious and inaccessible climes.

As to my reasoning in this matter, I have never hidden

*it, nor wished to hide it. I chose to educate my daughter as
I saw fit. And with what purpose in mind? For none other
than that she should live a life freed from the constrictive
influence of any particular village or nation, nor ever be
bound by the false constraints of custom, ideology, or
blood.*

And yet, despite its grandly stated purpose, *A View from
the Window* remained essentially a travelogue, though
one that detailed not only sights and sounds and historical
backgrounds, but the life Miss Channing and her father
had lived as together they'd roamed the world.

It had been a vagabond life, the book made clear, a
life lived continually in transit, with nothing to give it
direction save for Mr Channing's furious determination
to teach his daughter his own unique philosophy of life,
relentlessly driving it home by escorting young Libby, as
he called her, to bizarre and tragic sites, locations he'd
selected for the lessons he planned to teach.

Reading that philosophy on the bluff that afternoon,
I felt myself utterly swept away by a view of life so different from my father's, from the governing assumptions
of Chatham and of Chatham School, from any way of
seeing things I'd ever encountered before, that I felt as if
I'd suddenly entered a new galaxy, where, according to
Mr Channing, there should be 'no rules for the rule of
life', nor any hindrance whatsoever to a man's unbridled
passions.

It was a world directly opposite to the one I'd been
taught to revere, everything reversed or turned topsy-turvy.
Self-control became a form of slavery, vows and contracts
mere contrivances to subdue the spirit, the moral law no
more absolute than a passing fad. More than anything, it

was a world in which even the darkest evils were given a strange and somber dignity:

We took a boat from Sorrento, and disembarked a short time later at Marina Grande, on the eastern coast of Capri. The town was festive and welcoming, and Libby took great delight in its scents and in the winding labyrinth of its streets, skipping playfully ahead of me from time to time. She seemed captivated by the nearly tropical lushness of the place, particularly with the luxuriousness of its vegetation, forever plucking leaves and petals from the shrubs and flowers we encountered on the way.

But I had brought her to Capri for more than an afternoon's lark. Nor was it the quaint village byways and varied plant life I had brought her here to see. Mine was another purpose, as well as another destination, one I could but indistinctly glimpse from the town's narrow pathways.

And so we journeyed upward and upward for over an hour, baked in a nearly blinding summer heat, through the spectacular flowered hedges that lined both sides of the earthen walkway. The smell of flowers was everywhere, as were the sounds of small lizards, dozens of them, scurrying through the brush or darting like thin green ribbons across our path.

The walk was arduous, but the great ruin of the Villa di Giovi made infamous by Suetonius, loomed enticingly above, beckoning me with the same sinister and mysterious call the sirens had issued to Odysseus from the Bay of Naples far below. For like the ancient world of those mythic seamen, the place I journeyed to that morning had been bloody and perverse.

And yet there was something glorious here as well, something incontestably free in the wild pleasure gardens

*the emperor had designed, the human bodies he'd formed
into living sculptures, even in the heedless and unrestrained
delight he'd taken in their libidinous show. For it was
in this place that Tiberius had exalted physical sensual-
ity over spiritual aridness, breaking every known taboo,
pairing boys with boys, girls with girls, covering his own
wrinkled frame with the smooth bodies of the very young.
And though hideous and unnatural as it might seem, still it
remained the pagan world's most dramatic gesture toward
the truly illimitable.*

*And so I brought Libby here, to walk with her within
the bowers of this ruined yet still magnificent grove, and
once there, I sat with her in full view of the infamous Salto
di Tiberio and spoke to her of what life should be, the
heights it should reach, the passions it should embrace, all
this said and done in the hope that she might come to live
it as a bird on the wing. For life is best lived at the edge
of folly.*

An evening shade had fallen over the bluff, the deserted
beach beneath it, the whole small realm of Chatham,
when I finished *A View from the Window*. I tucked the
book under my arm and wandered back down Myrtle
Street toward home. On the way I saw Danny Sheen lop-
ing across the playing field, and Charlie Patterson lugging
a battered trunk along the front walkway of Chatham
School. Upstairs the lights were on, and I knew the boys
were either studying in the library or talking quietly in the
common room, that soon the bell would call them to their
dinner, my father dining with them as he always did on
Friday evenings, rising at the end of the meal, ringing his
little bell, then dismissing them with some quotation he
hoped might serve them in the years to come.

Thinking of all that, Myrtle Street like a flat, turgid stream flowing sluggishly ahead of me, I realized that I'd never known any way of life other than the one defined by Chatham School, nor felt that any other might be open to me. Certainly I'd never conceived of my destiny as anything but decided. I would graduate from Chatham School, go to college, make my living, have a family. I would do what my father had done, and his father before him. A different date marked my birth, and a different date would mark my death. Other than that, I would live as they had lived, die as they had died, find whatever joy or glory there might be in life along the same beaten path they'd trod before me through the misty ages.

But as I made my way home that evening, none of that seemed any longer as settled as it once had. The restlessness that seized me from time to time, the sullenness into which I fell, the way I cringed as my father offered his trusty platitudes to the assembled boys, the whole inchoate nature of my discontent began to take a certain shape and definition so that for the first time, I dimly began to perceive what I really wanted out of life.

It was simple. I wanted to be free. I wanted to answer only to myself, to strike out toward something. I didn't know at that moment how to gain my freedom, or what to do with it. I knew only that I had discovered what I wanted, and that with that discovery a great pall had lifted, a door opened. I didn't know where I was going, only that I had to go in a different direction than my father had gone, or that any of the other boys of Chatham School would likely go.

I ran down Myrtle Street, breathless, my mind glittering in a world of fresh ideas. Though night had nearly fallen by the time I reached home, it felt like dawn to me. I remember bounding up the stairs, stretching out on my bed, and reading Mr Channing's book again, cover to cover. One sentence held for all time: Life is best lived at the edge of folly.

I remember that a fierce exhilaration seized me as I read and reread that line in my bedroom beneath the eaves, that it seemed to illuminate everything I had ever felt. Even now it strikes me that no darkness ever issued from a brighter flame.

PART II

SEVEN

In old age and semiretirement I'd finally come to a time in life when I never expected to think of her again. By then years had gone by with little to remind me of her, save the quick glimpse of an old woman moving heavily across a wide wooden porch or rocking slowly in her chair as I drove by. And so Miss Channing had at last grown distant. When I thought of her at all, it was as a faded thing, like a flower crushed within the pages of an ancient, crumbling book. Then, suddenly, my own life now drawing to a close, she came back to me by a route I'd never have expected.

I'd come to my office early that morning, the village street still empty, a fog sweeping in from the sea, curling around the corner of Dalmatian's Cafe and nestling under the benches outside the town hall. I was sitting at my desk, handling the few cases that still came my way, when I suddenly looked up and saw an old man standing at my door.

'Morning, Henry,' he said.

It was Clement Boggs, dressed as he always was, in a flannel shirt and baggy pants, an old hat pulled down nearly to his ears. I'd known Clement all my life, though never very well. He'd been one of the local rowdies who'd smoked in front of the bowling alley, the type my father had always warned me against, a rough, lower-class boy who'd later managed to pull himself together, make a good life, even put away a considerable fortune. I'd handled quite a few of his legal affairs, mostly closings in recent years, as he'd begun to divest himself of the property he'd accumulated throughout his life.

He sat down in one of the chairs in front of my desk, groaning slightly as he did so. 'I've got an offer on some land I bought a long time back,' he told me. 'Out on Plymouth Road.' He hesitated, as if the words themselves held all the terror, rather than the events that had happened there. ''Round Black Pond. The old Milford cottage.'

As if I'd suddenly been swept back to that terrible summer day, I heard Mr Parsons say, *You often went to Milford Cottage, didn't you, Henry?* My answer simple, forthright, as all of them had been: *Yes, sir, I did.*

Clement watched me closely. 'You all right, Henry?'

I nodded. 'Yes,' I said. 'I'm fine.'

He didn't seem convinced, but continued anyway. 'Well, like I said, I've got an offer on that land 'round Black Pond.' He leaned back slowly, watching me intently, no doubt wondering at the scenes playing in my mind, the swirling water, a face floating toward me from the green depths. 'He wants to know if he can get a zoning variance. I thought you might look into it, see if the town might give him one.'

Clement sat only a few feet from me, but he seemed far way; Mr Parsons bore in upon me so closely I could almost feel his breath upon my face. *When were you last on Black Pond?* Matter-of-factly, with no hint of passion, and certainly none of concealment, my answer came: *On May 29, 1927. That would be a Sunday? Yes.*

'You'll have to go out there, of course,' Clement said, his gaze leveled upon me steadily, his head cocked to the right, so that for an instant I wondered if he might also be reliving my day in the witness box, listening once again to Mr Parsons' questions as they'd resounded through the crowded courtroom. *What happened on Black Pond that day?*

Clement's eyes narrowed, as if against a blinding light, and I knew that he could sense the upheaval in my mind no matter how hard I labored to contain it. 'I don't guess you've been out that way in quite some time,' he said.

'Not in years.'

'Looks the same.'

'The same as what?'

My question appeared to throw him into doubt as to what his answer should be. 'Same as it did in the old days,' he replied.

I said nothing, but I could feel myself helplessly returning to the days he meant. I saw an old car moving through the darkness, two beams of yellow light engulfing me as it came to a halt, a figure staring at me from behind the wheel, motioning now, whispering, *Get in.*

'Well, let me know what you find out,' Clement said, rising from his chair. 'About the variance, I mean.'

'I'll look into it right away.'

Once at the door, he turned back to face me. 'You don't have to stay out there for long, of course,' he told me, his way of lightening the load. 'Just get an idea of what the town might think of somebody developing it.'

I nodded.

He seemed unsure of what he should say next, or if it should be me to whom he said it. Finally, he spoke again. 'There's one more thing, Henry. The money. From the land, I mean. I want it to go to somebody in particular.' He paused a moment, then said her name. 'Alice Craddock.'

She swam into my mind, an old woman, immensely fat, her hair gray and bedraggled, her mind unhinged, the butt of a cruel school-yard poem I'd heard repeated through the years:

> Alice Craddock,
> Locked in the paddock
> Where's your mama gone?

'It just seems right that she should get whatever the land out there brings,' Clement said. 'I'm an old man. I don't need it. And they say Alice has come on bad times.'

I saw Alice as a middle-aged woman, slack-jawed, growing fat on potato chips and candy bars, her eyes dull and lightless, a gang of boys chasing after her, pointing, laughing, until Mr Wallace chased them away, his words trailing after them as they fled down the street: *Leave her alone. She's suffered enough.*

'Not much left of what was given her,' Clement said.

'Not much, no.'

He shrugged. 'Well, maybe this can help a little,' he said, then turned and walked through the door.

Once he'd gone, I went to the window and looked out. I could see him trudging toward the dusty old truck he'd parked across the street. But I could see him, too, as he'd looked years before, during the days of the trial, the way he'd stood with his cronies on the courthouse steps as Miss Channing had been rushed down them, jeering at her as she swept past, the dreadful word I'd heard drop from his mouth as he glared at her: *Whore.*

It was not something I'd ever expected to do, see Milford Cottage again, feel the allure I'd known there, the passions it had stirred. But once Clement's old truck had pulled away, I felt myself drawn back to it, not in a mood of youthful reminiscence, but as someone forced to look at what he'd done, view the bodies in their mangled ruin, a criminal returning to the scene of his crime.

And so I drove out to Milford Cottage only an hour later. It was still early, the streets deserted, with only a few people having breakfast at Dalmatian's Cafe. Driving along Main Street, it seemed to me that the village had changed very little since the days of Miss Channing's trial, when the crowds had swirled around the courthouse or milled about in front of Quilty's and Mayflower's, muttering of murder and betrayal.

Once outside the village, I followed the road that led along the seashore. There were bogs and marshes on either side, just as there'd always been, and from time to time I spotted a gull circling overhead, a crow skirting just over a distant line of trees.

A mile out of the village I turned onto Plymouth Road, taking the same route my father had taken the afternoon we'd first driven down it together, Miss Channing in the front seat, I in the back with her two valises. The forest thickness pressed in upon me no less thickly than it had that day, the green vines slapping once again against both sides of the car.

As I rounded the last curve, Milford Cottage swept into view.

It looked much smaller than it had the last time I'd seen it. But that wasn't the only change time had wrought. For the cottage had gone completely to ruin during the intervening years, the tar roof now ripped and curled, the screen door torn from its rusty hinges, the yard a field of weed and bramble, the whole structure so weathered and dilapidated that it seemed hardly able to hold its own against the changeless waters of Black Pond.

I stared at it, reviewing the story of its abandonment. I knew that no one would ever live there again, no young woman would ever rearrange the lanterns inside it or hang her father's picture on its walls. From the trial transcripts so generously quoted in Mr Parsons' book, I knew what had been said in its small rooms, what had been felt as well. But I also knew that there'd been other voices, too, other feelings, things Mr Parsons, for all his effort, had been unable to unearth. As if her lips were at my ear, I heard Miss Channing say, *I can't go on.* Then my reply, *What can I do to help?*

For a time I peered at the front door that had barred my father's way that first afternoon, remembering how Miss Channing had stood behind him, waiting silently in the rain as he'd struggled to unlock it. Then I walked up to it, gave a gentle push, and watched as it drifted back, revealing the emptiness inside.

I stepped into the cottage, my eyes moving along the leaf-strewn floor, settling for a moment on the old fireplace with its heap of gray ash. I heard Miss Channing say, *Get rid of this*, and closed my eyes abruptly, as if against a vision I expected to appear before them at any moment, Miss Channing standing at the hearth, staring into it with a steely glare, feeding letters into its leaping flames.

When I opened them again, the cottage was as empty as before, with nothing to give it sound or movement but the drama playing in my mind.

I glanced into the vacant bedroom, to where a little wooden bookshelf had once rested beside her bed. I could remember the books I'd seen collected there, the words of her father's heroes bound in dark vellum: Byron, Shelley, Keats.

A gust of wind slammed against the cottage, rattling what remained of its few dusty windowpanes. I saw a bare limb rake across the glass, a bony finger motioning me outside. And so I nodded silently, like someone agreeing to be led into another chamber, then walked to the back of the cottage, out the rear door, and across the yard to the water's edge.

The great willow still rose above the pond, the one Miss Channing had so often painted, its long, brown tendrils drooping toward the surface of the water. I wondered how many times during her first weeks in Chatham she'd stood beneath it, remembering the poems her father had so often read to her, sometimes in the very places where they'd been written, odes to nightingales and Grecian urns, pleasure domes and crystal seas, women who walk in beauty like the night. But there'd been other things as well, other titles on the shelf beside her bed, the speculations of Mesmer, the visions of Madame Blavatsky, the gruesome ravings of de Sade.

All of that, I thought, standing now where she had stood, my eyes fixed upon the motionless surface of Black Pond, *All of that was in her mind*. Then I looked out across the pond, and heard a voice, cold, lean, mouthing its grim question: *Do you want them dead?*

I was there when she saw him for the first time. Or, at least, I think I was. Of course, she'd already glimpsed him with the other teachers or disappearing into a classroom down the hall. But I don't think she'd actually *seen* him before, that is, picked him out from among the others, noticed something that distinguished him and drew her attention toward him more intently.

It was toward the middle of October, near the end of Miss Channing's first month at Chatham School. She was standing behind a sculptor's pedestal, as she often did, though this time there was no mound of clay. We were only to imagine it there, she said, shape it only in our minds.

'When you imagine the muscles, you have to feel their power,' she told us. 'You have to feel what is *beneath* the figure you're working with. What is *inside* it.' She picked up a large book she'd previously placed on her desk and turned it toward us, already open to the page she'd selected to illustrate her point.

'This is a picture of Rodin's *Balzac*.' She began to walk along the side of the room, the book still open, pressing the picture toward us. 'You can't see Balzac's body,' she added. 'He's completely covered in a long, flowing cape.'

She continued to move along the edge of the room, the boys now shifting in their seats to keep her in view. 'But if you opened the cape,' Miss Channing went on, 'you'd see this.' With a purposely swift gesture, she turned the page, and there before us, in full view, was a monstrously fat and bulging Balzac, immense and naked, his belly drooping hugely toward his feet.

'This figure is actually under the cape,' she said. 'Rodin added the cape only *after* he'd sculpted the body beneath it. The actual body of Balzac.'

She closed the book and for a moment stared at us silently. Then she lifted her hands and wriggled her fingers. 'You must imagine what's *beneath* the skin of the figure you're working on. Feel the muscles stretch and contract.' She swept her hands back until they came to a halt at the sides of her face. 'Even the smallest muscles are important, like the tiny ones that open and close your eyes.'

We stared at her in shocked silence, stunned by the naked figure she'd just displayed to us, but awed by it as well.

'Remember all that when you start to work on your figures in class tomorrow,' Miss Channing said just as the bell sounded our dismissal.

It was her last class of the day, and I remember thinking that her first month of teaching at Chatham School had gone quite well. Even my father had commented upon it, mentioning to my mother over dinner one evening that Miss Channing had 'gotten a grip on things right away', that teaching seemed to 'fit her nature'.

I was already at the door that afternoon, the other boys rushing by, when I turned back and saw her alone, standing behind her sculpting pedestal. It seemed the perfect time to approach her.

'Miss Channing,' I said, coming toward her slowly.

She looked up. 'Yes, Henry?'

I took her father's book from my bag and held it out to her. 'I thought it was great,' I said. 'I've read it quite a few times. Even copied things out of it. I thought he was right about everything. About "living on the run."'

She did not take the book, and I felt certain that she could sense the life I craved, how much I needed to bound over the walls of Chatham School, race into the open spaces, live on the edge of folly. For a moment she seemed to be evaluating me, asking herself if I had the will to see it through, possessed the naked ruthlessness such freedom might require.

'It isn't easy to live the way my father did,' she said, her blue eyes focused powerfully. 'Most people can't do it.'

'But everything else ... the way people *do* live ...' I stammered. 'I don't want to live like my father does. I don't want to be like him ... a fool.'

She didn't seem in the least shocked by my ruthless evaluation of my father. 'How do you want to be, Henry?'

'Open to things. To new things.'

She watched me a moment longer, and I could see that she was thinking of me in a way that no one else ever had, not merely as the boy I was, but as the man I might someday be. 'I've been noticing your drawing,' she said. 'It's really quite good, you know.'

I knew no such thing. 'It is?'

'There's a lot of feeling in it.'

I knew how strangely twisted my drawings were, how wreathed in a vampire blackness, but it had never occurred to me that such characteristics added up to 'feeling', that they might spring from something deep within me.

I shrugged. 'There's not much to draw around here. Just the sea. The lighthouse. Stuff like that.'

'But you put something into them, Henry,' Miss Channing said. 'Something extra. You should get a sketchbook and take it around with you. That's what I did in Africa. I found that just having it along with me made me look at things differently.' She waited for a response, then continued when I failed to offer one. 'Anyway, when you've done a few more drawings, bring them in and let me look at them.'

I'd never been complimented by a teacher before. Certainly none had ever suggested that I had a talent for anything but moodiness and solitude. To the other teachers I had always been a disappointment, someone tolerated because I was the headmaster's son, a boy of limited prospects and little ambition, a 'decent lad', as I'd once heard my father describe me in a tone that had struck me as deeply condescending, a way of saying that I was nothing, and never would be.

'All right, Miss Channing,' I said, immensely lifted by her having seen something in me the other teachers had not seen.

'Good,' she said, then returned to her work as I headed down the aisle and out the door.

I walked into the courtyard and drew in a deep, invigorating breath. It was autumn now, and the air was quite brisk. But my mood had been so heated up by Miss Channing's high regard that I could not feel its hint of winter chill.

A few hours later I took my seat for the final class of the day. I glanced out the window, then at the pictures that hung on the wall. Shakespeare. Wordsworth. Keats. My attention was still drifting aimlessly from one face to another when I heard the steady *thump ... thump ... thump* of the approaching teacher's wooden cane, soft and rhythmic, like the distant muffled beating of a drum.

Was he handsome, the man who came into the room seconds later, dressed, as always, in a chalk-smeared jacket and corduroy pants?

Yes, I suppose he was. In his own particular way, of course.

And yet it never surprised me that the people of the village later marveled that such fierce emotions could have stormed about in a so visibly broken frame.

He was tall and slender, but there was something in his physical arrangement that always struck me as subtly off kilter, the sense of a leaning tower, of something shattered at its base. For although he always stood erect, his back pressed firmly against the wall of his classroom while he spoke to us, his body often appeared to be of another mind, his left shoulder a few degrees lower than the right, his head cocked slightly to the left, like a bust whose features were classically formed yet eerily marred, perhaps distorted, the product of an unsteady hand.

Still, it was his face that people found most striking, the ragged black beard, lined here and there with gray, and the dark, deep-set eyes. But more particularly the cream-colored scar that ran crookedly from just beneath his left eye, widening and deepening until it finally disappeared into the thick bramble of his beard.

His name was Leland Reed.

I often recall my first glimpse of him. It was a summer afternoon several years before. I'd been slouched on the front porch of our house when I looked up to see a man coming down the street. He walked slowly, his shoulders dipping left and right like a little boat in a gently swelling sea. At last he came to a halt at the short metal gate that separated our house from the street. 'Good afternoon,' he said. 'I'm looking for Mr Arthur Griswald.'

'That's my father,' I told him.

He did not open the gate, but merely peered at me like someone who could see both my past and my future in a single glimpse, how I had been reared, what I would become as a result.

'He's inside the house,' I said, stung by his inspection.

'Thank you,' Mr Reed answered.

Seconds later I heard my father say, 'Ah, Mr Reed,' as he opened the door and let him in. Not long after that I found my father and Mr Reed in the parlor, my father so engrossed in interviewing Mr Reed that he never noticed me standing at the door, listening with a little boy's curiosity for the world of men.

Mr Reed had come from Boston, as it turned out, where he'd taught at the Boston Latin School for the past three years. He'd grown tired of the city, he said, then went on to provide other details in a self-confident, manly voice, but with something distant in it, too, a voice that later struck me as somewhat similar to his face, strong and forthright in its own way, but irreparably scarred.

'I'm surprised a man like yourself doesn't want to live in Boston,' my father said. 'I've always found it very stimulating.'

Mr Reed gave no answer.

'Would you mind if I asked your age?'

'Twenty-eight.'

I could tell that my father had thought him older, perhaps because of the wisps of gray visible in his beard, or, more likely, because his manner was so deliberative, his eyes so still.

'Twenty-eight,' my father repeated. 'And ... single?'

'Yes.'

They talked for well over an hour that afternoon, and although I drifted past the parlor's open door on several occasions, idly listening as their conversation continued, there was only one small fragment of it that later struck me as revealing of the kind of man Mr Reed actually was. It had come toward the end of the interview, my father's pipe now lying cold and smokeless in the ashtray beside his chair, Mr Reed still seated opposite him, both feet pressed firmly on the floor.

'And what about travel,' my father asked. 'Have you done much of that?'

Mr Reed shook his head. 'Only a little.'

'Where to, if I may ask?'

'France.'

My father seemed pleased. 'France. Now, that's a beautiful country. What part did you visit?'

'Only the countryside,' Mr Reed answered quietly, adding nothing more, so that my father had to finally coax him forward with another question.

'You were there on business?'

Mr Reed shook his head, and I saw one of his large hands move down to a right knee that had begun to tremble slightly.

'Just there on vacation, then?' my father asked lightly.

'No,' Mr Reed answered, a single coal-black eyebrow arching suddenly, then lowering again. 'The war.'

I remember that his voice had become strained as he'd answered, and that his eyes had darted toward the window briefly. At that, both my father and I suddenly realized that the casualness of my father's question had plumbed an unexpectedly raw aspect of Mr Reed's experience, miraculously revealing to us what Mr Reed himself must have seen some years before, an exploded shell lifting mounds of muddy earth, men hurling upward, then plummeting down, his own body spinning in a cloud of smoke, bits of himself flying away in surreal tongues of flame.

'Oh,' my father said softly, glancing toward the cane. 'I didn't know.'

Mr Reed drew his eyes back to my father but didn't speak.

'In your letter you didn't mention that you were a veteran. Most men do when they're applying for a job.'

Mr Reed shrugged. 'I find it difficult to do that,' he said.

My father reached for his pipe, though I noticed that he didn't light it. 'Well, tell me why you think you'd like to teach at Chatham School.'

I don't remember Mr Reed's answer, but only that my father had appeared satisfied with it, and that Mr Reed left the house a few minutes later, presumably walking back to the bus stop in Chatham center, then boarding a bus for Boston. I didn't see him again until almost two months later, and even then only briefly, a man moving down the corridor of Chatham School, one hand clutching a book, the other a cane, whose steady, rhythmic thump announced him like a theme.

As it still did when I heard it tapping down the hallway that autumn afternoon seven years later, followed by the inevitable cautionary whispers of, 'Shhh. Mr Reed is coming.'

However, on that particular day he didn't come into the room as he usually did, but stopped at the door instead, leaning one shoulder into it, so that he stood at a slant. 'There probably won't be many more days as pleasant as this one,' he said, nodding toward the window, the clear, warm air beyond it. 'So I thought we'd have class out in the courtyard this afternoon.'

With that, he turned and led us down the corridor to the rear of the school, then out into the little courtyard behind it. Once there, he positioned himself beside the large oak that stood near the center of the courtyard and motioned for us to sit down on the ground in a semicircle around him. Then, he leaned against the tree and glanced down at the book he'd brought with him. 'Today we're going to begin our study of Lord Byron,' he said, his voice a curious combination of something soft and rough, and which at times seemed almost physical, like the touch of a fine, unsanded wood. 'You should pay close attention, for Byron lived the poetry he wrote.'

As always, Mr Reed began by giving us the details of the poet's life, concentrating on his travels and adventures, a wild vagabond existence that Mr Reed clearly admired. 'Byron didn't settle for what the rest of us settle for,' he told us. 'He would find the lives we lead intolerably dull.'

During the next hour we learned that Byron had been raised in a place called Aberdeen, that as a child he'd been stricken with infantile paralysis, his right leg and foot so terribly contracted that he'd walked with a pronounced limp for the rest of his life. 'Like me,' Mr Reed said with a quiet smile, nodding toward his cane, 'except that he refused to let it hinder him, or change his life in any way.'

Byron had had what Mr Reed called 'an adventurous nature', throwing wild parties at his own castle, drinking burgundy from a human skull. 'He lived his ideas,' Mr Reed declared. 'Nothing ever stood in his way.'

Class was nearly over by the time Mr Reed finished telling us about Byron's life. But before releasing us completely, he opened the book he'd brought with him. 'I want you to listen now,' he said as he began flipping the pages briskly until he found the lines he'd been searching for. Then he looked toward us and smiled in that strange way I'd already noticed, a smile that seemed to require an undisclosed amount of effort. 'Words need to be heard sometimes,' he said. 'After all, in the beginning all poetry was spoken.'

With that he read the lines he'd selected for us, his voice low, almost a whisper, so that the words themselves sounded inordinately private, an intimate message sent by one whose peculiar sadness seemed at one with Mr Reed's.

Every feeling hath been shaken;
    Pride, which not a world could bow,
Bows to thee – by thee forsaken
    Even my soul forsakes me now;

But 'tis done – all words are idle –
    Words from me are vainer still;
But the thoughts we cannot bridle
    Force their way without the will.

His voice trailed off at the end of the recitation, though his eyes remained on the lines a moment longer, his head bowed wearily, as if beneath the weight of thoughts he himself could not bridle.

'I think it's sometimes a good idea to end class with a poem,' he said at last. Then he paused, watching us silently, perhaps hoping for a response. When none came, he closed the book. 'All right, you may go,' he said.

We scrambled to our feet quickly, gathering our books into our arms, and began to disperse, some heading back into the building, others toward the rear entrance of the courtyard and the playing fields beyond. Only Mr Reed stayed in place, his back pressed against the tree, the volume of Byron's poetry dangling from his hand. He looked as if he might crumple to the ground. But then I saw him draw in a long, reviving breath, straighten his shoulders, step away from the tree, and begin to make his way toward the building. 'Good night, Henry,' he said as he went by me.

'Good night, Mr Reed,' I answered.

I picked up my books and turned to the right. Miss Channing's classroom was directly in front of me, and when I glanced toward it, I saw that she stood at one of the three large windows that overlooked the courtyard. Her eyes were fixed upon Mr Reed with a clearly appreciative gaze, taking in the slight limp, the narrow cane, perhaps even the jagged cream-colored scar. I'd never seen a woman look at a man in exactly the same way, almost as if he were not a man at all, but a painting she admired for the boldness of its execution, the way the standard symmetries had been discarded in favor of jaggedness and instability, her earlier sense of beauty now adjusting to take it in, finding a place for mangled shapes.

EIGHT

From my place beneath the willow, staring out across the water, I could barely make out the house in which Mr Reed had lived so many years before, and so I stepped away from the tree and took a narrow footpath that hunters and swimmers and the occasional forest solitaire had maintained over the years, and which I knew to be the one Miss Channing had taken on that Saturday evening two weeks later, when she'd set out for Mr Reed's house on the other side of Black Pond. As I began to move down that same path, I heard Mr Parsons say, *So, from the beginning you were aware of their meetings?* My answer, *Yes, I was. And what were your impressions, Henry? I didn't see anything wrong with it. Do you now? Yes.*

A tangle of forest had surrounded Miss Channing that evening, and she might well have seen a lone white gull as it plummeted toward the surface of the pond. No doubt she heard the soft crunch of the leaves beneath her feet, but she may have heard an assortment of bird cries, too, or the scurrying of a field mouse, or the plop of a frog as it leaped into the water. For those were the things I saw and heard as I retraced her steps that morning, moving slowly, at an old man's pace.

Her dinner at Mr Reed's house had been arranged several days before. By then my father had told Miss Channing that it was getting a bit too cold for her to continue walking back and forth from her cottage to Chatham School. He'd gone on to inform her that there was another teacher who lived on Black Pond. It would be a simple matter for him to drop by for her each morning and return her to Milford Cottage in the afternoon.

And so at some point before the end of October, I saw Mr Reed escort Miss Channing to his car, a battered sedan, its wheels mud-spattered, its running board hardly more than a drooping sheet of rust, its windows streaked and scratched as if they'd been sandblasted with sea salt.

As to what they'd said to each other on that first drive, no one would ever have known had not Mr Parsons later been so insistent on learning every word ever spoken between them, requiring revelations so detailed that I could still hear their voices whispering in the air around me as I struggled to make my way along the edges of Black Pond.

I live just on the other side of the pond. You can probably see my house from your cottage.

Yes, I've seen it.

You may have seen me on the pond too. I go rowing on it occasionally.

Do you row at night?

Sometimes.

Then I think I saw you once. It was my first night in the cottage. I went out to stand by the pond. It was overcast, but I think I saw you for just a moment. Not you, exactly. Just part of the boat, and your hand. Why do you go out at night?

For the solitude, I suppose.

You don't live alone?

No. I have a wife and daughter. What about you? Do you live alone?

Yes.

You're not afraid? Living out here?

No.

Some people would be.

Then they should live elsewhere, I suppose.

Listening to their voices as I continued my journey around Black Pond that morning, I realized that such a statement had to have struck Mr Reed as amazingly self-possessed. How different she must have seemed from any other woman he had ever known.

I've seen you teaching. The boys seem very interested in your class.

I hope they are.

They look very attentive.

I've seen you with your class too. You were reading to them in the courtyard.

Oh, yes, a couple weeks ago. I wanted to take advantage of what I thought might be the last day we could go outside before winter sets in.

It was from Byron.

You recognized it.

Yes, I did. My father read a great deal of Byron. Shelley too. And Keats.

At that moment Miss Channing told him of her visit to the cluttered Roman apartment in which Keats had died. His books were still there, she said, along with pages written in Keats's own hand.

The interest Mr Reed by then had come to feel for Miss Channing can be gauged by what he did next.

I know this is rather sudden, Miss Channing. But I wonder if you'd like to have dinner with my family and me tomorrow evening?

I would like that very much, Mr Reed.

Around six, then?
Yes.
Shall I pick you up?
No. I like to walk. Besides, your house is just on the other side of the pond.

Only a ruin remained of Mr Reed's house, and even that was so overgrown, I nearly missed it as I made my way along the water's edge that morning. Hung with vines, its roof covered with forest debris, a scattering of shattered lobster traps strewn across its grounds, it gave off a forlorn sense of having been abruptly abandoned, then left to rot forever.

The stairs creaked loudly as I climbed them, grabbing a shaky railing as I went, then stood silently on the porch for a moment, looking into the house, thinking of the terrible words that had been said within its cramped few rooms, wondering if some element of all that might linger still, like a poison mold growing on the walls. A tiny voice pierced the air. *Mama. Mama.*

It was then that I glanced back out into the yard, where for a single visionary instant I saw a small girl in a white boat closely tethered to the shore, playfully pulling at the oars, her blond hair held in place by a thin red ribbon.

From behind me, a second, disembodied voice called her name. *Mary, Mary.*

I turned and saw Mrs Reed standing at the door of a house that was no longer overgrown with vines, its paint no longer peeling from wood gone black and sodden in the years since its abandonment. She seemed to stare directly through me, as if I were the ghostly one, she brought back to life. Then her eyes narrowed, and she brushed back a loose strand of red hair as she called to her daughter once again, her words echoing in the air, bounding and rebounding across the unresponsive surface of Black Pond. *Mary, come inside.*

I felt a cold wave rush through me, then saw Mary dart past her mother and into the house, laughing happily as she dissolved into its darkened space, her laughter growing faint in the distance, as if she were still running, though now down the passageway of a vast, unending tunnel.

Like a blast of arctic air, I felt all the terror of the past sweep over me in a breathless shiver, as if it were Mrs Reed and her daughter who had drawn me back into their world rather than I who had returned them unwillingly to mine.

I peered into the interior of the house, its front door long ago pulled down. The walls were now stripped and bare, the fireplace crumbling, the floor little more than a loose assemblage of sagging wooden slats. The kitchen was at the rear of the house, silent, empty, a dusky shaft of light pouring in from the rear window, and with nothing but four rust-colored indentations in the floor to indicate the heavy iron stove Mrs Reed had used to prepare dinner for her family.

From court testimony I knew that Mrs Reed had made a special meal for Miss Channing that night, that it had consisted of cabbage and boiled ham, deviled eggs, and a rhubarb pie. I knew that after dinner Mary Reed had busied herself in the front room while the Reeds and Miss Channing lingered over a pot of coffee whose phantom aroma I could almost smell, as if, down all the passing years, it had continued to waft out of the deserted kitchen, filter through the long-abandoned rooms, drift out onto the creaky, leaf-strewn porch where I stood.

Throughout dinner Mr Reed had kept the conversation

centered on Miss Channing, forever returning her to one place or another from her travels, so that during the course of the dinner she'd described everything from the look of Vesuvius as it loomed menacingly over the ruins of Pompeii to the tiny Danish village beloved by Christian Andersen. 'How interesting,' had been Mr Reed's repeated responses. 'How the boys at school must enjoy listening to you.'

As for Abigail Reed, she'd listened quietly, watching her husband as he watched Miss Channing, smiling politely from time to time, nodding occasionally, perhaps already beginning to sense that something unexpected had entered her life, a woman in a pretty dress, talking of the books she'd read, the things she'd seen, a world Mrs Reed had never known, nor thought it important to know. Mr Parsons' voice echoed in the air around me. *How well did you know Abigail Reed?* Her face appeared before me, floating wide-eyed in the green depths. *Not very well.*

The dinner had come to an end at around ten o'clock. By then Mary had drifted out of the front room and disappeared into the darkness surrounding the house. On the porch Miss Channing had politely thanked Mr Reed and Abigail for the dinner, then turned and headed down the stairs and out toward the narrow path that followed along the water's edge. From a distance she heard Mr Reed calling for his daughter, then Mrs Reed's assurance that there was nothing for him to be worried about, that she was only playing near the shed.

It had never occurred to me that it might still be there, but as I eased myself down the stairs of what was left of Mr Reed's house, I looked to the left and saw it. In contrast to the house, it was remarkably well-preserved, an unpainted wooden shed, tall and narrow, with a roof of corrugated tin. It stood in a grove of Norway spruce, perhaps a hundred yards on the other side of the Reed house. The trail that had once led to it was overgrown, and the tin roof was covered with pine needles, but the terrible weathering and neglect that had left the Reed house and Milford Cottage in such disrepair seemed hardly to have affected it.

I approached it reluctantly, as anyone might who knew the terror that had shivered there, the sound of small fingers clawing at its door, the whimpering cries that had filtered through the thick wooden slats, *Daddy, Daddy*.

It was windowless, its walls covered with tar paper, the heavy door trimmed in black rubber, creating a tight seal. Though very dark inside, it nonetheless gave off a sense of spaciousness because of the high roof, the great boards that ran its length nearly ten feet above, the large, rusty hooks that pierced the base of the boards and hung toward the floor like crooked red fingers. During Miss Channing's trial, Mr Parsons had repeatedly referred to it as a 'slaughterhouse', but it had never been any such thing. Rather, it was one of those outbuildings, common at the time, in which large slabs of meat were hung for smoking or salting or simply to be carved into pieces fit for cooking. The floor had been slightly raised, with half-inch spaces between the boards, so that blood could trickle through it, be soaked up by the ground beneath. Mr Reed had rarely used it, although it rested on his land, but Mary had often been seen playing both inside it and nearby.

It was this latter fact that had finally brought Captain Lawrence P. Hamilton of the Massachusetts State Police to its large gray door that afternoon. The captain had already searched Mr Reed's house by then, the little earthen basement beneath it, the cramped, unlighted attic overhead. That's where he'd found a battered cardboard box, a knife, and length of rope inside, along with an old primer curiously inscribed. But Captain Hamilton had not been looking for such things when he'd first come to the Reed house that day. His concerns had been far more immediate than that. For although Mrs Reed had already been found by then, Mary was still missing.

NINE

It was nearly ten in the morning when I returned to my car, pulled myself behind the wheel, and headed back toward Chatham. By then, the atmosphere of the places I'd just revisited – Milford Cottage, Mr Reed's house, the little shed Captain Hamilton had warily approached on that sweltering May afternoon – had sunk into my memory like a dark, ineradicable stain. I thought of all that had followed the events of that terrible day, some immediately, some lingering through all the intervening years. I remembered my father at his desk, desperately trying to reclaim some part of a dream already lost, my mother staring at him bitterly, locked in her own sullen disillusionment. I saw a young world grow old, the boys of Chatham School expanding into adulthood, then shrinking into old age just as I had, though with less than they had to show for my time on earth, wifeless, childless, a man known primarily for a single boyhood act.

Then, in the midst of all that dead or aged company, I glimpsed the youthful face of Sarah Doyle.

I remember that it was a Saturday afternoon in early November, only a week following Miss Channing's dinner with Mr Reed and his family. I was sitting on a bench at the edge of the coastal bluff. On the beach below I could see several people strolling about or lounging under large striped umbrellas. There was no one in the water, of course, the season for swimming having passed by then. But far out to sea, I could make out the white sail of a fifteen-footer as it skirted along the shore-line. Watching it drift by, I yearned to be on it, to be cutting across an illimitable blue vastness.

Sarah was wearing a long blue skirt and red blouse when she came up to me that morning, and she'd wrapped a flowered scarf over her shoulders, the knot tied loosely at her throat. Her hair was long and extraordinarily dark, and had a continually frazzled and unruly look to it, as if she'd just been taken by the heels, turned upside down, and shaken violently, her hair left in tangled disarray.

Still, for all that, she was quite a lovely girl, the same age I was, and I often found my attention drawn to her as she swept past my room or bounded up the stairs, but most particularly when I found her lounging on the porch swing, her arms at her sides, her eyes half-closed and languid, as if lost in a dream of surrender.

In those days, of course, the classes were more rigidly divided than they have since become, and so I knew that whatever my feelings for Sarah might be, they would always have to be carefully guarded. For unlike the other deadly sins, lust is sometimes joined to love, and such a prospect would no doubt have met with stern disapproval from my mother. And so, up until that day, I'd allowed myself only those hidden thoughts and secret glances that were within my sphere, thinking of Sarah at night, but by day returning her to the status of a servant girl.

'And hello to you, sir,' she said as she approached me, the Irish lilt now striking me as somewhat thrilling and exotic.

I nodded. 'Hi, Sarah.'

She smiled brightly, but seemed unsure of what to do next. 'Well, should I sit with you, then?' she asked.

'Sure,' I said casually, as if the nearness of her body meant no more to me than that of the lamppost a block away.

She sat down and looked out over the water. I did the same, careful to conceal the fact that all I could think of was her skin, the color of milk, her hair black as coal, the mysteries of her body infinitely enticing.

As to her history, I knew only the broad details. But from the bits and pieces of conversation I'd overheard as I roamed the house on Myrtle Street, I'd learned of her mother's early death in Limerick and had some picture of the bleak coastal village she'd grown up in after that. She'd had three brothers, two killed in the Great War, one an aimless drifter who'd disappeared into the dreary slums of East London. As to her father, he'd died of tuberculosis five years before, leaving her with only enough money to book passage to America. I'd heard my father speak grimly of that passage, the horrors of the steerage, the way the men had leered at her in the dank quarters of the ship's belly, the stale bread and dried beef that alone had sustained her until she'd finally disembarked at the Port of Boston.

After that Sarah had fallen upon the mercy of the Irish Immigrant Aid Society, who'd fed, clothed, and given her shelter until she'd landed a job as a serving girl in a great Boston house. It was there she'd met my father three years later, told him how much she longed for village life again, particularly if the village happened to be located near the sea. By all accounts she had spoken to my father with great earnestness, and my father, never one to remain deaf to such heartfelt solicitations, had first cleared it with

89

her employer, then offered her a place in our house at Chatham, one she'd taken without a moment's further thought and performed dutifully ever since.

But as I looked at her that morning nearly two years later, she seemed not altogether pleased with her earlier decision. There was a melancholy wistfulness in her eyes, a deep dissatisfaction.

'Something's bothering you,' I said bluntly, my own intense restlessness now spilling over into a general sense of radical impatience.

Her eyes shot over to me, as if I'd accused her of stealing the silverware. 'Now, why do you say that?' she asked in a sharp, defensive tone.

I gave her a knowing look.

She turned her head away, touched her cheek. 'I've nothing to complain about. I'll not be thought of as a whiner.'

I was too consumed with my own complaint to feel much tenderness toward Sarah's, so I said nothing more.

This seemed to jar her. 'Well I want you to know that I don't at all regret coming to Chatham. Not at all, that's for sure. I wouldn't ever want your father to think I wasn't grateful for what he's done for me. It's just that I didn't come to America to be a serving girl. I'm after more than that. I want to better myself, to break away from the cleaning and cooking. To *be* something, don't you know. Not just a serving girl ... like I am now.' She shook her head violently. 'It's no good, feeling like I do. Like I'm all tied up in ropes.'

I could see it in her face, a vast, billowing need to leap beyond the mundane and unglamorous life she otherwise seemed destined for, and which, since reading Mr Channing's book, I had also begun to feel far more

powerfully than I ever had before. Watching her agitation, the restlessness that swept over her, I suddenly felt
absolutely in league with her, the two of us castaways on
a narrow strip of land whose strictures and limitations
both appalled and threatened to destroy us. I saw my
father as grimly standing in our way, reading his ancient
books, mouthing their stony maxims. In my mind I heard
his steady drone: *Do this, do that. Be this, be that.* I had
never felt such a deep contempt for everything he stood
for.

'Maybe you should just take off, Sarah,' I told her. 'Just
take the train to Boston and disappear.'

Even as I said it, I saw myself doing it. It would be a
moment of wild flight, the real world dissolving behind
me, all its gray walls crumbling, the sky a vast expanse
before me, my life almost as limitless as the unbounded
universe.

'You should do whatever you have to, Sarah,' I continued boldly. Then, as if to demonstrate my zeal, I said, 'If
I can help you in any way, let me know.'

Her response came as a question that utterly surprised
me. For it had nothing to do with flight, with night trains
to Boston, or disappearing into the multitude. Instead, she
studied me intently, then said, 'Do you remember Miss
Channing? The lady that came to the house at the end of
summer, the one that's teaching art?'

'I'm in her class.'

'Such a fine lady, the way she talks and all. So smart,
don't you think?'

'Yes, she is.'

Sarah hesitated, now suddenly reluctant to ask what
she had perhaps come to ask me all along. Then the wall
fell, and she spoke. 'Do you think that such a fine lady as

Miss Channing is – talking so fine the way she does – that she might be of a mind to teach me how to read?'

We headed down Myrtle Street together the following Sunday morning, Sarah walking beside me, a basket of freshly baked cookies hanging from one arm, her offering to Miss Channing.

At the bluff we swung to the left, passed beneath the immense shadow of the lighthouse, then down the curving road that led into the village.

'What if Miss Channing says no,' Sarah asked. 'What if she won't teach me?'

'I don't think she'll say no, Sarah,' I said, though I know that part of me hoped that she would, wanted Sarah to be refused so that she would have to consider the other choice I'd already suggested, far bolder, as it seemed to me, edged in that frenzied sense of escape whose attractions had begun to overwhelm me.

'But what if she doesn't want to?'

I answered with a determination that was new to me, an icy ruthlessness already in my voice. 'Then we'll find another way.'

This appeared to satisfy her. She smiled brightly and took my arm with her free hand.

Still, by the time we'd turned onto Plymouth Road, her fear had taken root again. She walked more slowly, her feet treading very softly over the bed of oyster shells, as if it were an expensive carpet and she did not want to mar it with her prints.

'I hope I look all right, then,' she said as we neared Miss Channing's cottage.

She'd dressed as formally as she knew how, in what looked like her own schoolgirl version of the Chatham

School uniform. Her skirt was long and dark, her blouse an immaculate white. She'd tied a black bow at her throat and pinned a small cameo to her chest, one that had belonged to her mother, her sole inheritance, she told me.

It was not a look I admired, and even as I gazed at her, I imagined her quite differently, dressed like Ramona in *The Gypsy Band*, bare-shouldered, with large hoop earrings, a lethal glint in her eye, a knife clutched between her teeth as she danced around the raging campfire. It was as adolescent a fantasy as any I had ever had, and yet it was also tinged with a darkness that was very old, a sense of woman as most lusty and desirable when poised at the edge of murder.

At Milford Cottage Sarah glanced down at her skirt and frowned. 'There's dust all over the hem.' She bent forward and brushed at the bottom of her skirt. 'Sticks like glue,' she said, finally giving up. Then she lifted her head determinedly and I felt her hand tighten around my arm. 'All right,' she said. 'I'm ready.'

We walked down the little walkway that led to the door of the cottage. Without a pause Sarah knocked gently, glanced at me with a bright, nervous smile, and waited.

When no one answered, she looked at me quizzically.

'Try again,' I said. 'It's early. She must be here.'

Sarah did as I told her, but still there was no answer.

I remembered the occasion several weeks before, when I'd come to the cottage at nearly the same time, found it empty, as it now appeared to be, Miss Channing strolling along the edge of the forest.

'Sometimes she takes a walk in the morning,' I told Sarah confidently, although I could not be sure of any such thing. 'Let's look around.'

We stepped away from the door, walked to the far side of the cottage, then around it to the rear yard, toward the pond. A heavy morning mist still hung over the water, its lingering cloud rolling out over the edges of the land, covering it in fog.

For a moment Sarah and I stood, facing the pond, the impenetrable mist that drifted out from it covering the small area behind the cottage.

Nothing moved, or seemed to move, neither the air, nor the mist that cloaked the water, nor anything around us, until suddenly I saw a figure drift slowly toward us, the thick gray fog thinning steadily as she came nearer so that she appeared to rise toward us smoothly, like a corpse floating up from a pool of clouded water.

'Miss Channing,' Sarah said.

Miss Channing smiled slightly. 'I was out by the pond,' she said. 'I thought I heard someone at the door.' Dimly I could see the easel she'd set up at the water's edge, a large pad of drawing paper already in place upon it, all of it still shrouded in curling wisps of gray cloud.

'This is Sarah Doyle,' I told her. 'You may remember her from when you had dinner at our house the night you first came to Chatham.'

Sarah lifted the basket toward her. 'I brought you some cookies, Miss Channing,' she said nervously. 'I baked them special for you. As payment, ma'am.'

'Payment?' Miss Channing asked. 'For what?'

For an instant, Sarah hesitated, and I could see that she believed her entire future to be at stake at that moment in her life, all her limitless prospects to be placed in someone else's hands.

'For teaching me to read,' she said boldly, eyes on Miss Channing's face. 'If you'd be willing to do it, ma'am.'

Miss Channing did not pause a beat in her response. 'Of course I will,' she said, and stepped forward to take the basket from Sarah's trembling hand.

An hour later they were still at it. From my place at the edge of the water I could see Miss Channing sitting at a small table she'd brought from the cottage and placed beneath the willow tree. Sarah sat opposite her, a writing pad before her, along with a sheet of paper upon which Miss Channing had written the alphabet in large block letters.

I heard Miss Channing say, 'All right. Begin.'

Sarah kept her eyes fixed upon Miss Channing's, careful not to let them stray toward the page as she began. 'A, B, C ...'

She continued through the alphabet, stumbling here and there, pausing until Miss Channing finally provided the missing letter, then rushing on gleefully until she reached the end.

'Good,' Miss Channing said quietly. 'Now. Once more.'

Again Sarah made her way through the alphabet, this time stopping only once, at U, then plunging ahead rapidly, completing it in a flourish of pride and breathlessness.

When she'd gotten to the end of it, Miss Channing offered her an encouraging smile. 'Very good,' she said. 'You're a very bright girl, Sarah.'

'Thank you,' Sarah said, a broad smile lighting her face.

They continued their work until almost noon, when I heard Miss Channing say, 'Well, I think we had a very good lesson, Sarah.'

Sarah rose, then did a small curtsy, a servant girl once again, taking leave of her superior. 'Thank you, Miss

Channing.' Her earlier nervousness had now completely returned. 'Do you think we could have another lesson sometime, then?' she asked hesitantly.

'Yes, of course we could,' Miss Channing told her. 'Actually, we should have a lesson once a week. Would Sunday mornings be all right?'

'Oh, yes, ma'am,' Sarah burst out, a great relief and happiness sweeping over her. 'You can depend on it, Miss Channing. I'll be here every Sunday morning from this day on.'

'Good,' Miss Channing said. 'I'll be waiting for you.' She turned to me. I could see that something was on her mind. 'You didn't bring a sketchbook with you, Henry,' she said.

I shrugged. 'I guess I didn't ...'

'You should have it with you all the time,' Miss Channing told me. She smiled, then said a line I later repeated to Mr Parsons. 'Art is like love. It's all or nothing.'

With that she quickly walked into the cottage, then returned, this time with a sketchbook in her hand.

'Take one of mine,' she said as she handed it to me. 'I have a few left from my time in Africa.'

I looked at the book, the soft burgundy cover, the clean, thick paper that rested beneath it. Nothing had ever looked more beautiful to me. I felt as if she'd passed me a golden locket or a strand of her hair.

'Now, don't let me see you without a sketchbook ever again, Henry,' she said with a mocking sternness.

I tucked the book beneath my arm. 'I won't,' I told her.

She gazed at me a moment, then nodded toward the table and chairs. 'Would you mind taking all this back into the cottage?' she asked.

'Not at all.'

I grasped one chair in each hand and headed for the cottage. On the way I heard Sarah say, 'So you were painting this morning, were you?' And Miss Channing's reply, 'Yes. I often do in the morning.'

Inside the cottage I placed the chairs at the wooden table in the kitchen. Through the rear window I could see Miss Channing and Sarah as they strolled toward the easel that still stood at the water's edge, the pages of the drawing book fluttering slightly in a breeze from off the pond. Miss Channing had opened the drawing book and was showing one of her sketches to Sarah. Sarah had folded her hands before her in the way Miss Channing often did, and was listening attentively to her every word.

After a while I turned and walked back into the small living room at the front of the cottage. The picture of Miss Channing's father still hung in the same place. But since that time, several sketches had been added to the wall, carefully wrought line drawings that she had brought out of Africa and which portrayed vast, uncluttered vistas, borderless and uncharted, devoid of both animals and people, the land and sky stretching out into a nearly featureless infinity. This, I knew, was her father's world, unlimited and unrestrained.

I stared at her drawings a few seconds longer, then walked outside again, retrieved the table, placed it just inside the cottage door, and made my way over to where Miss Channing and Sarah still stood at the edge of the pond.

'I like that one,' Sarah said brightly, her eyes on one of the drawings Miss Channing had just displayed.

'It's not finished yet,' Miss Channing told her. 'I was working on it this morning.'

I peered at the drawing. It showed a body of water that only faintly resembled Black Pond. For it was much larger, as well as being surrounded by a world of empty hills and valleys that appeared to roll on forever. So much so, that the mood of the drawing, its immensity and sense of vast, unbounded space struck me as very similar to the ones I'd just seen inside the cottage. But there was something different about it too. For near the center of the drawing, hovering near the middle of a huge, unmoving water, Miss Channing had drawn a man at the oars of a small boat. His face was caught in a shaft of light, his eyes locked on the farther shore.

Sarah leaned forward, looking closely at the figure in the boat. 'That man there, isn't that—'

'Leland Reed,' Miss Channing said, the first time I'd ever heard her say his name.

Sarah smiled. 'Yes, Mr Reed. From Chatham School.'

Miss Channing let her eyes settle upon the painting. She drew in a deep breath and let it out slowly, a gesture which, months later, after I'd described it to Mr Parsons, he forever called 'a lover's sigh'.

TEN

I was still thinking of Miss Channing's drawing a few minutes later when I brought my car to a halt in front of Dalmatian's Cafe. It had long been my favorite place in Chatham, not only because it had been the place where the boys of Chatham School had sometimes gathered after a game or on the weekends, but because it had pretty much remained unchanged from that now-distant time. The grill and counter were still in the same place; so were the booths by the window. Even the old rusty plow blade that Mrs Winthrop, the cafe's first owner, claimed her great-grandfather had used to break ground on their family farm in 1754 still hung on the back wall, though now hemmed in by bright neon signs hawking beer and soft drinks.

I took my usual seat in the booth farthest from the door, the one that nestled in a corner by the window, and from which I could look out and watch the village's activities. And without warning I saw Dr Craddock pull up in front of our Myrtle Street house just as he had on that night so long ago, driving the sleek black sedan in which he paid house calls in the twenties, saw him as he walked through the rain to where my father stood gloomily on the porch. The doctor had been dressed in a black suit, and had taken off his hat as he came up the stairs, his question delivered almost like a plea. *I'm sorry to trouble you, Arthur, but could we talk about the little girl?*

And as I sat there hearing the doctor's voice, time reversed itself, old buildings replacing more recent ones, the blue pavement of Main Street suddenly buried beneath a stretch of earth marked by both wooden wagon wheels and the narrow rubber tread of clanging Model A's.

Far in the distance I saw an old iron bell materialize out of the motionless air of the long-empty bell tower of what had once been Chatham School, then begin to move, as if it had been pushed by an invisible hand, its implacable toll reverberating over the buildings and playing fields of Chatham School summoning us to our classes in the morning, and releasing us from them in the afternoon, ringing matins and vespers with an authority and sense of purpose that had little diminished from the time of monks and kings.

And then, as if from some high aerie where I sat perched above them, I saw the boys pour out of the great wooden doors at the front of the school, sweep down its wide cement stairs, and fan out into the surrounding streets, myself among them, the gray school jacket now draped over my shoulders, its little shield embroidered on the front pocket, along with the single phrase, *Veritas et Virtus*, truth and virtue, the words my father had long ago selected as the motto of Chatham School.

It was a Friday afternoon in late November, around three weeks after I'd taken Sarah to Miss Channing's cottage for her first reading lesson. By then Sarah and I had become somewhat closer, she no longer simply a servant girl, I no longer simply the son of her master. Her yearning to make something of herself fired my own emerging vision of living an artist's life, a life lived 'on the run', as Jonathan Channing had called it, and whose vast ambitions Sarah's own great hope seemed to mirror in some way.

We were on our way to the lighthouse that afternoon, Sarah in a cheerful mood, strolling almost gaily over a carpet of red and yellow leaves, Sarah with a new purse she'd bought at a village shop, I with my sketchbook tucked firmly beneath my arm.

'I just want you to look at them before I show them to Miss Channing,' I told her as we strode across the street, then onto the broad yard that swept out from the white-washed base of the lighthouse. 'And if they're bad, Sarah, I want you to tell me so. I don't want Miss Channing to see them if they're bad.'

Sarah flashed me a smile. 'Give them to me, Henry, and stop going on so about it,' she said, playfully snatching the sketchbook from my hand.

'It's just pictures of places around here mostly,' I added as she opened it. 'Just beaches and stuff.'

But to me they were anything but local scenes. For what they portrayed was not Chatham, but my view of it. As such, they were moody drawings of shrouded seascapes and gloomy woods, each done with an unmistakable intensity, everything oddly torn and twisted, as if I'd begun with an ordinary scene in mind, some commonplace beach or village lane, then dipped it in black ink and put it through a grinder.

And yet, for all their adolescent excess, they'd had a certain sense of balance and proportion, the intricate bark of a distant tree, the grittiness of beach sand, drawings that suggested not only the look of things, but their physical textures. There was a vision of the world in them as well, a feeling for the claustrophobia of life, so that even the vistas, wide though they seemed, appeared pinched and walled in at the same time, the earth, for all its spinning vastness, no more than a single locked room from which nothing seemed able to escape.

Sarah remained silent while she flipped through my sketchbook. Then, with a quick flick of her hand, she closed it, a wry smile on her lips.

'I like them, Henry,' she said happily. 'I like them a lot.'

She no doubt expected a smile to burst onto my face, but nothing of the sort happened. Instead, I stared at her with a decidedly troubled look. 'But do you think Miss Channing will like them?' I demanded.

She looked at me as if the question were absurd. 'Of course she will,' she said. She gave me a slight nudge. 'Besides, even if Miss Channing didn't like your drawings, all she'd want to do is teach you how to make them better.'

'All right,' I said, drawing the sketchbook from her hand as I got to my feet.

I walked a short distance away from her across the lighthouse grounds, then stopped and glanced back to where she remained seated on the little cement bench. 'Thank you, Sarah,' I said.

She watched me closely, clearly sensing my insecurity, her teasing, carefree mood now entirely vanished. 'Do you want me to come with you, Henry?'

I knew she'd read my mind. 'Yes, I think I do.'

'All right,' Sarah said, coming to her feet with a sweep of her skirt. 'But only as far as the courtyard, not into Miss Channing's room. When you show her your drawings, you should do it on your own.'

I'd expected to find her alone, doing what she normally did at the end of the school day, washing the tables and putting away her supplies. It was only after I'd reached the door of her classroom and peered inside that I realized she was not. Even so, I don't know why it surprised me so, finding Mr Reed in her room, leaning casually against the front table while she stood a few feet away, her back to him, washing the blackboard with a wet cloth. After all, I'd often seen them arriving at school in the morning and leaving together in the afternoon, Mr Reed behind the wheel of his sedan, Miss Channing seated quite properly on the passenger side. I'd seen them together at other times as well, strolling side by side down the school corridor, or sitting on the steps, having lunch, usually with a gathering of other teachers, yet slightly off to the side, a mood surrounding them like an invisible field, so that even in the midst of others, they seemed intimately alone.

'Hello,' Miss Channing said when she turned away from the blackboard and saw me standing at the door. 'Please, come in, Henry.'

I came into her room with a reluctance and sense of intrusion that I still can't entirely explain, unless, from time to time, we are touched by the opposite of aftermath, feel not the swirling eddies of a retreating wave, but the dark pull of an approaching one.

'Hello, Henry,' Mr Reed said.

I nodded silently as I came down the aisle, sliding the sketchbook back slightly, trying to conceal it.

'I thought you'd be at the game,' Mr Reed said, referring to the lacrosse match that had been scheduled for that same afternoon. 'It's against New Bedford Prep, you know.' He glanced toward Miss Channing. 'Traditionally, New Bedford Prep has been our most dreaded opponent.'

I said nothing, tormented now with second thoughts about showing my drawings to Miss Channing since Mr

Reed would be there to see them too. I'm not sure I would have shown them at all had not Miss Channing's eyes drifted down to the sketchbook beneath my arm.

'Did you bring that for me?' she asked.

She could see my reluctance to hand it over. To counteract it, she smiled and said, 'You know, my father used to stand me in front of a bare wall. He'd say, "Look closely, Libby. On that wall there is a great painting by someone who was afraid to show it." If no one ever sees your work, Henry, then what's the point of doing it at all? Let's see what you've done.'

I drew the sketchbook from beneath my arm and handed it to her.

She placed it on the table and began to turn the pages, studying one drawing at a time, commenting from time to time, mentioning this detail or that one, how the trees appeared to bulge slightly, something in them trying to get out, or the way the sea tossed and heaved.

'They have a certain – I don't know – a certain *controlled uncontrol* about them, don't you think?' she asked Mr Reed.

He nodded, his eyes on her. 'Yes, I do.'

She drew in a long breath. 'If we could only live that way,' she said, her eyes still on one of my drawings.

She'd said it softly, without undue emphasis, but I saw Mr Reed's face suddenly alter. 'Yes,' he said, his voice little more than a whisper, yet oddly charged as well, as if he were responding not to an idle remark made in an open room, but to a note slipped surreptitiously beneath his chamber door.

I left Miss Channing's room a few minutes later, reasonably satisfied with her response, but in other ways somewhat troubled and ill at ease, as if something had been denied me, a moment alone with her.

'I knew she'd like them,' Sarah said firmly when I told her what had happened.

She'd waited for me at the back of the school, the two of us now moving down its central corridor, other boys brushing past us, a few turning to get a better look at Sarah after she'd gone by.

Once outside, we returned to our little cement bench beside the lighthouse. From it we could see Chatham School just across the street.

'I wish I could leave here,' I said abruptly, almost spitefully, my mind turning from my drawings to the escape route they represented for me. Not art, as I know now, but an artist's life as I then imagined it.

Sarah looked surprised by the depth of my contempt. 'But you have everything, Henry. A family. Everything.'

I shook my head. 'I don't care. I hate this place.'

'Where do you want to go?'

'I don't know. Somewhere else, that's all.'

She looked at me knowingly. 'There are lots of places worse than Chatham,' she said.

It was then that Miss Channing and Mr Reed came out the front door of the school and began strolling slowly toward the parking lot. Despite the formal distance they maintained, the fact that they at no point touched, there was something in the way they walked along together that drew my attention to them, called forth those first small suspicions that would later grow to monstrous size.

'I'll bet they'd like to go someplace else too,' I said.

Sarah said nothing, but only turned toward the school and watched as Mr Reed and Miss Channing continued toward Mr Reed's car. When they reached it, he opened the door for Miss Channing, waited until she'd gotten in, then closed it once again.

The car rumbled past us a few seconds later, Mr Reed at the wheel as always, and Miss Channing seated beside the passenger door. A late afternoon chill had settled over the village by that time, and I noticed that she'd rolled her window up to shut it out. Her face, mirrored in the glass, seemed eerily translucent as the car swept by.

More than anything, I remember that she appeared to sit in a great stillness as the car drifted by. Just as she would some months later, after the verdict had been rendered, and she'd been hustled down the courthouse stairs and rushed into the backseat of a black patrol car. She'd sat next to the window on that occasion too, staring straight ahead as the car inched through the noisy, milling crowd, slowly picking up speed as it continued forward, bearing her away.

ELEVEN

I found that I couldn't go directly to my office after leaving Dalmatian's Cafe that morning. For there was yet another place that called to me even more darkly than Milford Cottage or Mr Reed's house or the silent reaches of Black Pond. For although the final act had occurred there, its tragic origins lay somewhere else, a different conspiracy entirely from the one Mr Parsons felt so certain he'd unmasked in the courtroom the day I took the stand.

And so, after a second cup of coffee at Dalmatian's Cafe, I walked back to my car, pulled out of the parking space, and headed up the steadily ascending coastal road that curved along the outerbank to Myrtle Street.

At the top of the bluff I wheeled to the right. The lighthouse gleamed in the bright morning air as I drove past it, a vast blue sky above, with only wisps of skirting clouds to suggest the tearing wind and rain that had rocked us during most of the preceding week.

Dolphin Hall rose just down the street from the lighthouse, and even at that early hour there were a couple of cars parked in its lot. One of them, a sleek BMW, bright red with thin lines of shimmering chrome, was parked beneath the same ancient oak that had once shaded the battered chassis of Mr Reed's old Model T.

I pulled in next to it and stopped. Through my windshield I could see the gallery a few yards away, its red brick portico little changed since the days when the building had housed the boys of Chatham School.

Other things had been altered, of course. The tall, rattling windows had been replaced by sturdy double-paned glass, and a wide metal ramp now glided up the far right side of the cement stairs, granting access to the handicapped.

But more than any of these obvious changes, I noticed that a tall plaster replica of the lighthouse had been placed on the front lawn in almost exactly the spot where Miss Channing's column of faces had briefly stood, my own face near the center of the column, my father's near the bottom, where a circular bed of tulips had been planted.

On the day the school's governing board ordered it battered down, my father had stood with his arms folded over his chest, listening to the ring of the hammer as it shattered the plaster faces one by one. Standing rigidly with his back to the small group of people who'd come to observe its destruction, clothed in his neatly pressed black suit, he'd watched it all silently and with complete dignity. It was only after it had been done, the faces gathered in a dusty pile, that he'd glanced back toward me, his head cocked at an angle that allowed the morning sun to touch his face, its brief glimmer caught in the tears of his eyes.

The cement walkway to the gallery had been replaced by a more attractive cobblestone, but the path itself was still as straight and narrow as before.

At the door, a small cardboard sign read simply WELCOME, so I opened the door and walked inside, entering what had once been Chatham School for the first time in all the many years that had passed since its closing.

From the foyer I could see the wide central corridor that had led from the front of the school all the way to the rear courtyard, the stairs that rose toward the second floor dormitory, and even the door of what had once been my father's office, its brass knob reflecting the newly installed halogen lights.

Beside the front window there was a little table filled with information about the various exhibitors represented in the gallery. I reached for the one nearest me and moved down the corridor, more or less pretending to read it, acting quite unnecessarily like some secret agent who'd been sent from the past to bring back news from the present, inform the ghostly legions as to how it had turned out.

I'd gotten only a little way down the corridor before I was intercepted.

'Well, Mr Griswald. Hello.'

I recognized the man who greeted me as Bill Kipling, the gallery's owner, and whose grandfather, Joe Kipling, had once played lacrosse for Chatham School. Joe had been a lanky, energetic boy, later a town selectman and real estate baron, more recently an old man who'd swallowed handfuls of vitamins and food supplements before he'd finally died of liver cancer in a private hospital room in Hyannis.

'Well, what made you decide to drop by after all this time?' the younger Kipling asked cheerily.

'Just thinking about old times, I guess. When Chatham School was here.'

'My grandfather went to Chatham School, you know.'

'Yes, I remember him.'

And saying that, I saw Joe Kipling not as a boy rushing forward with a lacrosse stick raised in the air, but as he'd stood beside the gray column, a sledgehammer in his hand, swinging it fiercely at the plaster faces Miss Channing had fashioned, a layer of dust gathering upon the shoulders of his school jacket.

'My father loved Chatham School,' his grandson told me now.

'We all did.'

Some few minutes of small talk followed, then he left me to browse through the gallery undisturbed, knowing that I had not really come to see the pictures he'd hung from its walls, but to hear the shouts and laughter of the boys as they'd tumbled chaotically down the wide staircase at seven-thirty sharp, some fully dressed, others still looping their suspenders over their shoulders or pulling on their jackets, but always under the watchful eye of my father. For each morning he'd taken up his position at the bottom of the stairs, his arms folded over his chest like a Roman centurion, greeting each boy by name, then adding a quick 'Work well, play well.' I could still remember how embarrassed I'd felt at such a scene each morning, the boys rushing by, trying so hard to please, to be what my father wanted them to be, sturdy, upright 'good citizens'. At those times he'd appeared almost comical to me, a caricature of the Victorian schoolmaster, an artifact from that dead time, bloodless as a bone dug out of an ancient pit. Of all the mired and passionless things I did not wish to be, my father was chief among them. As for the 'good life' about which he sometimes spoke, standing before the boys in his Ciceronian pose, it struck me as little more than a life lived without vitality or imagination, a life hardly worth living, and from which death could come only as a sweet release.

His office had faced the staircase, and its great mahogany door was still in place. Stepping up to it, I could almost hear him uttering the ominous words I'd overheard as I'd swept down the stairs that faced his office on that drizzly afternoon in May of 1927. The door had still been fully open when I'd begun to make my way from the upper landing, but he'd begun to close it, his attention so focused on the people already inside his office that he hadn't seen me descending the stairs. 'This is Mr Parsons, the commonwealth attorney,' I'd heard him say as he stepped farther into his office, slowly drawing the door behind him.

I'd been able to glance inside the office and see a man in a dark suit, a homburg held in his hand. He stood in front of my father's desk, a large cardboard box in the chair beside him. 'Please sit down, Miss Channing,' I heard him say.

Through the narrowing space that remained open as I reached the bottom of the stairs, I could see Miss Channing standing stiffly before Mr Parsons, her hands folded together at her waist, her hair in a tight bun. As the door closed, I heard her reply to him, her words spoken softly, but in a tone that struck me as deathly cold. 'I prefer to stand,' she said.

The door to what had formerly been my father's office now had a little sign tacked to it, one that read 'Private', so I could not go in. I stood, facing it, remembering that a completely different sign had once been there, one that had read 'Arthur H. Griswald, Headmaster'.

My father had removed that sign himself, placed it in a shoe box, and kept it in the cellar of the little house we rented after leaving Chatham School. But it was not very difficult for me to imagine that it was still in place, and that beyond the door his desk was still there too, along with the crystal inkwell my mother had given him on their tenth anniversary, the ceremonial quill pen he'd used to sign important documents, even the brass lamp with the dark green shade that had given the room an indisputable authority.

I knew that a whole world had once held its ground in that small room, made what amounted to its last stand. How fully all of that had been visible in my father's face the day he'd marched onto the front lawn of the school, then instructed Joe Kipling to take his place before Miss Channing's carved column of faces. He'd paused a moment, his gaze lingering on the column, then turned to Joe and given the order with a single word: *Begin*.

I felt my eyes close against the awesome spectacle of that moment, the sound of the hammer as it slammed into the column, the severe and unsmiling faces of the people who watched as Joe Kipling pounded it into dust.

I turned away from the door. On either side, large rooms were filled with paintings of more or less modern design, the paint splattered upon the canvas or lathered over it in chaotic swirls, fragments of color pressed jaggedly one against another. I could only imagine how their disharmony would have offended my father, how much he would have preferred the idyllic scenes and passive landscapes he'd scrupulously selected for these same corridors during his tenure as headmaster, works governed by order and design, harmony and the laws of reason, a vision of life he'd striven to maintain at Chatham School ... and failed.

Toward the rear of the corridor I stepped into the room that had once been Mr Reed's. Able to accommodate no more than ten or twelve student desks, its large windows looked out into the courtyard. Through them he had been able to see the little converted storeroom where Miss

Channing taught. How often he must have glanced out those windows and caught her in his eyes, a slender young woman with raven black hair and light blue eyes, standing behind a sculpting pedestal or before an easel, spinning stories of fabled lands and tragic people while she worked with paint and clay. Although I never saw it happen, I'm sure that from time to time Miss Channing must have glanced toward her own window and caught Mr Reed watching her from across the courtyard, at first through veils of autumn rain, then through swirls of windblown snow, and finally through the shimmering air of that final spring, their eyes now locked in a dreadful stare, a look as desperate and harrowing as the words I'd heard them speak: *How do you want to do it? Without looking back.*

I didn't remain in Mr Reed's classroom for very long. For I could feel a heat and sharpness in the air, as if it had begun to sizzle.

And so I turned and fled to the courtyard where the outbuilding that had once been Miss Channing's classroom still stood, though it had long been converted into the gallery's framing shop.

The door was open, and standing at its threshold I could see the wide counter that ran along the rear of the building, stacks of empty frames leaning against the wall behind it. Frame samples of various colors and materials – brass, wood, aluminum – hung from a large square of pressed board. To the right, where I'd once sat at the front of the room, a work space had been created, complete with a large table and circular saw. A layer of sawdust and wood chips coated the floor beneath the table, and a bright red metal toolbox rested alongside.

Clearly, of the several places I visited that day, it was Miss Channing's room that had been most transformed. No trace remained of the tables and chairs where the boys had sat watching her sculpt and paint, nor of the sculpting pedestals and easels and canvases we'd used to fashion our own crude works of art; nor the cabinet where she'd returned the room's modest supplies before joining Mr Reed for their drive home each afternoon; nor even the portraits of Washington and Lincoln that had watched us from the room's opposite walls, their faces stern but kindly, like two old-fashioned fathers.

And yet, for all that, I sensed Miss Channing's presence more within that transformed and cluttered space than in any of the other places I'd revisited. And I could feel Mr Reed as well, the two of them together as I had found them on that long-ago afternoon, she behind the front table, he at the far door, moving toward her irrevocably, his words spoken so softly that I'd barely been able to hear them: *Because I love you, I can do it.*

It was more than I could bear. And so I wheeled around and walked back through the courtyard and down the central corridor of the building, then swiftly out of it, like someone in flight from a surging fire.

At last I came to a halt at the little cement bench where Sarah and I had sat together years before, the lighthouse behind us, the school in front. In my mind I saw Miss Channing and Mr Reed walk once again to the car beneath the oak, Mr Reed open the door, Miss Channing slip inside, the car begin to move, turning out of the parking lot and onto Myrtle Street, finally drifting by me as it had that day so many years before, Miss Channing staring straight ahead, so silent and so still, with nothing but a dark strand of loosened hair to leave its mark upon her face.

*

I returned to my office, sat down at my desk, my eyes involuntarily drifting over to the archive my father had long ago assembled, perhaps as something to remind him of his fall, though without in the least knowing that it had been mine as well.

I rose and walked to the file cabinet beneath my father's portrait. Glancing up at it, I heard his voice in old age, hung with the bleakness of his final years, perhaps even the deepest of its disappointments: *So there'll never be a wife, Henry? Never a child?* My answer as stark as it had always been: *No.*

I turned away from the portrait, opened the cabinet, and pulled out the forms I would need to begin my work for Clement Boggs, already considering what the last phase of that work would inevitably require, the cruel lyrics of a dreadful song playing in my mind as I made my way back to my desk:

> Alice Craddock
> Locked in a paddock
> Where's your daddy gone?

PART III

TWELVE

During the final years of his life, with my mother gone, and few means of passing the idle hours, my father took to walking through the countryside. I was a middle-aged bachelor by then, with little to engage me but my legal practice. And so I often accompanied him on his rambles, the two of us first driving to a particular spot, then setting off into the woods. Usually we went to Nickerson State Park, where the trails were easiest. But from time to time we would wander into some more remote area, park the car along the road, then follow a less well-defined path around a nearby hill or up a gently angled slope.

Most of these walks were routine affairs, my father talking quietly about whatever he'd read most recently, a book or magazine article that had briefly held his attention. The past, particularly his years at Chatham School, seemed nearly to have disappeared from his consciousness altogether.

Then, one afternoon only a year before his death, we found ourselves on a hilltop outside Chatham, the spires and roofs of the village in the distance, and down below, like a dark, sightless eye, the unruffled waters of Black Pond.

He remained silent for a time, but I could see that he was struggling to say something, release some pronouncement he'd long kept inside. It was a struggle that surprised me.

For except for those times when my mother had insisted upon bringing up the subject, my father had seemed more than satisfied to let all thought of the Chatham School Affair sink unmourned into oblivion.

'So much death, Henry,' he said finally. 'Down there on Black Pond. So much destruction.'

I saw bodies swirling in green water, small hands clawing at a strip of black rubber, a boat lolling in an empty sea, a middle-aged woman rocking on her front porch, her eyes vacant and emotionless, staring into nowhere, her hair a sickly yellow streaked with gray.

My father continued to peer down at the pond, his hands behind his back, two wrinkled claws. 'I sometimes forget that I ever really knew them. Miss Channing and Mr Reed, I mean.' He shook his head. 'How about you, Henry? Do you ever think of them?'

I glanced about, recalling the slow trudge we'd all made up the hill that morning, Mr Reed in the lead, Miss Channing just behind him. I could still feel the cold November air that had surrounded us, how we'd had to brush snowflakes from our eyes.

'I came up here with them,' I said. 'To the top of this same hill. Sarah came with us too.' My eyes settled on the very place where we'd stood together and looked out over the pond. 'It all seemed harmless at the time.'

I remembered Miss Channing and Mr Reed strolling through Chatham, pausing to gaze in shop windows, or standing beside the fence at London Livery, Miss Channing stroking the muzzle of one of the horses. Once I'd come upon them in Warren's Sundries, Mr Reed with a model boat in his hand, turning it at various angles, pointing out its separate parts, the mast, the spinnaker, the fluttering sail, his words spoken quietly, bearing, at the time, no grave import. *It wouldn't be hard to do it.*

My father's eyes searched the near rim of the pond. The thick summer foliage blocked the spot I knew he was looking for.

'Why did you go to Milford Cottage so often?' he asked, still peering down the hillside.

'Because of Sarah. I went to her reading lessons.'

'But why?'

'I don't know.'

My father kept his tone matter-of-fact, but I knew how charged his feelings were, how many questions still plagued him. At last he asked one he'd kept inside for a long time. 'Were you in love with her, Henry?'

I remembered the night I'd gone to her room, how gently she'd received me, her eyes shy and downcast, her body beneath a white nightgown, a satin ribbon dangling just above her chest. 'She was a lovely girl,' I said. 'And living in our house the way she did, I might have—'

'I wasn't talking about Sarah,' my father said, interrupting me. 'I was talking about Miss Channing.'

I heard rain batting against the windowpanes of Milford Cottage as it had that night, wind slamming at the screen door, saw candles burning in her bedroom, a yellow light pouring over her, the stillness in her eyes when she spoke. *Will you do it, Henry?* Then my reply, obedient as ever, *Yes.*

'I always thought that was the reason you took it so hard,' my father added. 'Because you had a certain ... feeling for Miss Channing.'

Her face dissolved in a haze of yellow light, and I saw her as she'd appeared the day we'd stood there on the hill, snow clinging to her hair and gathered along the shoulders of her long blue coat. 'I wanted her to be free,' I said.

'To do what?'

'Live however she wanted to.'

He shook his head. 'It didn't turn out that way.'

'No, it didn't.'

I felt my father's arm settle on my shoulders, embrace me like a child. 'Never forget, Henry,' he said, offering his final comment on the Chatham School Affair, 'never forget that some part of it was good.'

I'm not sure I ever fully believed that, though I couldn't deny that there'd been good moments, especially at the beginning. One of those moments had been the very day we'd all gone up the hill and stood together in the first snow of the season.

Sarah and I had walked to Milford Cottage that November morning, Sarah eager to get on with her lessons, confident that she would soon master the skills she needed to 'better' herself, childlike in her enthusiasm, adult in her determination.

Not long after we'd left Chatham it had begun to snow, so that by the time we'd finally reached Milford Cottage we were cold and wet.

As we neared the cottage, I saw Miss Channing part the plain white curtains of one of its small windows and peer out. She was wearing a white blouse, the sleeves rolled up to the elbow, and her hair fell loosely over her shoulders. From the look on her face, I could tell that she was somewhat surprised to see us.

'You didn't have to come, you know,' she called to us as she opened the door. 'I would have understood that the weather—'

Sarah shook her head vigorously. 'Oh, no, Miss Channing,' she said, 'I wouldn't think of missing a lesson.'

Miss Channing eased back into the cottage and motioned us inside. 'Well, come in quickly, then,' she said. 'You must be frozen stiff.'

We walked into the cottage, and I realized that it looked considerably different from when I'd last been inside. Some of Miss Channing's older sketches had been replaced by more recent ones, quiet village scenes, along with intricate line drawings, beautifully detailed, of various leaves and vegetation she'd found in the surrounding woods, some of which now rested in a large glass vase on her mantel.

'You've made it very cozy inside the house here,' Sarah said. She glanced about the room, taking in other changes, the hooked rug in front of the fireplace, the bookshelf in the far corner, the small red pillows that rested against the wooden backs of the room's two chairs. 'You've made it look like a regular house,' she added, drawing her scarf from her head. 'It's quite grand, Miss Channing.' She lifted the basket she'd brought with her from Myrtle Street. 'I brought a fruitcake for you. There's a bit of spirits in it though.' Her mischievous smile flickered. 'So we shouldn't be having too much of it, or we won't stay clearheaded, you know.'

Miss Channing took the cake and deposited it on the small table by the window. 'We'll have some after the lesson,' she said.

They got down to their lessons right away, Miss Channing opening the notebook Sarah had brought along, peering at the writing inside, evaluating it closely before commenting. 'Good,' she said warmly. 'Very good, Sarah.'

After that they went to work in the usual way, Miss Channing writing short, simple sentences which Sarah then read back to her. From my place in a chair not far away, I could see how well they got along, how much Sarah admired Miss Channing, perhaps even dreamed of being like her, 'a fine lady,' as she'd always said.

I suppose it was something in that 'fineness' that made me take out my sketchbook that morning and begin to draw Miss Channing, concentrating on the way she leaned forward, her head cocked slightly, her hair falling in a dark wave across her shoulders. I found that I could capture her general appearance, but that there was something else I couldn't get, the way her eyes sometimes darkened, as if a small light had gone off behind them, and which Mr Parsons later described as 'sinister', the very word he used at her trial.

She was still working with Sarah when I heard a car coming down Plymouth Road, its engine rattling chaotically as it slid to a halt in the driveway of the cottage.

Miss Channing rose, walked to the window, and looked out.

'We have a guest,' she said. There was a hint of excitement in her voice, something Sarah must have heard too, for her eyes swept over to me with a quizzical expression in them.

By then Miss Channing had walked to the door and opened it, a gust of wind sweeping her black hair across her face.

'Well, good morning,' she called, waving her arm. She turned toward Sarah and me. 'It's Mr Reed,' she said.

I walked to the window. At the edge of the yard I could see Mr Reed as he got out of his car. He was wearing a heavy wool coat, brown boots, and a gray hat he'd pulled somewhat raffishly to the left. He waved to Miss Channing, then came tramping down the walkway, the snow nearly an inch deep by then.

'You're just in time for fruitcake,' Miss Channing told him as he neared the door.

'Fruitcake,' Mr Reed said. 'Well, it's certainly the right weather for it.' For a moment he stood on the threshold of the cottage, facing Miss Channing from the bottom of the stairs, his eyes lifted toward her, gazing at her. 'I wanted to—' he began, then stopped when he saw Sarah and me inside the cottage. 'Oh, I see you have company,' he said, his manner now stiffening slightly.

'Yes, I do,' Miss Channing said. 'Sarah's here for her reading lesson. She made the fruitcake I mentioned.'

Mr Reed appeared at a loss as to what he should do next, whether he should come into the cottage or leave immediately. 'Well, I wouldn't want to disturb Sarah's lesson,' he said.

'No, no. We've just finished it,' Miss Channing told him. She stepped back into the room. 'Please, come in.'

Mr Reed hesitated a moment, but then came into the cottage and took a seat by the window as Sarah and Miss Channing disappeared into the kitchen to serve the cake.

For a time Mr Reed said nothing. I could tell that my presence disturbed him. Perhaps at that time he thought me an informer, certain that I'd rush back to Chatham, tell my father about his visit to Miss Channing's cottage. Then he glanced at me with a certain apprehensiveness I'd never seen in him before. 'Well, Henry, are you enjoying your classes this year?'

'I guess so,' I answered.

He smiled thinly and returned his attention to the window.

He was still staring out of it a few seconds later, when Miss Channing and Sarah came back into the room. Miss Channing placed the cake on the table in front of him and

began to cut. The first piece went to Sarah, the second to
Mr Reed. Then, turning to me, she said, 'Would you like
a large piece?'

I shook my head, trying to be polite.

She smiled, no doubt sensing my hunger, then spoke a
line that life forever proves to be a lie. 'Take as much as
you want, Henry. There is plenty.'

A few minutes later the four of us walked out of Miss
Channing's cottage, swung to the left, and followed Mr
Reed as he led us down Plymouth Road, then up a gentle
slope to a clearing at the top of a nearby hill.

Once there, we sat down on a fallen tree, the four of us
in a single line, facing back down the hill toward Black
Pond. The snow had thickened by then; a layer of white
gathered on the leafless trees and settled onto the brim of
Mr Reed's hat.

'A snow like this,' Miss Channing said. 'The flakes so
small, but so many of them. Like confetti.'

Mr Reed smiled at her. 'Is that how you'd paint it,
Elizabeth? As confetti?'

She smiled, but didn't answer him. Instead, she walked
a few paces farther on, while Mr Reed remained in
place, watching her as she reached the crest of the hill,
then stood, peering out over the pond. For a moment she
remained very still, as if lost in thought. Then she lifted
her arms and drew them around her shoulders. It was a
gesture made against the cold, quite unselfconsciously, I
think, but one Mr Reed must have experienced as a vision
so beautiful and so brief that it remained with him forever after that, set the mark against which everything else
would ultimately be measured.

We stood in a ragged line at the crest of the hill, facing

east, across Black Pond, to where a curl of chimney smoke could be seen rising from the trees along its most distant bank.

'That smoke must be coming from your house, Mr Reed,' Sarah said, pointing to it.

Mr Reed nodded, his manner now strangely somber. 'I should be getting back home,' he said, glancing toward Miss Channing. 'Abigail is waiting.'

'It looks just like a Christmas card, if you ask me,' Sarah said happily. 'The house by the pond. The snow. Just like a Christmas card, don't you think so?'

Mr Reed smiled, but with a curious wistfulness, as if it were something he remembered fondly from a distant past. 'Yes,' he said, his eyes now fixed on the far bank of the pond. 'Yes, it looks just like a Christmas card.' Then he turned away and I saw his eyes light upon Miss Channing, linger upon her profile for a moment.

'And are you going away for the Christmas holiday then?' Sarah asked him. The cold air had caused the color to rise in her cheeks and her eyes sparkled with excitement.

He seemed reluctant to answer, but did so anyway. 'Yes,' he said. 'I'm going to Maine for a couple of weeks. We always do that, go to Maine.'

With that, he turned quickly and led us back down the hill to Miss Channing's cottage.

Mr Reed stopped when he reached his car. 'I'll be getting home now,' he said, his eyes on Miss Channing.

'I'm glad you dropped by,' she told him, her voice quite soft, almost inaudible.

'Perhaps I'll come again,' Mr Reed said in a tone that struck me as subtly imploring, as if he were asking for some sign from her that he should return.

If she gave him one, I didn't see it. Instead, she shivered slightly. 'It's really quite cold.'

'Yes, it is,' Mr Reed answered, his voice now entirely matter-of-fact. 'Would you like a ride into the village?' he asked Sarah and me.

We accepted his offer and climbed into the car. Mr Reed remained outside it, facing Miss Channing, the snow falling between and around them. He spoke to her again, words I couldn't hear, then stepped forward and offered his hand. She took it, held it for just an instant, then let it go, smiling quietly as he stepped away. It was then I saw it in all its naked force, the full measure of the love that had begun to overwhelm Mr Reed, perhaps even some hint of the exquisite agony that was inseparable from it, not yet fierce, and certainly not explosive, but the fuse already lit.

Instead of going directly to Chatham, Mr Reed swung to the right and drove to his own house on the other side of the pond. 'I should tell my wife that I'm going to the marina,' he told us.

'The marina?' Sarah asked.

Mr Reed nodded. 'Yes,' he said. 'I rented a boathouse there a few years ago. I'm building a boat in it. A fifteen-footer.'

Sarah stared at him admiringly, the thought of such a grand endeavor playing in her eyes. 'When will it be finished?' she asked.

'With a little help, I could probably finish it by summer,' Mr Reed answered.

Impulsively, without giving it the slightest thought, I suddenly made an offer that has pursued me through the years, following me through time, like a dog through the night, its black muzzle forever sniffing at my heels.

'I could help you finish it,' I said. 'I'd like to learn about boats.'

Mr Reed nodded, his eyes fixed on the road ahead. 'Really, Henry? I didn't know you were interested in that sort of thing.'

'Yes, I am,' I told him, though even now I don't know why I felt such an interest. I do know that it had not come from the seafaring adventure novels I often read, though that was the reason I offered Mr Parsons the day we walked through the boathouse together. More likely, it had sprung from a voyeur's dark urge, the allure of the forbidden already working like a drug in my mind.

We reached his house a few minutes later. Sarah and I remained in the car while Mr Reed went inside.

'He's such a nice man,' Sarah said. 'Not an old fogy like some of them at Chatham School.'

I nodded. 'Yes, he is.'

He came back out of the house almost immediately, a long roll of white paper beneath his arm, bound with twine, like a scroll. I watched as he made his way across the yard, his daughter Mary rushing down the stairs behind him while Mrs Reed stood at the edge of the porch, wiping her hands on her apron as she watched him trudge back toward us through the falling snow. She was still in that position when he pulled himself into the car, but Mary had bounded toward us, then stopped, smiling mischievously as she attempted to roll a snowball in her hands.

Once inside the car, Mr Reed started the engine and began to pull away. We'd drifted back only a few feet, when Mary suddenly rushed forward and hurled the snowball toward us. It landed on the hood and exploded just at the base of the windshield, sending a flurry of white onto the glass. Mr Reed turned on the wipers, and as they swept across the windshield, I saw Mrs Reed still standing on the porch, watching motionlessly as Mr Reed continued backward, away from her, leaving two dark cuts in the snow.

I told my father about that scene as we stood together on the hill overlooking Black Pond.

'Do you think she'd already sensed it?' my father asked me when I'd finished the story. 'I mean, before Christmas. Before they all went to Maine together? Do you think Mrs Reed already suspected something?'

I shrugged. 'I don't know.'

His eyes shifted to the left, and I could tell he was gazing in the general direction of where Mr Reed had once lived with his wife and daughter. 'If she did know, or if she already suspected something by that time, then she had to have dealt with it for a long time before ...'

'Yes, she had,' I said. And with those words I saw her again, Abigail Reed standing beside me as she had in the boathouse that day, her eyes staring down into a cardboard box, fixed on the things that lay inside it – the rope, the knife, a nautical map with a route already drawn in red ink.

'So what finally broke her, I wonder. Sent her over the edge, I mean.'

I said nothing.

He looked at me, his puzzlement returning once again. 'We'll never get to the bottom of it, will we, Henry? We'll never know what she was thinking in the end.'

I did not answer him, but in my mind I saw her in that final moment, a face pressing toward me out of the murky depths, her red hair waving behind her like a shredded banner.

THIRTEEN

But despite those times when I was forced to consider the end of it, as I had that day on the hill with my father, I found that I more often hearkened back to its beginning, particularly to a story Miss Channing told in class only a few days after we'd all had fruitcake and gone for a walk in the snowy woods.

At Chatham School, the lunch break was one hour, from twelve to one, and after having lunch in the upstairs dining hall I'd walked into the village, made my way to Peterson's Hardware Supply, idly fiddled with a fancy new fishing pole, then headed back up the snow-covered hill toward the school.

As I neared Myrtle Street, I saw Miss Channing sitting on a wooden bench near the edge of the cliff, Mr Reed standing behind her, leaning on his cane, the wind blowing back his jacket and riffling through his hair, so that he seemed momentarily captured in that passionate wildness Mr Parsons would later describe as the origins of murder. I saw his hand touch her shoulder, then leap back, as if from a red-hot stove. Then he said something, and she glanced back at him and smiled.

That's when she caught me with her eye, peered at me an instant, then rose and began to stride toward me.

She was wearing a long, dark coat, and as she moved toward me from the crest of the bluff, the high collar raised up against the back of her neck, I remember thinking that she looked like someone from an earlier century, one of those women we'd read about in Mr Reed's literature class the previous year, Eustacia Vye, perhaps, or Madame Bovary, wild and passionately driven, capable of that lethal wantonness Mr Parsons later described to the jury, and in whose presence, he said, Mr Reed was 'little more than a piece of kindling before a raging flame.'

And yet, on that particular morning Miss Channing hardly looked wanton. She had dressed herself conservatively, as she usually did, her hair tied with a dark blue ribbon, a cameo at her throat.

It was Mr Reed who appeared somewhat emboldened, standing very erect beside her, his face full of purpose as he spoke.

'Have you seen Sarah?' he asked.

I shook my head. 'Not since this morning.'

Miss Channing drew a book from beneath her arm. It was old, with a peeling cover and frayed yellow pages, its spine long ago broken, so that some of the pages were barely held in place. 'I wanted to give her this,' she told me.

'It's my primer,' Mr Reed explained. 'From grade school. I've kept it all these years, and now Miss Channing thinks she can use it in her lessons with Sarah.'

I looked at Miss Channing. 'If you want, I could give it to her when I go home after school.'

'Thank you, Henry,' Miss Channing said. She handed me the book. 'Just tell Sarah to bring it when she comes for her lesson next Sunday.'

I nodded.

'Thank you again, Henry,' Miss Channing said. Then she turned, and the two of them walked back to the bench beside the cliff, Mr Reed now sitting beside her, though still at a discreet distance, his cane resting between them like a strictly imposed divide.

I didn't see Miss Channing again until that same afternoon, this time as she stood behind the table at the front of her classroom.

'Today we're going to start something new,' she said. 'Landscapes.' She turned and made a broad arc over nearly the entire length of the blackboard, then flattened its upper reaches with a few quick strokes. 'This is the general shape,' she said, 'of a volcano.'

With that, her face took on the curious intimacy I'd become accustomed to by then, the odd intertwining of her teaching and her life. 'Nothing on earth, not even the sea, will ever make you feel as small as a volcano makes you feel,' she said.

Then she told us the story of the day her father had taken her to Mount Etna. Its immensity could hardly be grasped by anyone who had not seen it firsthand, she said. It soared from its base to a height of nearly two miles, and the railway that circled it was over ninety miles long, roughly the same distance from Chatham School to Boston. 'My father was in awe of the violence of Etna,' she said. 'Of how powerful it was, and how indifferent to everything but itself. He wanted me to see how the lava from one of its eruptions had once flowed all the way to the sea, destroying everything in sight.'

She seemed to envision that vast smoldering flow as it had rolled down the slopes, then flowed across the valley, devouring everything in flames, consuming whole villages as it swept toward the sea.

Then, rather suddenly her face brightened. 'But what I

remember best about Mount Etna,' she said, 'is that there were flowers everywhere. On the slope and in the valley. So many of them that even near the rim, where I could see smoke and steam rising from the crater itself, even at that point, where everything else was so desolate, I could still smell the flowers down below.' She appeared genuinely amazed at the process she described. 'Flowers grown from ash.'

During all the years since then, I've thought of the Chatham School Affair in exactly opposite terms, the whole process utterly reversed, something that flowered briefly, gave off an exquisite sweetness, then, in a harrowing instant, turned everything to ash.

And so, just as my father later said, some part of it was good. Especially for Mr Reed, since, as I later learned, he'd never before experienced that form of passion that turns our eyes to the far horizon, erases the past like chalk dust from a board, raises us from the dead as surely as it consigns all others to the grave.

I showed up at his rented boathouse just after Miss Channing's class that day, images of smoldering volcanos still playing in my mind, my sketchbook already filled with my own attempts at rendering an explosive and primeval violence I was certain I would never experience.

Mr Reed was sitting at the little wooden desk he'd placed in the corner, a pile of papers spread out across it. He turned to face me as I came through the door.

'Hello, Henry,' he said.

'I wondered if you still needed help on the boat.'

He smiled. 'So, you're still interested?' he asked, already reaching for his cane.

'Yes.'

'Well, there she is,' he said, indicating the boat. 'What do you think?'

The boat rested on a wooden frame that stretched nearly the entire length of the room. The inner shell had only been partially fitted, so I could see into its still-unfinished interior. Hoisted upon the frame, without a mast, and with slats missing from its outer wrapping, it looked more like the skeleton of some ancient beast than a boat.

'As you can see,' Mr Reed said, 'there's still a lot to do. But not as much as you might think. Toward the end, it all comes together rather suddenly.' He paused, gauging my response. Then he said, 'We can start now, if you're still interested.'

We set to work right away, Mr Reed giving me my first basic lesson in boat-building, the patience it required, the precision of measurement. 'You have to go slowly,' he said at one point. 'Just let things fall into place.' He offered a wry smile. 'It's like a woman who can't be rushed.'

As we continued to work that afternoon, it struck me that something had fallen away from Mr Reed, some part of the impenetrable weariness I'd seen during all the years I'd known him, and which had served to cloak him in a melancholy that seemed inseparable from his character. A new and vital energy had begun to take its place. It was as if a fire were slowly burning off the detritus of his former life, making him more alert and animated than I'd ever seen him, a sense of buoyancy replacing the ponderousness that had so deeply marked him until then, and which I have since come to recognize not as the product of a dream already fulfilled, but only of a hope precariously revived.

We worked together all that afternoon, Mr Reed more talkative than he'd ever been outside the classroom. He spoke of writers he admired, quoted lines from their works, though not so much in the manner of a teacher as simply of a man whose mind and heart had been informed and uplifted by his reading. He talked about his boat as well, its speed and durability, what its capacities were. 'A boat this size, built this way,' he said at one point, 'you could sail it around the world.' He thought a moment, as if considering such a possibility. 'You'd have to sail along the coastline and skip from island to island,' he added. 'But it could be done.'

Only once did the old melancholy appear to settle over him again. 'Just one life, Henry,' he said, staring out the window of the boathouse, his eyes fixed on the bay, and, beyond it, the open sea. 'Just one life, and no more chances after that.' He turned back to me. 'That's the whole tragedy, right there.'

It seemed the perfect moment to add my own comment. 'That's what Miss Channing's father says,' I told him. 'In his book. He says that if you look back on your life and ask What did I do?, then it means that you didn't do anything.'

Mr Reed nodded thoughtfully, and I could tell he was turning the line over in his mind. 'Yes, that's true. Do you think Miss Channing believes that?'

With no evidence whatsoever, I answered, 'Yes, I do.'

He seemed pleased by my answer. 'Well, it *is* true, Henry. Absolutely true. Whether most people want to believe it or not.'

I suppose that from then on I felt in league with Mr Reed, willing to work on his boat every afternoon and weekend if that's what it took to finish it, willing to listen to him in all the weeks that followed, his tone bright and buoyant at first, then darkening steadily until, toward the end, he seemed mired in endless night.

It was nearly evening when I finally headed back toward home. And I remember that as I walked up the coastal road, the autumn drizzle felt more like a spring rain, the bare limbs not destined for a deeper chill, but on the very brink of budding.

The table had already been set for dinner by the time I reached home, my mother and father in their usual places at opposite ends of it, Sarah moving smoothly from one to the other, humming softly under her breath so my mother could not hear her.

My father glanced at his pocket watch as I took my seat. 'Are you aware of the time, Henry?'

I wasn't, but said I was, then gave him a reason that I knew would justify my tardiness. 'I was down at the marina, helping Mr Reed.'

'Helping Mr Reed?' my mother asked doubtfully. 'To do what?'

'He's building a boat,' I answered. I glanced toward Sarah, saw her give me a quick conspiratorial smile. 'He's been working on it for a long time,' I added. 'He wants to finish it by summer.'

My mother could not conceal her disapproval. 'It's his house over on the pond that could use a little work, if you ask me,' she sniffed. 'More than some fool boat down at the marina.'

'Now, Mildred,' my father cautioned, always careful that teachers at Chatham School not be criticized in front of me. 'What Mr Reed does in his spare time is his own business. But being on time for dinner is your responsibility, Henry, and be sure you look to it from now on.'

'Yes, sir,' I said, glancing once again toward Sarah, her smile even broader now, her eyes gleaming with a quick, mischievous fire.

*

Her room was in the attic.

The tap at the door must have surprised her. 'Who's there?' she asked, a hint of apprehension in her voice.

'It's me, Henry,' I said, standing in the utter darkness of the narrow stairway. 'Miss Channing wanted me to give you a book.'

She opened the door slightly, her face in candlelight. 'You shouldn't be up here, Henry,' she whispered. 'What if your ...'

'They're asleep,' I told her. I smiled mockingly. 'I know they are. I can hear my mother snoring.'

She laughed sharply, and swiftly covered her mouth. 'Be quick about it, then,' she urged as she opened the door.

The room was tiny, with a slanting ceiling, her bed pressed up against the far wall, a small desk and a chair at the other end, along with a short bureau with a porcelain wash basin and china pitcher on top. Now, when I recall that room, it seems smaller still, particularly compared to the aspirations of the girl who lived there, the life she yearned for.

'Miss Channing asked me to give you this,' I said, handing her Mr Reed's primer.

She stepped over to her bed and sat down upon it. I stood a few feet away, watching as she opened the book and began to leaf through the pages.

'It's Mr Reed's primer,' I said. 'The one he had in grade school. Miss Channing wants you to bring it with you on Sunday.'

She continued to glance through the book until she reached the end. Then she turned back to its beginning. 'Look, Henry,' she said, her eyes on the book's front page.

I walked over to the bed and sat down beside her.

'Look at what Mr Reed wrote to Miss Channing,' she said.

The words were in dark blue ink, Mr Reed's small, tortured hand immediately recognizable, though the words seemed far more tender than Mr Reed himself ever had.

My dear Elizabeth,

I hope that you can make some use of this book, even though, like the owner of it, it is an old and worn-out thing.

With love,
Leland

Sarah's eyes lingered on the inscription for a time before she lifted them to me, her hand suddenly brushing mine very gently, almost silkily, with no more weight than a ribbon. 'Have you ever been in love, Henry?' she asked, the words coming with an odd hesitancy, her eyes upon me with a softness and sense of entreaty that have never left me since then, and which I often recall on those nights when the wind blows and drifts of snow climb toward the window, and I am alone with my memories of her.

My answer was quick and sure. 'No.'

I saw her shoulders fall slightly, felt her hand draw away. She closed the book and placed it on the bed beside her. 'You'd better go now,' she said, her eyes now averted.

I walked to the door, opened it, and stepped out onto the narrow landing. 'Well, good night, Sarah,' I said as I turned to close the door again.

She did not look up, but kept her head bowed slightly so that a dark curtain of black hair fell over the right side of her face. 'Good night, Henry,' was all she said.

I closed the door and returned to my room. I don't recall thinking of Sarah again that night. But I have thought of her often since then, wondered if things might have turned out differently on Black Pond had I lingered a moment longer in her room. Perhaps I might finally have grasped the ribbon that dangled from her gown, given it a slow, trembling pull, and thus come to know both the power of that first encounter, and then the later pleasures of enduring love. I don't know if Sarah would have given herself to me that night, but if she had, I might have gone to her from then on rather than to the boathouse or Milford Cottage. I might have experienced love up close and through all its changing seasons, and by doing that, come to feel spring as something other than a cruel deception, winter the dreadful truth of things.

FOURTEEN

But in the end, I chose to think of life rather than to live it.

I said as much in my office one afternoon. I'd been talking to Mr Parsons' son, Albert Parsons, Jr., the two of us in our middle fifties by then, with the elder Mr Parsons now impossibly old and senile, a figure rooted on a bench outside the town hall, muttering to himself and flinging crumbs to the pigeons.

'So many books, Henry,' he said in a tone that seemed vaguely accusatory. 'Have you read them all?'

I offered him a mirthless smile. 'They're what I have instead of a wife and children.'

Albert laughed. 'You're a pistol, Henry. A real barnyard philosopher.' He sat back and let his eyes roam the bookshelves in my office, squinting at the titles. 'Greeks and Romans. Why them in particular?'

'They were my father's favorites.'

'Why's that?'

I shrugged. 'Maybe because he thought they saw it more clearly.'

'Saw what?'

'Life.'

He laughed again. 'You're a pistol, Henry,' he repeated.

We'd just come to a settlement that each of us felt our clients would accept, his being the aggrieved party in a construction contract dispute, mine, a local contractor named Tom Cannon.

'You know, Henry, I was a little surprised that Tom ever got named in a lawsuit like this,' Albert said. 'He's done plenty of work for me, and I've never had any trouble with him.' He took a sip of the celebratory brandy I'd just poured him. 'He even built that little office my father used when he was working on his memoirs.'

Some part of the old time abruptly reasserted itself in my mind, and I saw Mr Parsons as he'd stood before the jury on the last day of Miss Channing's trial, a man in his early forties then, still young and vigorous, no doubt certain that he'd found the truth about her, revealed for all to see the murderous conspiracy she'd hatched with Leland Reed.

'How is Mr Parsons these days?' I asked.

'Oh, he's as good as can be expected, I guess,' Albert answered. 'Of course, the way he is now, there's not a whole lot he can do but sit around.' He took a greedy sip from the brandy. 'He likes to hang around the courthouse for the most part. Or on that bench in front of the town hall.' He shrugged. 'He mutters to himself sometimes. Old age, you know.'

I saw Mr Parsons on his lonely bench, his hand rhythmically digging into a paper bag filled with bread crumbs or popcorn, casting it over the lawn, a circle of pigeons sweeping out from around him like a pool of restless gray water.

Albert took a puff on his cigar, then flicked the ash into the amber-colored ashtray on my desk. 'He talks about my mother, of course, along with my sister and me,' he went on absently. 'Some of his big cases too. They come to mind once in a while.'

Before I could stop myself, I blurted, 'The Chatham School Affair.'

Albert looked at me, perhaps surprised that it had leaped into my mind so quickly. 'Yes, that one in particular,' he said. 'He got quite a shock from that woman ... what was her name?'

'Channing,' I said. 'Elizabeth Channing.'

Albert shook his head. 'Nobody could have imagined that that woman would cause so much trouble,' he added with a short laugh. 'Not even your father.'

Inevitably I recalled how the people of Chatham had finally laid a large portion of the blame for what happened on Black Pond at my father's feet. It was the price he'd paid for hiring Miss Channing in the first place, then turning what everyone considered a blind eye to her behavior, a delinquency that his neighbors had never been able to forget, nor his wife forgive.

'You think he ever suspected anything, Henry?'

I remembered the look on my father's face as he'd closed the door of his office that day, with Mr Parsons in his dark suit, reaching into the box he'd placed on the chair beside him, drawing out a book with one hand, a length of gray rope with the other, Miss Channing standing before him in a white dress. 'Not of what they thought she did. No, I don't think he ever suspected her of that.'

'Why, I wonder,' Albert said casually, as if he were discussing no more than a local curiosity, 'I mean, she was pretty strange, wasn't she?'

For a moment I thought I saw her sitting silently on the other side of the room, staring at me as she had that last time, her hair oily, matted, unwashed, her skin a deathly pale, but still glowing incandescently from out of the surrounding shadows. In a low, unearthly whisper I heard her repeat her last words to me: *Go now, Henry. Please.*

'No, she wasn't strange,' I said. 'But what happened to her was.'

Albert shrugged. 'Well, I was just a little boy at the time, so really, about all I remember is that she was very pretty.'

I recalled my father's eyes the day she'd approached him across the summer lawn of Milford Cottage, her bare feet in the moist green grass, then the look on Mr Reed's face as he'd gazed at her on the hill that snowy November morning. 'She was beautiful,' I told Albert Parsons, my eyes now drifting toward the window, then beyond it, to the lighthouse she'd fled from that terrible afternoon. 'But she couldn't help that, could she?'

'Well, one thing's for sure,' Albert said. 'It was the man who was the real shocker in the whole thing. The other teacher, I mean.'

'Leland Reed.'

'That's right.' Albert released a quick, mocking laugh. 'I mean, God almighty, Henry, who'd have thought that a man like him would interest a young woman as pretty as that Channing woman was?' He shook his head at the curiousness of human beings, their woeful randomness and unpredictability, the impenetrable wilderness they make of life. 'Why, hell, that Reed fellow looked like a damn freak, as I remember it, always limping around, his face all scarred up. Just a rag of a man, that's what my father said. His very words. Just a rag of a man.'

I drew my eyes away from the lighthouse and settled them on the old oak that stood across the way, its bare limbs rising upward, twisting and chaotic, a web without design. Beyond it, down a distant street that led to the marina, I could make out the gray roof of the old boat-house where Mr Reed and I had labored to build his boat. In my memory of those days I could see him working frantically through the night, painting, varnishing, making the final preparations for its maiden voyage. Like someone whispering invisibly in my ear, I heard him say, *Disappear, disappear*, the grim incantation of his final days.

'Of course that Channing woman certainly saw something in him,' Albert said. He smiled. 'What can you say, Henry? The mysteries of love.'

But the nature of what Miss Channing might have seen in Leland Reed seemed hardly to matter to Albert, Jr. He crushed his cigar into the ashtray. 'They didn't get away with it though,' he said. 'That's the main thing. I once heard my father say that he'd never have gotten to the bottom of it – that he'd have just thought it was all some kind of terrible accident – if it hadn't been for you.'

I felt something give in the thick wall I'd built around my memory of that time. In my mind I saw Mr Parsons standing in front of me, the two of us on the playing field behind Chatham School, facing each other in a blue twilight, Mr Parsons suddenly twisting his head in the general direction of Black Pond before returning his gaze to me, his hand coming to a soft paternal rest upon my shoulder. *Thank you, Henry. I know how hard it is to tell the truth.*

The newspaper headline stated the fact baldly: STUDENT TESTIFIES IN CHATHAM SCHOOL AFFAIR.

There'd been a photograph beneath the headline, a young man in dark trousers and a gray jacket, his black hair now slicked back and neatly combed, a figure that had not in the least resembled the wild-eyed boy who'd stood at the top of the lighthouse some weeks before, madly drawing one frenzied portrait after another, rendering Chatham as a reeling nightmare world.

Others in the village have no doubt forgotten what I said upon the stand, but I never have, nor ever will. So that on that day over forty years later, when I'd sat in my office with Albert Parsons, Jr., watching him light his second cigar, I'd seen it all unfold once again, myself in the witness box, dressed in the black trousers and gray jacket of Chatham School, my hair neatly combed, all my wild ideas of flight and freedom now brought to heel by Mr Parsons' first question: *When did you first meet Elizabeth Channing?*

After that he'd continued gently, pacing back and forth while I sat rigidly in the witness box, a bright morning sun pouring in from the high windows, flashing rhythmically in the lenses of his glasses as he moved through blinding shafts of light.

Mr Parsons: Now, you are a student at Chatham School, are you not, Henry?

Witness: Yes, sir.

Mr Parsons: And you took English with Mr Leland Reed, I believe, and art with the defendant, Miss Elizabeth Channing?

Witness: Yes.

Mr Parsons: And would you say that Mr Reed took a special interest in you?

Witness: Yes, he did.

Mr Parsons: And Miss Channing too?

Witness: Yes.

Mr Parsons: How would you describe the interest Miss Channing took in you, Henry?

Witness: Well, mostly she was interested in my draw-ing. She told me that she thought I had talent, and that I should get a sketchbook and draw in my spare time.

Sitting in the witness box, listening to my own voice, I remembered all the times I'd tucked that same sketch-book beneath my arm and set out from my house on Myrtle Street, a lone figure marching solemnly into the village or strolling down the beach, fired by the idea of an artistic life, of roaming the world as Miss Channing's father had, a creature with no fixed abode.

Mr Parsons: And did you do a great deal of drawing at this time?

Witness: Yes, I did.

Mr Parsons: But that was not your only activity at this time, was it, Henry?

Witness: Activity?

Mr Parsons: Well, you also became involved in another project during that year at Chatham School, didn't you? With Mr Reed, I mean.

Witness: Yes, I did.

Mr Parsons: And what activity was that?

Witness: I helped him build his boat.

Even as I'd said it, I recalled how often I'd gone down to the boathouse Mr Reed had rented near the harbor, the two of us drifting down the coastal road in his old car, Mr Reed talking quietly, I listening silently, my fingers drum-ming incessantly on the sketchbook in my lap, increasingly extravagant visions playing in my mind, the vagabond life I so desperately wanted, trains hurling through mountain tunnels, night boats to Tangier.

But it hadn't been my boyish fantasies, nor even my

relationship with Mr Reed, that Mr Parsons had been intent upon exploring the day he'd questioned me in court, and I remember how my body had tensed as he began to close in upon what I knew to be his sole intended prey:

Mr Parsons: So during this last year you spent at Chatham School, you came to know Miss Channing well?
Witness: Yes, I did.
Mr Parsons: And sometimes you visited her at her cottage on Black Pond, isn't that so?
Witness: On Black Pond, yes, sir.
Mr Parsons: In the company of Sarah Doyle, is that right?
Witness: Yes.

I saw all those many occasions pass through my mind as the questions continued, my answers following, Mr Parsons now beginning to lead the silent courtroom spectators into a steadily more sinister tale, my own mind working to avoid that part of it Mr Parsons had not yet discovered, trying not to see again what I'd seen that fateful day, a woman seated on a porch, snapping beans from the large blue bowl that rested on her lap, dropping their severed ends into a bucket at her feet, then rising slowly as I came toward her from the distance, peering at me intently, a single freckled hand lifting to shield her eyes from the bright summer sun.

Concealing all of that, my answers had continued to take the form of Mr Parsons' questions, adding nothing, going along with him, responding to questions that sounded innocent enough but which I knew to be lethally aimed at the only villain in the room.

Mr Parsons: Did you have occasion to meet with Miss Channing in her classroom at Chatham School on Friday afternoon, December 21, 1926?

Witness: Yes.

Mr Parsons: Could you tell the court the substance of that meeting?

It had happened during the last week of school before the Christmas break, I told the court, nearly a month after the time I'd come up the coastal road and noticed Miss Channing and Mr Reed talking together at the edge of the bluff. I had left her class later that same afternoon, feeling rather low because she'd not seemed terribly enthusiastic about some of the drawings I'd shown her, wide seas and dense forests, suggesting that I try my hand at what she called 'a smaller canvas', a vase of flowers or a bowl of fruit.

During most of the next day I'd brooded over her suggestion. Then an idea had occurred to me, a way of regaining some measure of the esteem I so craved at that time. With that goal in mind, I'd returned to Miss Channing's classroom at the end of the following day.

Mr Parsons: Miss Channing was alone when you came to her classroom?

Witness: Yes, she was.

Up until that moment in my testimony I'd answered Mr Parsons' questions directly and with little elaboration. Then, rather suddenly, I began to supply unnecessary details. I'd gone to Miss Channing's room with a particular purpose in mind, I told him, my eyes fixed directly on Mr Parsons, my voice low, almost a whisper, as if I'd convinced myself that whatever I said from then on would be kept strictly secret between Mr Parsons and me, that there was no jury present, no benches filled with spectators, no reporters to record the things I said and send them out into the larger world.

Miss Channing had been preparing for the next day's classes, I told the court. I'd come through the door silently, so that she'd been slightly startled when she saw me.

Mr Parsons: Startled? Why was she startled?
Witness: Probably because she'd been expecting someone else.
Mr Parsons: Who?
Witness: Mr Reed, I suppose.
Mr Parsons: What happened after that?
Witness: She spoke to me.
Mr Parsons: What did she say?

'Henry?' she said.

I stood at the door, facing her. From the way she looked at me, I could tell that she hadn't expected to see me there.

'What is it, Henry?' she asked.

I wanted to answer her directly, tell her frankly why I'd come to see her at that hour, but the look in her face silenced me.

Mr Parsons: What look was that, Henry?
Witness: Well, Miss Channing had a way of looking at you that made you ... made you ...
Mr Parsons: Made you what?
Witness: I don't know. She was different, that's all. Different from the other teachers.

Mr Parsons: In what way was she different?

Witness: Well, she taught her classes in a different way than the other teachers did. I mean, she told us stories about the places she'd been to, about things that had happened in these places.

Mr Parsons: These 'things that had happened', were they pleasant things?

Witness: Not always.

Mr Parsons: In fact, many of them were often very cruel things, weren't they? Stories about violence? About death?

Witness: Sometimes.

Mr Parsons: She told the class about a certain Saint Lucia, isn't that right? A woman who'd gouged out her own eyes?

Witness: Yes. She told us about the church in Venice, where her body is.

Mr Parsons: Another one of her stories involved the murder of children, didn't it?

Witness: Yes. The little princes. That's what she called them.

Mr Parsons had continued with similar questions, unearthing other of Miss Channing's stories, tales of children who'd been buried alive, women who'd been drowned, before returning at last to the afternoon I'd gone to her room.

Mr Parsons: All right. Now, tell me, Henry, did you finally tell Miss Channing why you'd come to her classroom?

Witness: Yes, I did.

Mr Parsons: What did you tell her?

'I want to draw you,' I told her.

'Draw me?' she asked. 'Why?'

'I tried to do it once before,' I said, concealing my true purpose in wanting a portrait of her. 'But it didn't come out very well.' I lifted the sketch pad I'd tucked beneath my arm. 'I thought I'd try again if you wouldn't mind.'

'You want me to pose for you, Henry?'

I nodded. 'Just until you ... go to Mr Reed.'

I could see that the expression I'd used, the way I'd said 'go to Mr Reed', had sounded suggestive to her, but I added nothing else.

Mr Parsons: And so you could tell, even at that early time, that Miss Channing was already aware that you were suspicious of her relationship with Mr Reed?

Witness: I think so, yes.

Mr Parsons: And how did she react to the fact that she might be coming under suspicion?

Witness: Like she didn't care.

Mr Parsons: What gave you that impression?

Witness: What she said, and the way she said it.

She lifted her head in a gesture that made her look very nearly prideful, and said, 'As a matter of fact, Mr Reed will be here in just a few minutes.'

'I could draw you until he comes,' I told her. 'Even if it's only for a few minutes.' I took a short, uneasy step toward her, the afternoon light flooding over me from the courtyard window. 'Just for practice.'

'Where do you want me?' she asked.

I nodded toward the wooden table that served as her desk. 'Just sitting at your desk would be fine,' I said.

Mr Parsons: And so Miss Channing posed for you that afternoon?

Witness: It wasn't exactly a pose. She just sat at her desk, working, while I drew.

Mr Parsons: How long did she do that?

Witness: For about an hour, I guess. Until Mr Reed came for her. By then it was getting dark.

Mr Parsons: As a matter of fact, it was already dark enough for you to turn on the light in the room, isn't that right, Henry?

Witness: Well, I could see her, but I needed more light, yes.

Mr Parsons: What I'm trying to make clear is that it was very late in the afternoon by the time Mr Reed came to Miss Channing's room.

Witness: Yes, it was.

Mr Parsons: Could it reasonably be said that all the other teachers had left Chatham School by then?

Witness: Yes.

Mr Parsons: And where were the other students?

Witness: In the dormitory, most of them. On the second floor. It was almost time for dinner.

Mr Parsons: And so, when Mr Reed arrived at Miss Channing's room, he probably expected to find her alone, is that right?

Witness: Yes.

Mr Parsons: And when Miss Channing saw Mr Reed come into her room, did you notice any reaction from her?

Witness: Yes, I did.

Mr Parsons: What was that reaction?

Miss Channing's eyes suddenly brightened, I told the

court, and she smiled. 'I thought you'd forgotten me,' she said, her eyes gazing toward the front of the room.

I glanced over my shoulder and saw Mr Reed standing at the door, leaning on his cane.

'Am I interrupting something, Elizabeth?' he asked as he stepped farther into the room, his eyes drifting over to me, then back to Miss Channing.

'No,' she answered. 'Henry just wanted to practice his drawing.' She rose and began to gather up her things. 'We'll have to continue this some other time,' she said to me.

I nodded and started to close the sketchbook, but by that time Mr Reed had come down the aisle, his eyes on my drawing.

'Not bad,' he said, 'but the eyes need something.'

He looked at Miss Channing. 'It would be hard to capture your eyes.'

She smiled at him softly. 'I'm ready,' she said as she walked toward the front of the room. Mr Reed stepped back and opened the door for her, then watched as she passed through it. 'Coming, Henry?' he asked, glancing back into the room. I closed my sketchbook and walked out into the courtyard, where Miss Channing stood beside the tree, a few books hugged to her chest.

'Well, good night, Henry,' she said as Mr Reed joined her, the two of them now moving through the courtyard and into the school, I trailing behind at a short distance.

Mr Parsons: So you were more or less following Miss Channing and Mr Reed, is that right?

Witness: Yes. But I stopped at the front door of the school. They went on to the parking lot. Toward Mr Reed's car. Then they drove away.

Mr Parsons: Do you know where they went?
Witness: I later found out where they went.
Mr Parsons: How did you find that out, Henry?
Witness: Mr Reed told me. The next day. On the way to Boston.
Mr Parsons: So by this time you and Mr Reed had developed the sort of relationship that allowed him to confide such things in you?
Witness: Yes, we had.
Mr Parsons: Could you describe the nature of that relationship?

It was in answer to that question that I told my only lie upon the witness stand, one whose enduring cruelty I had not considered until I told it. 'Mr Reed was like a father to me,' I told Mr Parsons, then glanced over to see my own father staring at me, a mournful question in his eyes. *Then what was I to you, my son?*

FIFTEEN

Despite the answer I gave to Mr Parsons that day, Mr Reed was never really like a father to me. Nor like a brother nor even a friend. Instead, we seemed to move forward on parallel conspiracies, the two of us lost in separate but related fantasies, his focused on Miss Channing, mine upon a liberated life, both of us oblivious of what might happen should our romantic dreams converge.

It had developed rapidly, my relationship with Mr Reed, so that only a few weeks after we'd begun to work on the boat together, it had already assumed the ironclad form that would mark it from then on, Mr Reed still vaguely in the role of teacher, I in the role of student, but with an unexpected collusion that went beyond all that, as if we were privy to things others did not know, depositories of truths the world was too cowardly to admit.

To the other teachers and students of Chatham School during those last few months, we must have seemed a curious pair, Mr Reed walking slowly with his cane, I trailing along beside him with a sketchbook beneath my arm, the two of us sometimes making our way up the lighthouse stairs, to stand at its circular iron railing, Mr Reed pointing the tip of his cane out to sea, as if indicating some far, perhaps impossible place he yearned to sail for. 'Past Monomoy Point, it's open sea,' he told me once. 'There'd be nothing to stop you after that.'

We drove to Boston together the day before he was set to leave for Maine with Mrs Reed and his daughter. He'd wanted to buy a breastplate for the boat, along with some rigging. 'The really elegant things are in Boston,' he explained. 'Things that are made not just to be used, but to be ... admired.'

We took the old route that curved along the coast, through Harwichport and Dennis, past Hyannis, and farther, until we reached the canal. It was no more than a muddy ditch in those days, Sagamore Bridge not yet built, so that we rumbled across the wooden trellis that had been flung over the water years before, a rattling construct of steel and timber, functional but inelegant, as Mr Reed described it, the way much of life appeared to be.

Once over the bridge, the Cape receding behind me, I looked back. 'You know what Miss Channing said when she saw the Cape for the first time?' I asked.

Mr Reed shook his head.

'That it looked tormented,' I told him. 'Like a martyr.'

'Yes, she would say something like that,' he said with a quiet, oddly appreciative smile. He grew silent for a moment, his eyes fixed on the wider road that led to Boston. 'I guess you noticed Miss Channing and me leaving school together yesterday afternoon.'

I pretended to make nothing of it. 'You always leave together.'

He nodded. 'I usually take her straight home,' he said. 'But yesterday we went to the old cemetery on Brewster Road.' He waited for a question. When none came, he continued. 'We wanted to talk awhile. To be alone.' He stared at the road, the strand of dark hair that had fallen across his brow now trembling slightly with the movement of the car. 'So we went to the cemetery. Just to get away from ... other people.' He smiled. 'I promised Miss Channing that I'd have her home before dark.'

The landscape swept by on either side. I had not been off the Cape in well over a year, and I felt an unmistakable exhilaration in the forward thrust of the car, the unfolding of the landscape, the vast, uncharted world that seemed to lie just beyond my grasp.

'I don't know why I picked that cemetery,' Mr Reed went on as if he were circling around something he was not sure he wanted to reveal. 'Something about it, I suppose. Probably the quiet, the solitude.'

'Did Miss Channing like it?' I asked.

'Yes, she did. There's a little grove near the center of it. Some evergreen trees, with a little cement pool.' He forced a small laugh. 'I did most of the talking. You know, about my life.'

After that Mr Reed told me a great deal of what he'd said to Miss Channing in the cemetery the previous afternoon, how he'd been born in a working class section of Boston, a noisy, pinched world of clattering factories and grimy tenements where people lived beneath clouds of industrial vapor and coal dust.

'My father left when I was just a boy. My mother was a ... well ... not like your mother, Henry.' He smiled. 'She looked a little like Sarah, though. With long black hair, I mean, and a light complexion. Black Irish, we call it. My mother wanted me to be a clerk of some sort. In a bank, something like that. To wear a white shirt and tie, that's what she wanted me to do, look respectable.' He peered down at the brown jacket, its worn sleeves, the chalk dust. 'But it didn't turn out that way.'

'How did you happen to become a teacher?' I asked.

'Just by reading books, I guess. There was a school

158

in Braintree. That's where I went. The war interrupted things, but when I got back, I got a job at Boston Latin School.' I saw his fingers draw more tightly around the steering wheel. 'It's funny how you have to make so many decisions before you're prepared to make them. All the important ones, I guess. About your life. Your work. The person you marry.' Suddenly he looked at me with a striking earnestness. 'I hope you make all the right decisions, Henry. If you don't, life can be so ... treacherous ... You can end up wondering why you should even bother to live it through.'

No one had ever talked to me so intimately, nor with such urgent regard for my own future happiness. It seemed to me that my father had spoken only of the rules of life, never of its possibilities, his world a straight, unbending road, Mr Reed's a narrow lane of pits and snares and hairpin curves, a place I should be warned about before it was too late and I had become not what I wanted to be, but what my father already was.

'The main thing is not to settle too quickly,' Mr Reed added after a moment. 'In life ... or in love.'

An immense longing swept into his face, as if he'd recognized for the first time just how lonely and bereft he was. I wanted to offer him something, a token of the high regard I had for him. 'Chatham School would be very different without you, Mr Reed,' I said.

He appeared wholly unmoved by what I'd said. 'Yes, of course,' he replied dryly. 'What would the boys do without me?'

I said nothing else, but only watched as Mr Reed continued to stare toward the road ahead, his face fixed in that intense yearning I'd wanted to ease somehow, and which I remembered in all the years to come, so that it finally seemed to me that we were not created in God's image at all, but in the image of Tantalus instead, the thing we most desire forever dancing before our eyes, and yet forever beyond our grasp.

Once in the city, Mr Reed led me through a series of shops, picking up the items he'd come to buy, brass knobs and hinges that he often touched softly before buying, moving his fingers lightly over the smooth surface of the metal, or holding it up to the light, staring at it wonderingly sometimes with an admiring smile, like a pirate of the old time, his eyes feasting on a gold doubloon.

It was noon by the time we'd finished buying what Mr Reed had come for. Bundled up in our winter coats, we had lunch on a bench in the Common, near the botanical gardens, facing the great facade of the Ritz Hotel, the two of us munching sandwiches Mrs Reed had prepared for us, and which Mr Reed took from a metal lunch pail, along with a thermos of lemonade.

'I was tired of Boston before I moved to Chatham,' Mr Reed told me. 'But now—'

'Now what?' I asked.

'Now I think I'm tired of Chatham.'

'Where do you want to go?'

He shrugged. 'Anywhere,' he said.

'Is Mrs Reed tired of Chatham too?'

'No, she's quite content to live in Chatham,' he said, his eyes taking on a strange agitation. 'She always has been ... content.' He thought a moment, then added, 'She's afraid of things, Henry.' His eyes drifted toward me. 'Even afraid of me sometimes, I think.'

With that, he turned away, placed the thermos in the lunch pail, and snapped it shut. 'We'd better be on our way,' he said as he got to his feet, determined, or so it seemed, to end any further conversation about Mrs Reed.

It was then I realized that Mr Reed had already removed his wife to some remote and inaccessible place in his life, locked her in an imaginary attic or down in a dark cellar, where she sat in the shadows, isolated and alone, listening with whatever combination of anticipation or fear to his footsteps on the stairs.

On the way back to the car, Mr Reed suddenly stopped at the window of a jewelry store on a side street not far from where we'd parked. 'Look how beautiful that is, Henry,' he said, pointing to a necklace made of colored glass. He stared at it as if it were a talisman, something that could magically transform an all too lusterless world.

'It's pretty expensive,' I said, my eyes on the small white price tag.

He looked at me as if I'd offered him a challenge. 'Maybe once in a while you have to do something foolish,' he said. 'Just to prove that you're still alive.' With that, he smiled and walked into the shop.

I followed him inside, then stood at the counter while the shopkeeper retrieved the necklace from the window and handed it to Mr Reed. He turned it slowly, so that the colored glass in his hands glinted in the light. 'I'll take it,' he said.

The shopkeeper wrapped it in a piece of tissue and placed it in a small red box. Mr Reed thanked him and put the box in his jacket pocket.

We were on the road a few minutes later, Mr Reed's spirits suddenly quite high, as if he'd proved himself in some way by buying the necklace, his hand from time to time crawling into the pocket of his jacket, moving slowly inside it, turning the box over delicately, fondling it with his fingertips, a curious excitement in his eyes.

It was nearly nightfall by the time we got back to Chatham. Mr Reed drove me directly to my house on Myrtle Street, the old car shaking violently as it came to a halt in my driveway.

'Thanks for coming along, Henry,' Mr Reed said.

I nodded, then glanced toward the house. I could see my mother peering down at me from behind the parlor curtains. 'I'd better get inside,' I said. 'My mother's suspicious.'

'Of what?' Mr Reed asked.

I gave him a knowing smile. 'Everything.'

He laughed. 'Most people are, Henry,' he said.

I got out of the car and headed toward the stairs. I'd almost reached them when I heard Mr Reed call to me. 'Henry? Are you going to Milford Cottage with Sarah tomorrow?'

'I guess.'

'Tell Miss Channing I'll drop by when I get back from Maine.'

'All right,' I answered, then turned and moved on up the stairs.

The rest of that evening went along routinely. I had dinner with my mother and father, then went for a short walk with Sarah, the two of us sitting on the bench by the bluff for a few minutes before the cold drove us back inside.

'I don't like winter on the Cape,' she said with a shiver.

'I don't either,' I told her. 'Or the fall or spring or summer.'

She laughed and gave me a playful nudge with her shoulder. 'You should have more patience, Henry,' she said. 'You'll be off to college soon enough. You don't ever have to come back here after that.'

I looked at her squarely. Only half jokingly, I said, 'If I do come back here, kill me.'

Her face darkened. 'Don't say things like that, Henry. Not even as a joke.' Then she said a line that has never left me since that time. 'I wish we could be happy just to be alive.'

A few minutes later, now alone in my room, I went back over the day I'd spent with Mr Reed, my affection for him growing, along with my admiration, particularly for the boldness I could see rising in him, making it possible that he might actually break free from whatever it was that bound him so. I thought of the necklace he'd impulsively bought, then of the fact that Christmas was coming on. It struck me that I wanted to give Mr Reed a present. I thought of something for the boat, a brass nameplate, perhaps, or a lantern for the small cabin we'd nearly completed by then. Then I noticed my sketchbook lying on top of my desk, and knew what the perfect gift would be.

But several months later, near the conclusion of my first hour of testimony, it was clear that Mr Parsons was not interested in what I'd later decided to give Mr Reed for Christmas. He was interested in another gift entirely. The necklace brought back from Boston.

Mr Parsons: What happened after Mr Reed bought the necklace?

Witness: He put it in his pocket and we walked back to his car and came back to Chatham.

Mr Parsons: Did Mr Reed ever tell you who the neck-lace was for?

Witness: No, he didn't.

Mr Parsons: Well, did you ever see it again?

Witness: Yes, I saw it again.

Mr Parsons: Where did you see it?

Witness: At Milford Cottage. In Miss Channing's bed-room. It was lying on the bookshelf beside her bed.

Mr Parsons: How did you happen to see it?

Witness: It was the Friday night before … the deaths. Miss Channing went into her bedroom. That's where I saw it. She took it off the bookshelf, and gave it to me.

Mr Parsons: What did she say when she gave it to you, Henry?

Witness: She said, 'Get rid of this.'

Mr Parsons: And did you do that for her?

Witness: Yes.

Mr Parsons: What did you do with the necklace?

Witness: I threw it into Black Pond.

I will always remember the low murmur that rose from the people in the courtroom when I said that, then the rap of Judge Crenshaw's gavel, calling them to order. It was late in the afternoon by then, and so he adjourned the court for the day.

At dinner later that night, my father and mother and I sat silently at the table for a long time, a newly hired serv-ant girl flitting in and out of the dining room, her hair a dazzling red. Then, her eyes aflame, my mother suddenly glanced at me. 'They thought they were above everything,' she said with that bitterness that would mark her life from then on, 'that woman and Mr Reed. They thought they could do anything, and no one would ever know.'

My father's head jerked up from his plate, his eyes nearly bulging. 'Mildred, please.'

'Above all the rest of us, that's what they thought,' my mother went on relentlessly, her glare now leveled directly upon my father. 'They didn't care who they hurt.'

'Mildred, please,' my father repeated, though with little force. 'This is not the time or place to—'

'But they started in death and they ended in death,' my mother declared, referring now to the meeting in the cemetery I'd described in the courtroom only hours before. I could hear again the things I'd said, the answers I'd given, always careful to tell nothing but the truth, yet all the while listening as one truth followed another, the body of evidence accumulating one answer at a time, until, truth by truth, it assumed the shape of a monstrous lie.

My mother lifted her head proudly. 'I'm proud of you, Henry,' she said. 'For remembering the ones they murdered.'

I heard my father gasp. 'Mildred, you know perfectly well that—'

She raised her hand and silenced him. Her eyes fell upon me with a lethal force. 'Don't ever forget the ones that died, Henry.'

I never did. But in remembering them, I also remembered Miss Channing and Mr Reed in a way my mother would have abhorred. For despite everything, and for a long, long time, I persisted in thinking of them as romantic figures, modern-day versions of Catherine and Heathcliff, standing together on a snowy hilltop or strolling beside a wintry sea rather than rushing toward each other across a windswept moor.

And yet, for all that, there were other times when I'd glimpse a row of marble headstones in the same cemetery where they'd gone to be alone that long-ago afternoon, and see Mr Reed and Miss Channing as they'd appeared that final spring, Mr Reed staring toward the courtyard, his eyes trained on Miss Channing as she worked on her column of faces.

But that had been toward the end of it, the curtain poised to close, all the characters already beginning to assume their positions for the final scene: Abigail Reed, scratching at her hands as she peered out across Black Pond; little Mary at the bottom of the stairs, her eyes trained on the distant, darkened shed; I trudging grimly down Plymouth Road through the sweltering summer woods, a single phrase circling in my mind, taken from William Blake and quoted by Mr Reed, facing the courtyard when he said it, Miss Channing at work on her column only a few short yards away. *Sooner murder an infant in its bed than nurse unacted desire.*

PART IV

SIXTEEN

Mr Reed and his family returned to Chatham from Maine on the third of January in the new year of 1927. I'd just come out of Warren's Sundries, a cup of hot apple cider steaming in my hand, when his car swept past me. Mrs Reed was seated in the front seat, Mary in the back, an old trunk lashed to the top of the car, olive green, and with one of its corners slightly battered in.

Mr Reed didn't see me as he drove by, nor did Mrs Reed, for both were staring straight ahead, Mr Reed's face cast in shadow beneath the brim of a floppy gray hat, Mrs Reed's locked in stony silence, Mary's eyes drifting toward me as the car went by, a frail smile on her lips, her small hand lifted in a faint gesture of recognition. *Hi, Henry.*

It had been nearly two weeks since Mr Reed's departure, and the sight of him returning to Chatham filled me with anticipation, as if, after a long intermission, the curtain had risen again on the adventure in which I'd joined him.

When I rushed home and told Sarah that I'd just seen Mr Reed drive past Warren's Sundries, she'd seemed to share my excitement about his return. 'You can get on with the boat now,' she said, smiling. 'Maybe finish it by summer.'

During the Christmas break Sarah and I had often found ourselves alone in the house, my mother working at the church, helping other local women prepare for the Nativity play, my father busy in his office at Chatham School. The school vacation had given us a chance to talk more intimately and for longer periods than we ever had before. Sarah spoke eagerly of one day going to college, her glowing ambition no longer satisfied with attaining the most basic skills, but now set resolutely upon mastering the highest ones. In later years I sometimes thought that it was she who should have been my father's child, a proud and grateful graduate of Chatham School, I an illiterate boy shipped in from far away, the future author of its ruin.

For by then my own character and ambitions had moved very far from my father's teaching. It was Mr Reed to whom I was drawn, particularly to the passionate discontent I could sense in him, his need to do more, be more, break free of Chatham, discover some new world, as if life were a horn of plenty, vast and infinite, rather than a small basket, inadequately stocked, and from which, in choosing one fruit, we must forever lose another.

I found him in the boathouse the day after his return to Chatham. Coming through the door, the Christmas gift I'd brought for him held firmly beneath my arm, I'd expected to find him as I usually did, planing spruce for the rigging, caulking seams, or simply at work with sandpaper, paint, varnish.

But instead, he was sitting idly at the stern of the boat, his hands in his lap, the cane propped up against the bare, unpainted rail to his left.

He looked up sharply at my entrance, like someone pulled abruptly from a long period of deep concentration, his face still cast in that mood of troubled thoughtfulness I'd seen in it the day before.

'I thought you might be here,' I said. 'I saw you drive through town yesterday.'

He smiled faintly. 'Go warm yourself,' he said, pointing to the stove. 'Then we can start to work.'

I walked over to the stove, then stood with my back to it, watching silently as Mr Reed began to apply a coat of sealant to the inner frame of the boat. He seemed pre-occupied, very nearly distracted, his eyes narrowing from time to time, his lower lip moving very slightly, as if he were reciting lines beneath his breath.

'Did you enjoy your trip to Maine?' I asked, though I could tell he hadn't.

He shook his head, his eyes following the brush. 'Not much.'

I offered a possible reason, though one I doubted. 'It's probably even colder there than it is here in Chatham.'

Mr Reed didn't look up from his work to answer me. 'I don't care for Maine. I'd rather have stayed here.' He added nothing else for a while. Then he said, 'Did you go over to Milford Cottage during the break?'

'Once,' I told him. 'With Sarah.'

The brush stopped. 'And Miss Channing ... how is she?'

'Fine, I guess.'

And yet, even as I answered him, I recalled that there'd been something in Miss Channing's manner that had seemed somewhat different from the other times I'd accompanied Sarah to Milford Cottage, more subdued than she'd been before, locked in what appeared the same concentration that I now noticed in Mr Reed. Throughout the lesson she'd occasionally glanced out her front window, peering through the parted curtains to the empty lawn, her eyes filled with a subtle but detectible agitation, the way I imagined the wives of sailors to have gazed out from their widow's walks, apprehensively scanning the horizon for their husbands' ships. I now had no doubt that it was Mr Reed she'd been thinking of at those moments.

Mr Reed returned to his work, the brush moving rhythmically right and left.

I watched him for a few moments, knowing that he was thinking about Miss Channing. I could feel the present I'd made for him still cradled under my arm. It seemed the perfect time to give it to him.

'I have something for you,' I said, rising from the chair. 'A Christmas present. I finished it while you were in Maine. I hope you like it. Merry Christmas, Mr Reed.'

I'd wrapped it in bright green paper and bound it together with a red ribbon. 'Thank you,' he said, lifting it slightly, smiling. By its shape he must have known that it was a drawing, although when he opened it, I could tell that what I'd done both surprised and pleased him.

'Miss Channing,' he murmured.

I'd drawn her with pen and ink, though in a pose far different than Mr Reed would have expected, her hair falling over her bare shoulders in a tangled mass, her eyes intense and searching, lips full and slightly parted, her head tilted forward, but her gaze directed straight ahead, a figure both real and unreal, ethereal, yet beckoning, rendered in an unmistakable attitude of seduction.

'It's beautiful, Henry,' Mr Reed said, his eyes fixed on the portrait. He gazed at it a moment longer, then walked over to the small table in the corner. 'I'll hang it here,' he said. He took a nail from his jacket pocket and drove it into the wall above the desk. But before he hung the portrait, he paused, as if another thought had come to him. 'You know, Henry, we should show it to Miss Channing.'

'Do you think she'd like it?'

'Of course she would.'

I was not so sure, but Mr Reed seemed certain, so a few minutes later we were backing out of the driveway of the boathouse, headed for Milford Cottage, Mr Reed's spirits considerably higher now, the framed portrait of Miss Channing pressed against his side.

And so, as it turned out, I didn't do any work on the boat that day. But during the next few weeks I often returned to the boathouse to do what remained of the caulking and sealing, construct the mast and the boom, assemble the rigging. Enough work so that, four months later, after the Coast Guard had found the boat adrift in Cape Cod Bay, towed it back to Chatham, and moored it in the harbor, I could still walk down to the water's edge, look out beyond the other boats to the far side of the marina, and see the white prow of the *Elizabeth* lolling emptily in the distance, my eyes forever focused upon that part of it, the naked mast, the rolled-up sail, that I had helped to make.

Miss Channing was standing at the edge of Black Pond when we pulled into the driveway, a place where Sarah and I would sometimes find her when we arrived at Milford Cottage on a Sunday morning, and where, in my mind, I still see her, dressed in white, her back to me, framed by a swath of dark water.

She'd turned as Mr Reed's car came to a halt, rushed toward it briefly, then glimpsed me in the passenger seat, and instantly reined herself in, so that she was walking slowly by the time she reached us.

'Hello, Elizabeth,' Mr Reed said softly as he got out of the car.

'Hello, Leland,' Miss Channing answered. It was the first time I'd ever heard her call Mr Reed by his given name.

He drew the picture from beneath his arm. 'I want to show you something. It's a Christmas present. Henry gave it to me.'

She stared at the portrait much longer than I'd expected her to. Now I realize that she could not possibly have cared for the way I'd drawn her, that it was only a nakedly romantic vision of herself, fervidly adolescent, and as she'd continued to study it that afternoon, she might well have been thinking those very words she would later say to Mr Parsons, her eyes downcast, staring at her hands. *It was never me.*

'Very nice,' she said softly at last. She looked at me, smiled thinly, then handed the portrait back to Mr Reed. 'Would you like some tea?'

Mr Reed didn't hesitate in his reply. 'Yes. Thank you.'

We went directly into the cottage.

'When did you get back?' Miss Channing asked Mr Reed after she'd prepared the tea and served us.

'Just yesterday,' Mr Reed answered.

'And how was Maine?'

'Like always,' Mr Reed muttered. He took a quick sip, then said, 'And you? What did you do while I was away?'

'I stayed here,' she replied. 'Reading mostly.'

Mr Reed drew in a slow breath. 'Tell me, Elizabeth ... do you sometimes think that you're living only in your head?'

She shrugged. 'Is that such a bad place?'

Mr Reed smiled gravely. 'It depends on the head, I suppose.'

'Yes, of course,' Miss Channing said.

There was an interval of silence before Mr Reed said, 'The boat will be finished by summer.'

Miss Channing said nothing, but only raised the cup to her lips, her eyes on Mr Reed.

'After that it would be possible to' – he stopped, as if cautioning himself against speaking too rashly, then went on – 'possible to go anywhere, I suppose.'

Miss Channing lowered the cup to her lap. 'Where would you like to go, Leland?'

Mr Reed stared at her intently. 'Places you've already been, I suppose.'

For an instant, they stared at each other silently, but with an unmistakable intensity and yearning that made the shortest distance between them seem more than they could bear. It was then I first recognized the full depth of what they'd come to feel for each other. It had emerged slowly, incrementally, building every day, word by word, glance by glance, until, at last, it had broken the surface of their long decorum, something irresistibly powerful now blazing up between them, turning all show of mere friendship into a lover's ruse.

We walked out of the cottage a few minutes later, Mr Reed and Miss Channing just ahead of me as we strolled out toward the pond, then turned to the right and walked to the end of the old wooden pier that stretched out over the water.

'In the spring we'll go rowing,' Mr Reed said. 'On the Bass River. All of us together.'

I could see his house in the distance, the small white boat pulled up on dry land. I remembered that only a few weeks before, as we'd stood in the snow on the hill, the sight of his own house had appeared to disturb Mr Reed, work in his mind like an unpleasant memory. Now it seemed very nearly invisible to him.

It did not seem so to Miss Channing, however, and as she looked across the water toward it, I saw something in her eyes darken, a little light go out. 'You should be getting home, Leland,' she told him.

'Yes, I should,' he said, though he made no effort to do so. 'That was the first boat I ever built, that little rowboat you can see on the bank there,' he said, his words now turned deeply inward, as if it had been in the process of building it that he'd discovered some abandoned part of himself, a part that had grown steadily since then, and was now poised to consume him. 'I guess I wanted something that would let me drift by things,' he added. 'Not sail toward them. But just drift by. Hardly make a mark.' He drew in a slow, troubled breath. 'Your father would have despised me, Elizabeth,' he said.

Her eyes flashed toward him. 'Don't ever think that, Leland,' she told him. 'It isn't true.' She glanced at me, then away, clearly trying to determine exactly what she could do or say in my presence. Then, as if suddenly alarmed by the fact that I was there at all, she said sharply, 'You'd better go, Leland.'

Mr Reed nodded silently, turned, and headed off the pier, Miss Channing at his side, the two of them moving slowly across the yard toward where his car rested in the driveway, I off to the right at a little distance, trying to give them all the privacy I could, knowing that it was far less than they desired.

'Well, I'll come for you on Monday morning,' Mr Reed said to Miss Channing when we reached the car. 'We'll drive into school together, just like always.'

Miss Channing smiled very faintly, then, in a gesture that seemed to come from deep within her, she suddenly stepped forward and pressed her hand against the side of his face. 'Yes,' she whispered. 'Monday morning.'

It was the only act of physical intimacy I ever saw between them. And yet it was enough so that when Mr Parsons asked his question several months later – *Was it your impression, Henry, that Miss Channing was in love with Mr Reed at this time?* – I could answer, as always, with the truth:

Witness: Yes.

SEVENTEEN

And so it never surprised me that in the photograph taken nearly two months later, they were still together, standing side by side, Mr Reed holding to his cane, Miss Channing with her arms at her sides, the trees that tower over them still locked in the grip of that long winter, their limbs stripped and frigid, as bare and fruitless as a bachelor's life can sometimes be.

Mr Reed and Miss Channing are not alone in the picture, however. To Mr Parsons' dismay, no photograph of them alone was ever located. Instead, they stand amid a throng of teachers and students from Chatham School, along with its office and janitorial staff, everyone assembled on the school's front lawn, with my father standing proudly in front of them, the lordly captain of their tidy ship, dressed, as always, in his black suit and starched white shirt. The boys fan out to the left and right behind him, all of them dressed in their winter uniforms, shoes shined brightly, wool scarves around their necks, dark blue with gold fringes, the colors of Chatham School. I stand near the end of one flank, my sketchbook pressed manfully against my chest, a warrior behind his sturdy shield.

In every way, then, it was a picture typical of the time, a group photograph artlessly taken and presumed to have little value save to the people pictured in it. Nor would

I ever have specifically recalled it had my father not cut it out of the school annual some months after its publication, then added it to his little archive, his reason for doing so made obvious by what he wrote on the back: *Chatham School, 7 March 1927, Last known photograph of Leland Reed.*

But for Mr Parsons, the principal importance of the photograph was that it showed Mr Reed and Miss Channing standing beside each other as late as the first week of March 1927, their 'illicit affair', as he called it, still clearly going on. For their arms are touching lightly, as he noted for the jury, a fact that indisputably suggested, as he said in his closing argument, 'that Elizabeth Channing and Leland Reed remained united in a relationship whose adulterous and malevolent nature witness after witness has already made clear.'

The testimony of those witnesses was dutifully recorded in Mr Parsons' book, but even had I never read it, I would have remembered what they said, a catalogue of random sightings that stretched through the winter and nosed into the following spring, a scattering of words snatched from longer conversations, often innocent in themselves, but within the context of what later happened on Black Pond, as profoundly sinister and unnerving as a trail of bloody footprints around a scene of slaughter.

Trial Transcript, Commonwealth of Massachusetts vs. Elizabeth Rockbridge Channing, August 16, 1927.

Witness: Well, I was sitting on one of the dunes there on First Encounter Beach. That's when I saw two people coming up the beach, a man and a woman.

Mr Parsons: Is it unusual for people to be on the beach in late January, Mr Fletcher?

Witness: Yes, sir. The cold pretty much keeps people in. But I probably wouldn't have made much of it, except that the man had a cane, and you don't usually see a cripple like that out on the beach no matter when it is.

Mr Parsons: What did these two people do on the beach that morning?

Witness: They walked on a little ways, then they sat down at the bottom of one of the dunes.

Mr Parsons: And what did you observe at that point?

Witness: Well, they talked awhile, but I couldn't hear what they said, of course. They were sort of snuggled up together, with the man's arm around the woman's waist, pulling her up against him. They sat that way awhile, then I saw the man take a piece of paper out of his coat pocket. It was all rolled up, but he unrolled it, and they both looked at it. The man was talking and pointing out things on the paper.

Mr Parsons: Do you remember the color of that paper?

Witness: It was greenish looking. Sort of light green.

Mr Parsons: Did you recognize either the man or the woman you saw that morning?

Witness: No, I didn't recognize them until later. That is, when I saw their pictures in the paper.

Trial Transcript, Commonwealth of Massachusetts vs. Elizabeth Rockbridge Channing, August 17, 1927.

Mr Parsons: Now, as the harbor master of Chatham harbor, Mr Porter, you're in charge of maintaining various buildings and storage areas that are rented to people who use the harbor, are you not?

Witness: Yes.

Mr Parsons: Do you remember renting such a building to Mr Leland Reed in November of 1923?

Witness: Yes, I do. He planned to build a boat.

Mr Parsons: Did he subsequently build that boat?

Witness: Yes, he did. He finished it toward the end of this last May.

Mr Parsons: During the last weeks of the boat's construction, did you sometimes have occasion to step inside the building Mr Reed rented?

Witness: I went in sometimes. To see how things were going.

Mr Parsons: Did you ever happen to see a piece of paper unfolded on the desk inside that building?

Witness: Yes, sir. It was a nautical map is what it was. Of the East Coast, and down through the Caribbean.

Mr Parsons: Did you notice anything about the map that struck you as unusual?

Witness: Well, I noticed that somebody had drawn a route on it. In red ink.

Mr Parsons: Now, this route, this nautical route, it went from where to where?

Witness: From Chatham to Havana, Cuba.

Mr Parsons: Do you remember the color of the paper?

Witness: It was the usual color for nautical maps. It was pale green.

Mr Parsons: Now, Mr Porter, did you ever see the defendant, Elizabeth Channing, with Mr Reed in the building where he was building his boat?

Witness: Not in the building, no, sir. But I saw them out walking through the marina one time.

Mr Parsons: And when was this?

Witness: Around the same time I saw the map, I guess. Early February, I'd say. Mr Reed was pointing out into the bay there, sort of wheeling his cane around, like he was telling Miss Channing directions.

Mr Parsons: And if a boat followed that route out of Chatham harbor, where would it go, Mr Porter?

Witness: Into the open sea.

Mr Parsons: On that occasion, did you notice anything else about Miss Channing and Mr Reed?

Witness: Only that when they turned back toward the boathouse, Miss Channing sort of threw her head back and laughed.

Trial Transcript, Commonwealth of Massachusetts *vs.* Elizabeth Rockbridge Channing, August 19, 1927.

Mr Parsons: What is your occupation, Mrs Benton?

Witness: I teach Latin at Chatham School.

Mr Parsons: Are you familiar with the defendant?

Witness: Yes, sir. Her place ... her room at the school, I mean ... it's just across the courtyard from mine.

Mr Parsons: So you have a good vantage point to see what goes on in that classroom, is that correct?

Witness: Yes, sir.

Mr Parsons: Did you ever see Mr Leland Reed in that room?

Witness: Yes, sir.

Mr Parsons: Often?

Witness: Just about every day. He would come there and have lunch with Miss Channing. Then he'd come again in the afternoon.

Mr Parsons: Tell me, Mrs Benton, situated as you were, so close to Miss Channing's room, did you ever hear any conversation pass between the defendant and Mr Reed?

Witness: Yes, I did.

Mr Parsons: How did that come about?

Witness: Well, I was coming along the side of Miss Channing's room, and I heard voices.

Mr Parsons: Do you recall the approximate date when you heard the voices?

Witness: It was March fourth. I know because I had bought a birthday present for my son, and I was taking it home that afternoon.

Mr Parsons: And the voices you heard that day, they were coming from Miss Channing's classroom?

Witness: Yes, they were, and so I looked in, just as I was passing, and I saw Miss Channing sort of turned away, facing the wall over there by the cabinets, and Mr Reed was standing behind her.

Mr Parsons: Did you hear any conversation at that time?

Witness: A little. 'We'll find another way.' That's what Mr Reed said.

Mr Parsons: And that was all?

Witness: Yes.

Mr Parsons: Did Miss Channing reply to that?

Witness: Well, she kept her back to him, but I heard her say, 'There is no other way.'

Trial Transcript, Commonwealth of Massachusetts vs. Elizabeth Rockbridge Channing, August 20, 1927.

Mr Parsons: Now, Mrs Krantz, you're a clerk in Peterson's Hardware, is that right?

Witness: Yes, sir.

Mr Parsons: I want to show you a receipt for a purchase made at Peterson's Hardware on March 15, 1927. Do you recognize this receipt?

Witness: Yes, sir.

Mr Parsons: What items were purchased, according to the receipt?

Witness: Well, the first one is a bottle of arsenic.

Mr Parsons: Do you recall the person who purchased that arsenic on March fifteenth?

Witness: Yes, I do.

Mr Parsons: Who was it, Mrs Krantz?

Witness: Mr Leland Reed.

Mr Parsons: Could you read the other items that Mr Reed purchased that day?

Witness: It says here, a knife and twenty feet of rope.

Trial Transcript, Commonwealth of Massachusetts vs. Elizabeth Rockbridge Channing, August 20, 1927.

Mr Parsons: What is your job, Mrs Abercrombie?

Witness: I'm Mr Griswald's secretary.

Mr Parsons: By 'Mr Griswald', you mean Arthur Griswald, the headmaster of Chatham School?

Witness: Yes, sir.

Mr Parsons: Mrs Abercrombie, did you ever see or hear anything transpire between the defendant and Mr Leland Reed that indicated to you that the nature of their relationship was somewhat beyond what might be expected of two professional colleagues, or even two friends?

Witness: Yes, I did.

Mr Parsons: Could you tell the court, please.

Witness: One afternoon – this was during the last week of March, I think – anyway, I was walking through the parking area. It was late. I mean, it was night already. Everybody had gone home. But Mr Griswald had been preparing next year's budget, so I'd stayed late to help him. Anyway, I saw that Mr Reed's car was still parked in the parking area, there beside the tree, where he usually put it, and as I went on by, I saw that he was sitting behind the wheel, and that Miss Channing was in the car with him.

Mr Parsons: Miss Channing was sitting in the front seat, was she?

Witness: Yes, she was. And she had her hands sort of at her throat, and I saw Mr Reed lean over and take her hands and pull them away.

Mr Parsons: Now, Mrs Abercrombie, in your capacity as assistant to Mr Griswald, did you ever have a conver-sation with the headmaster about the behavior of Miss Channing and Mr Reed, the very scene that you witnessed that evening in the parking lot of Chatham School?

Witness: Yes, I did. I felt like it was something he needed to know about. So I told him about what I'd seen that night in Mr Reed's car, and I also told him that there was a lot of talk about Miss Channing and Mr Reed among the other teachers.

Mr Parsons: How did Mr Griswald respond to what you told him?

Witness: He said he wasn't much for gossip.

Mr Parsons: And that was the headmaster's only re-sponse to what you reported to him?

Witness: The only one I know of, yes.

But it had not been the only response my father made, as I had known long before Mrs Abercrombie took the stand. For one day during the very next week, he dropped in on Mr Reed's afternoon class.

I remember how I'd entered Mr Reed's room to find my father already stationed in one of the desks at the back. He nodded to each of us as we came into the room, then silently watched as Mr Reed began his lesson, leaning back, trying to appear casual, but with a clearly visible sense of vigilance in his eyes.

My father remained in that position during the entire

class, his gaze only occasionally drawn toward the court-yard, Miss Channing's room at the far end of it. Instead, he kept his attention intently focused upon Mr Reed, no doubt listening not only to what he said, but how he said it, observing not just a teacher going through the motions, but the man behind the teacher, looking for that broken part of Mr Reed that he so deeply feared and distrusted, not the part that had been shattered in the war, but long before, as he conceived it, in Adam's dreadful fall.

When the class was over, my father rose quietly and walked to the front of the room. He said something to Mr Reed, nodded politely, then walked down the corridor to his office. I watched as he made his way down the hallway, his dark, ponderous frame like an ancient ship cutting through a stream of youthful, darting boys, silent, meditative, a melancholy figure in a black coat, head bowed, shoulders slumped, as if beneath the burden of our lost and implacable hearts.

EIGHTEEN

Spring came at last, and toward the middle of April, we went rowing, just as Mr Reed had promised we would on that cold January day when the three of us stood at the end of the pier together and looked out over Black Pond.

It was a Saturday, warm and sunny, with what my father called 'the glow of Easter' everywhere around us. During the preceding months I'd worked on the boat with Mr Reed and attended classes with Miss Channing, but I'd actually seen them together only during their accustomed arrivals and departures from Chatham School. All their other 'secret rendezvous', as Mr Parsons later called them, had been discreetly held outside my view.

I'd gotten to the boathouse early that morning, already at work when Mr Reed arrived, fully expecting that we'd labor through the day, as we always did, finish up toward the end of the afternoon, then take a long walk on the beach near the marina.

Mr Reed had arrived at the boathouse with a very different plan in mind, however, one he announced as soon as he opened the door and peered inside.

'It's too pretty to be cooped up in here,' he said, one foot inside the boathouse, the other still on the walkway outside it. He stepped out of the door and into the warm spring air. 'Come on, Henry,' he said, motioning me to follow after him.

I followed him out the door, then down the wooden walkway toward the road. In the distance I could see his car, half-concealed behind one of the marina's old outbuildings, but enough of it visible so that I could make out the small white rowboat roped to its top.

Mr Reed was already pulling himself behind the wheel by the time I rounded the corner of the building. 'Come on, Henry,' he said, motioning me forward, hurrying me along. 'We want to get an early start.'

It was then I saw Miss Channing sitting on the passenger side, a large basket in her lap, her pale blue eyes like distant misty lights behind the dusty windshield.

'Hello, Miss Channing,' I said as I climbed into the backseat of the car.

She nodded but didn't answer, and I suppose that it was precisely at that moment I first noticed the peculiar tension and uneasiness that would never leave her after that, a sense of being trapped or constricted, the world's former breadth and expansiveness now drawing around her like a noose.

Mr Reed leaned forward and hit the ignition. 'We're off to the Bass River,' he said in a cheerful tone that struck me as somewhat forced, as if he were trying to lift Miss Channing's spirits. He looked at her for a moment, offering a slender smile. 'We'll have the whole day, Elizabeth,' he told her. 'Just like I said we would.'

It took nearly an hour to reach the Bass River, a spot Mr Reed had already selected, one he'd 'chosen for its remoteness and seclusion', as Mr Parsons later described it, surrounded by high grass and at the bottom of a sloping embankment, so that neither the car nor the boat was visible from the main road a short hundred yards or so away.

'At this point in the river, it's nearly a mile from bend to bend,' Mr Reed told us as he began to untie the ropes that bound the boat to the top of the car. 'We can row downstream, then come back with the tide.'

Miss Channing walked to the bank of the river, and stood, watching, as the current swept past her, bearing bits of wood and marsh debris, its slowly moving surface reflecting a cloudless sky.

Once the boat had been untied, Mr Reed grasped the bow, pulled it toward him, then down, so that it slid off the roof of the car at a deep angle, its bow nosing into the soft ground. 'All right, Henry,' he said, 'take hold of the back there.'

I did as he told me, the two of us lugging the boat toward the water, then setting it down in the moist earth that bordered the river.

Miss Channing remained in place, still facing the water, her eyes fixed on a yellow film of pollen gathered in a pool on the farther shore.

'Are you ready, Elizabeth?' Mr Reed asked gently, almost delicately, as if her mood were a fragile thing, a rare vase he feared breaking.

She nodded without turning around, and Mr Reed offered her his hand. She took it and stepped inside the boat. 'Thank you,' she said as she released it.

'You're next, Henry,' Mr Reed said.

I climbed into the boat, then looked back just as Mr Reed pushed it forward again, drawing himself up and over the rail as he did so, a movement that struck me as very smooth and agile, his cane left on the bank behind us, the river lapping softly at its curved end.

*

I will always remember the few hours that followed, the slow drift of the boat down the narrow channel of the river, a wall of grass on either side, Mr Reed at the oars, Miss Channing facing him from the opposite end of the boat, her right hand lowered toward the water, a single finger slicing it silently, leaving a glistening trail across its otherwise smooth surface.

At that moment she seemed as beautiful as any woman had ever been or would ever be. I picked up my sketch-book and began to draw, hoping to please her this time, to draw her as she really was. She was staring just off to the left as I began, her face in profile as she watched a gull prance along the far embankment. Turning back, she saw the sketchbook open in my lap, the drawing pencil in my hand, my eyes intent upon her. Her face suddenly grew taut, as if she thought I'd been sent to record her presence in the boat, use it later as evidence against her. 'No, Henry,' she said.

'But I was just ...'

She shook her head determinedly, her eyes locked in that steeliness Mr Parsons would later associate with the cold-ness of her heart. 'No,' she repeated firmly. 'Put it down.'

I glanced at Mr Reed, saw him turn away from me, fix his attention on the stream ahead, clearly unwilling to go against her.

'Yes, Miss Channing,' I said, then closed the book and placed it on the seat beside me.

There was an interminable silence after that, Miss Channing motionless on her seat as we drifted onward, the boat now moving through a labyrinth of narrow chan-nels, Mr Reed suddenly tugging more fiercely at the oars, as if already in flight from some grim, pursuing hand.

*

After a time we came to a bend in the river, but rather than rounding it, Mr Reed rowed us to shore.

Once on the riverbank, we spread a checkered cloth a few feet from the water, the wind billowing it up briefly as we lowered it to the ground. Mr Reed sat at one corner, Miss Channing at another, removing fruit and sandwiches from the basket.

We ate slowly, in what I later recognized as the kind of silence that falls when the last resort has been reached, all debate now closed, nothing to be taken back or reconsidered, the final decision irrevocably made, though perhaps still unstated.

In an effort to lighten that very atmosphere, Mr Reed suddenly looked at Miss Channing and said, 'Tell us a story, Elizabeth.'

She shook her head.

Mr Reed leaned forward slightly. 'Something from your travels,' he said softly, almost gingerly as if her feelings were a red-hot coal he feared to touch.

She shook her head again.

'Just one, Elizabeth.' Mr Reed's tone was now so imploring it seemed almost beggarly.

Without a word she got to her feet and strode away from us, down along the water's edge, to where a tangle of driftwood lay on the bank, its limbs rising like fleshless bones from the moist ground.

Mr Reed watched her leave us, then, moving slowly and unsteadily without his cane, walked down to where she stood.

I tried to turn away, but I found myself continually drawn back to them, their bodies so fully surrounded by walls of grass and coils of water, they looked utterly ensnared, like two animals captured in an invisible net, thrashing about, desperate to break free, and yet with every thrust and movement growing more fatally entangled. I thought of the delight in Mr Reed's eyes as he'd bought the glass necklace in Boston, then of the look on Miss Channing's face as she'd pressed her hand against his cheek, traced its jagged scar, and finally of the hopelessness and futility that appeared to have overwhelmed them since that time. That the passion I was certain I'd seen between them should now be in the process of disintegration seemed inconceivable to me, and watching them, as they continued to talk intently only a few yards away, I felt a scalding surge of anger against the whole design of life, its web of duties and obligations, Chatham like a dark pit in which Miss Channing and Mr Reed were now imprisoned, Mrs Reed standing on its rim, grim and unrelenting, dressed in black, her implacable arms folded over her chest, the female version of my father.

'Well, Henry, I suppose we'd better be on our way now,' Mr Reed told me solemnly when he and Miss Channing rejoined me. I helped them gather up the cloth and the basket.

At the boat Mr Reed offered Miss Channing his hand. She grasped it lightly, stepped inside, and took her seat again at the stern.

'It'll be quick going back,' Mr Reed told her as he pushed us off. 'The tide's coming in now.' He pulled himself over the rail and took hold of the oars, his gaze upon Miss Channing as he said, 'Parting is such sweet sorrow, and all that.'

It was a line from *Romeo and Juliet*, of course, and it must have lingered in Miss Channing's mind, for when the bend in the river had disappeared behind us, she broke her silence. 'I went to Juliet's house in Verona when I was sixteen,' she said. 'There were lots of people there. It was like a shrine.' She gathered her arms more tightly around the basket that rested in her lap. 'My father pointed to the balcony and told me to stand where Juliet had, looking down at Romeo.' Her eyes took on an unmistakable intensity, as if she were reliving the moment again, she on the stone balcony, her father in the courtyard below, their eyes fixed upon each other. 'That's what he was searching for, I think,' she said. 'An ideal love.'

Mr Reed drew back the oars slowly. 'If he'd ever found a love like that,' he said, 'I'm sure he'd have found a way to keep it too.'

Miss Channing said nothing, but only stared rigidly ahead as the boat moved swiftly inland, the nightbound tide now exerting its vast pull. No one ever looked more tortured by a grave resolve.

It was nearly night when we reached Milford Cottage. An evening mist drifted over the pond. I sat in the car while Mr Reed walked Miss Channing to her door. They lingered on the threshold, Mr Reed on the step beneath Miss Channing, she looking down at him. Finally, he took her hand, held it very briefly, then released it and headed back toward where I sat.

She'd lit a candle by the time Mr Reed got into the car, a soft yellow glow now coming from the windows of the front room.

'It's so hard, Henry,' Mr Reed said, his eyes on the cottage as he began to back away. 'It's the hardest thing in the world.'

I never mentioned his words to Mr Parsons, since they'd seemed directed toward something larger than the

Chatham School Affair, not the crime of forbidden love, which was Mr Parsons' sole interest, but some deeper one, plotted at the core of life, and which inflexibly decrees that one love in flower must leave another in decay.

When we arrived at Mr Reed's house on the other side of the pond, Mary was playing in the front yard, building a house of sticks and leaves as she sat near the water, nearly obscured in a blue twilight. She ran toward the car as we got out, then stood watching while we unlashed the boat and carried it toward its usual mooring by the tree at the water's edge.

'Did you catch a fish?' she asked Mr Reed brightly as she skipped along beside him.

'We didn't go fishing,' he told her. 'Just rowing.' He glanced back toward me. 'Just Henry and me,' he added.

We set the boat down, and Mary climbed into it as Mr Reed tethered it to the tree, taking a seat at the bow, bouncing slightly, her small hands clapping rhythmically to some beat in her mind.

'Where's your mother?' Mr Reed asked her once he'd secured the boat.

Mary pointed to the porch. 'She's been sitting there all day.'

I turned toward the house. In the evening shade I had not seen her, but now I could make her out quite clearly. She sat in the far corner of the porch, rocking quietly, her green eyes peering dully out of the shadows like two small, unpolished stones.

NINETEEN

After the Chatham School Affair, my father always believed that the deepest tragedies inevitably unfolded slowly, reached their climaxes in seizures of violence and grief, then lingered on forever in the minds of those who were near enough to feel their lethal force and yet survive.

Some, of course, do not survive at all.

Those who perished return to me most often in a newspaper photograph published during the trial, which I saw lying on my father's desk at Chatham School one evening, my father at his office window, his hands clutched behind his back, staring out into the courtyard, where the remnants of Miss Channing's sculpture had been gathered into a pile of gray rubble, an almost surreal mound of shattered faces.

In the photograph Mrs Reed is seated in her husband's small white boat. Mary is on her wide lap. Both smile happily in a picture taken, according to the newspaper, by Mr Reed during what it called 'happier times'.

I can still remember how wrenching I found that photograph the evening I first saw it. Because of that, it never surprised me that I sometimes took it from the little archive I inherited at my father's death, staring at it by the fire, letting it remind me of Mrs Reed and her daughter, what they'd been, no longer were, and thus warn me away from the temptation I occasionally felt to find a wife, have children of my own.

Of course, there'd been plenty of testimony to remind me of them at the time, particularly of Mrs Reed, neighbors and relatives who'd come at Mr Parsons' bidding, and who, by answering the questions he put to them, had labored to bring her back to life, consistently portraying her as a dutiful and, for the most part, cheerful woman, faithful and hardworking, a good mother and a good wife, incontestably entitled to her husband's unswerving devotion.

I remembered Mrs Hale, the coroner's wife, talking quietly of how well Mrs Reed had taken care of her parents in their illness and old age. Then Mrs Lancaster after her, speaking no less quietly about Mrs Reed's kindness toward her feebleminded sister, the way she'd never failed to bring her a cake and a jar of apple cider on her birthday.

But of all the people who testified about Abigail Reed, the witness I most remember was my mother.

As it turned out, she'd known Mrs Reed almost all her life, remembered her as Abbey Parrish, the only daughter of William and Dorothy Parrish, he a fisherman who moored his boat in Chatham harbor, she a fisherwife of the old school, who hauled tubs of lobster and baskets of quahogs and slabs of smoked bluefish to the local market every day. As a child, Abigail had often accompanied her mother there, standing at her side, helping her sell the day's catch from behind a wooden table that had been placed beneath a tattered canvas roof, her hands made rough by the work, scarred by scales and fins.

On the stand, my mother had spoken in a somewhat more agitated manner than either Mrs Hale or Mrs Lancaster. Her voice took on an unmistakable edginess as she answered Mr Parsons' questions, her eyes sometimes involuntarily flitting over to Miss Channing, little sparks of anger glinting in them, especially as she related the afternoon Mrs Reed had turned up at our house on Myrtle Street, her manner quite desperate by then, as my mother described it, a chilling terror in her red-rimmed eyes.

Still, for all the impact of her testimony, my mother didn't do or say anything on the stand that stunned me as much as what happened only a few minutes after she left it.

'Walk your mother home, Henry,' my father told me as she stepped from the witness box and began to make her way down the aisle toward the back of the courtroom.

She was already passing through its large double doors by the time I caught up with her, moving at that brisk, determined pace she often assumed, as if something were chasing after her, she trying to outrun it.

'Are you thirsty, Mother?' I asked her as we made our way through the dense crowd that had gathered on the courthouse steps. 'Do you want to stop and have something to drink?'

She stared straight ahead as she answered, roughly elbowing her way through the mob, her eyes glaring hotly toward the street. 'No, I want to go home,' she said.

At the bottom of the stairs, she wheeled to the right and strode up Main Street at the same nearly frantic pace, taking short, quick steps, her heavy black shoes thumping loudly along the walkway.

For nearly a block she kept silent, then, suddenly, under her breath, in a kind of bitter hiss, I heard her say, 'That woman should be hung.'

My eyes widened in dreadful horror at what she'd said. 'Miss Channing?' I gasped, my complicity in her fate sweeping over me in a bitter wave. 'But she didn't ...'

My mother waved her hand, silencing me, as she continued forward at the same merciless pace, her eyes now glowing furiously.

I could tell by the hard look in them that she had no intention of saying more. So I simply rushed along beside her, glancing at the bustling crowds, the knots of people that had gathered on every street corner and in front of every shop. It looked as if the whole world had suddenly descended upon our village, all drawn by the dark specter of the Chatham School Affair.

'I don't understand why everybody is so caught up in this,' I said to my mother as she surged forward along the crowded street, an observation I only half believed but felt safe in making, so utterly neutral, as it seemed to me, edging neither toward my mother's testimony nor my own, neither to the error of her suspicions, nor the unbearable actuality of my crime.

Still she said nothing, oblivious, or so it appeared, not only of my last remark, but of the steady stream of traffic in the streets, the cars and people moving past us, the scores of men and women who spread out over the broad lawn of the town hall.

In that ceaselessly agitated surrounding, it seemed equally safe to offer another observation, one I'd desperately clung to during the previous weeks, as if, by clinging to it, I could stay afloat above the tragedy that had by then engulfed so many others. 'It's the love story that attracts them, I guess. Just that it's basically a love story.'

At that, my mother came to a halt so abrupt and violent, she appeared to have run into an invisible wall.

'A love story?' she asked, her eyes igniting with a fire I had never seen in them before and of which I had not believed her capable.

'Well, that's what Miss Channing and Mr—'

'You think it's a love story, Henry?' My mother's words burst from her mouth like puffs of steam.

I could feel the air heat up around us, my mother's body begin to smolder.

'Well, in a way it is,' I said. 'I mean, Miss Channing just—'

'Miss Channing?' my mother cried. 'What about Mrs Reed? What about her love for her husband? Isn't *that* a love story too?'

It seemed the sort of question Mr Parsons might have posed to the twelve jurors who'd been asked to judge Miss Channing, and ultimately to condemn her, and I realized that I had no answer for my mother, that I had never known the kind of love she had just spoken of, one based on ancient vows and meant to last forever, the 'love story' of a marriage.

'All you do is think about that woman,' my mother said. 'That Miss Channing. How romantic it all is. Her and Mr Reed. Walking on the beach. Sailing in the boat. Where do you think Mrs Reed was while all that was going on?'

In my mind I suddenly saw Mrs Reed as she'd appeared on the porch the day we'd returned from the Bass River, heard her daughter's words again, the vast suffering and loneliness they now so powerfully conveyed. *She's been sitting there all day.*

'I'm ashamed of you, Henry,' my mother snapped angrily, her words hitting me like small iron pellets. 'Ashamed of the way you think.'

Staring at her mutely, I realized that I'd never understood how from the moment the trial began, my mother had done nothing but consider not the tale spun by my willful romantic imagination, but the dreadful anguish of

Abigail Reed, the unbearable fear and rage and sense of betrayal that must have overwhelmed her as she'd watched her husband slip away.

'I'm sorry, Mother,' I whispered.

What she said next stunned me with its uncompromising force. 'You're all alike, Henry, all you men.'

She stared at me for one long, ghastly moment, then turned and walked away, leaving me in a world that had begun to move again, though differently than it had before, filled with greater complications, a weave of consequences and relations that seemed larger than romance, deeper and more enduring, though still distant from my understanding, a world I'd only just briefly glimpsed, as it were, through my mother's eyes.

My mother never again spoke to me directly about the Chatham School Affair. And I remember that a few hours later, after a nearly silent dinner, I went upstairs to my room, lay down upon my bed, and tried to think about Mrs Reed, not in the panic and despair of her last seconds, as I'd continually thought of her throughout Miss Channing's trial, but before that, when she'd been a wife and mother.

Toward dawn I awoke, and there she was before me. Abigail Reed, as if she were alive again, with red hair and green eyes, watching me silently from the ruins of her shattered faith. And for the first time, as I lay in the shadowy early morning light, I found that I was able to imagine what it must have been like for her during those weeks when Mr Reed had begun to drift from her, spending long hours with me in the boathouse, the two of us working deep into the night to complete his boat, while she remained at home, tending to their daughter, bathing her, clothing her in thick flannel sleeping gowns, putting her to bed.

I saw all those many nights when the hour had grown late, and still Mr Reed had not returned. How she must have wondered about the changes that had come over her husband, how preoccupied and distracted he had become, as if he could not keep his mind from wandering away from her, and toward some distant attachment whose nature she could not let herself consider.

And yet she had to have considered it, had to have noticed that he no longer touched her with the same affection, nor with any great desire, and that although he still frolicked with Mary, he more often preferred to be alone with his daughter, taking her on long walks or even rowing her out into the center of Black Pond, where, bundled up against the cold of that long winter, they fished in the icy water.

Perhaps, in order to escape the unbearable implications of the changes she noticed in him, Mrs Reed had sometimes recalled the moment when she'd first seen him, a tall, slender man, leaning on a cane as he bought his weekly supplies at the village store, the way they'd walked out together, he holding the door for her, nodding quickly as she passed, then falling in behind her for a little distance before she'd stopped, turned toward him and asked him bluntly if he was not Leland Reed, the new teacher at Chatham School.

But where had he gone, this man who'd lived with her for more than five years, who was the father of her daughter, and who'd provided for her and loved her as no man ever had or ever would again, but who now seemed to have receded, perhaps even beyond the promised gravity of home.

How Mrs Reed must have suffered during all those long nights, I thought as the air lightened outside my bedroom window that morning. How she must have yearned to regain Mr Reed once again, not just for a night, but forever.

But as I well knew, Mr Reed had never returned to her. So that as the days passed one after the other, and the nights deepened and grew colder, I knew that she must have walked to the window at regular intervals, parted the curtains, and peered out into the darkness, her eyes now fixed on the empty road, searching for some sign of his approaching car. At such a moment, locked in dread, Mrs Reed's face could not have looked at all like the women of romantic myth, Iseult beneath her billowing white sail, or Guenevere waiting heroically to be burned alive. And yet, for all that, she now seemed heroic to me somehow, as my mother had certainly thought of her when she fled the court that day, convinced, as she had every right to be, that no man, her son included, could ever conceive or even remotely comprehend the depth of her long pain.

TWENTY

Nor do I think that my father ever really understood it. At least not at that time. For although he must have felt the deepest sympathy for Mrs Reed, I believe that he remained captured in a different orbit, one that spun around Miss Channing, had *her* life, *her* loss, as its central star.

And so it never surprised me that he labored to defend her on that August afternoon when it came his turn to take the stand.

Mr Parsons: Now, you hired Miss Elizabeth Rockbridge Channing as a teacher at Chatham School, did you not, Mr Griswald?

Witness: Yes, I did.

Mr Parsons: And early on, did you have any reason to doubt the wisdom of choosing Miss Channing for her post at Chatham School?

Witness: No, I did not.

Mr Parsons: Well, at a later time, did you begin to have reservations about Miss Channing's character?

Witness: Not exactly.

Mr Parsons: But as you have already heard, Mr Griswald, an earlier witness has testified that she told you about certain rumors having to do with Miss Channing's relationship with Leland Reed.

Witness: Yes, I was informed that certain people felt that way.

Mr Parsons: But you chose to ignore their warnings?

Witness: I had no proof of anything, Mr Parsons.

Mr Parsons: But you had observed some rather odd behavior, had you not? In regard to both Mr Reed and Miss Channing. Certain alarming behavior?

Witness: I wouldn't call it alarming.

Mr Parsons: Well, isn't it true that both Mr Reed and Miss Channing appeared extremely strained during the final weeks of the school year?

Witness: Yes, they did.

Mr Parsons: And didn't this strain become obvious at one point in your own house, Mr Griswald? At a party on, I believe, April twenty-third.

Witness: Yes, it did.

Mr Parsons: Did Miss Channing and Mr Reed come to that party together?

Witness: No. Miss Channing came into my office the afternoon before the party and asked if I might pick her up.

Mr Parsons: You, Mr Griswald? She didn't wish to be picked up by Mr Reed?

Witness: Evidently not.

Mr Parsons: And did you agree to do that, to bring Miss Channing to your house that evening?

Witness: Yes, I did.

And so, as he had so many times in the past, my father demanded that I come with him to Milford Cottage that evening, the two of us driving through a soft blue twilight to retrieve her. On the way, I remember that he had a certain agitated look in his eyes, like someone pressed into a service he'd rather have avoided but felt it his duty to perform. By then, of course, he must have known that something very grave had begun to darken the atmosphere of Chatham School, something he found it difficult to confront, or simply knew no way of confronting. I have often wondered what I might have said had he turned to me that evening and asked me bluntly what I knew about Miss Channing and Mr Reed. Perhaps I would have lied to him, as I later did, claiming an innocence I did not deserve.

But he talked of the party instead, the long tables that had been placed on the back lawn, the Chinese lanterns he'd hung over them, how festive everything looked.

It was not until we neared Milford Cottage that he grew silent.

Miss Channing came out immediately, dressed in a long black skirt and a dark red blouse, her hair bound tightly in a bun. Her eyes seemed feverish and her skin was very pale.

I got out of the car, and held the door open for her. 'Thank you, Henry,' she said as she got into the front seat beside my father.

'Good evening, Miss Channing,' my father said.

She nodded softly. 'Good evening, Mr Griswald.'

They hardly spoke for the first few minutes of the drive back toward Chatham. Then, out of nowhere, my father suddenly blurted out, 'I was thinking of offering you a commission, Miss Channing. A private commission, that is. A portrait of myself.' He glanced toward her, then back to the road. 'Do you do portraits?'

'Yes,' she said. 'I've done a few. My uncle. His wife. When I was in Africa.'

'So, do you think you'd like to take a crack at it?'

She smiled slightly. 'Yes, I would.'

My father seemed pleased. 'Splendid.'

They went on to arrange various times when my father would be available to sit for her, and during the next few weeks I saw them often in his office together, the door always open, of course, Miss Channing in her gray smock, standing behind her easel, my father posed beside the window, looking out onto the courtyard, his body caught in a shaft of light.

During the rest of the drive, my father talked rather absently about the spring term, how brief it always seemed compared to fall and winter, warning Miss Channing that the boys would become 'increasingly rambunctious' as the end of the school year approached. 'So keep a firm hand on them,' he told her, 'because they'll certainly need it.' It was not until we'd turned onto the main road back to Chatham that he suddenly said, 'By the way, Mr Reed may not be able to join us this evening.'

My attention sprang to Miss Channing, and I saw her body grow tense at the mention of Mr Reed's name.

'It seems that Mrs Reed has taken ill,' my father went on. 'Something to do with her stomach.'

Miss Channing turned away from my father and toward the window at her side, a quick reflexive gesture made, or so it seemed to me at the time, in order to shield her face from his view. Watching her, I recalled the way she'd sat so stiffly in the boat as we'd made our way down the Bass River only a week or so before, her manner now even more enclosed than it had appeared that day, so that she seemed oddly frightened of the very movement her life had taken, as if it were a blade swinging above her head.

It was warm enough for my father to have rolled the

window down on the driver's side, and as we made our way along the coastal road he peered out over the fields of sea grass that rose from the marshes and the bogs. 'I love the spring on Cape Cod. Summer, too, of course. Do you plan to stay here on the Cape for the summer, Miss Channing?'

'I haven't really thought about the summer,' she murmured as if such a possibility had not occurred to her.

'Well, there's still plenty of time to think about it,' my father told her, then let the subject drop.

We pulled into the driveway of our house seconds later. I got out and opened the door for Miss Channing. 'Thank you, Henry,' she said as she stepped out of the car.

Some of the other teachers had already arrived, the rest coming only a few minutes later, everyone serving themselves from the plentiful buffet my mother and Sarah had arranged on a long table in the backyard, then sitting in small groups on chairs my father and I had placed throughout the grounds earlier that afternoon.

It was my job to help Sarah serve the guests at the buffet table, and from that position I could see Miss Channing as she sat with a group not far away, my mother facing her directly, Mr Corbett to her right, Mrs Benton, the Latin teacher, to her left, and finally Mrs Abercrombie, my father's assistant, just a bit outside the circle, her long, thin legs requiring somewhat more room.

My mother was doing her best to be sociable that evening, talking in that slightly rapid way of hers about whatever matter she thought might interest the people gathered around her.

At one point I heard her say, 'Well, Chatham is small, but I think there must be quite a few eligible young men.' Then she turned to Miss Channing, the only unmarried woman in the group, and asked, 'Don't you think so, Elizabeth?'

I remember that Miss Channing seemed unable to answer my mother's question, perhaps suspecting that she had some ulterior motive in asking it.

In that brief silence, I saw my mother's eyes narrow slightly as she added, 'I mean to say, I was wondering what your experience had been.'

Still, Miss Channing did not answer, and in that interval of silence I noticed Mrs Benton glance knowingly at Mrs Abercrombie.

Finally, Miss Channing said, 'I wouldn't know about that.'

I expected my mother to let the answer go, but she didn't. 'You wouldn't?' she said, clearly surprised. 'So you've not become acquainted with any of the young men in Chatham since you arrived?'

Miss Channing shook her head. 'No, I haven't.'

My mother gave her a slow, evaluating look. 'Well, I'm sure someone will come along,' she said with a stiff smile.

They went on to other topics after that. Each time I glanced Miss Channing's way, she appeared fixed in the same position, her hands in her lap, her back erect, a plate of uneaten food nestled in the grass beside her chair.

By nine most everyone had departed. It was April, a chill still present in the evening air, and so my father invited the few guests who remained to join him in the parlor.

My mother took her usual chair by the fireplace, my father the wooden rocker a few feet away. Mrs Abercrombie and Mrs Benton shared the small settee, while Miss Channing chose a chair somewhat off to the side. I pulled out the piano stool and sat by the window.

I don't remember what they talked about for the next few minutes, only that Miss Channing said very little, her face more or less expressionless as she listened to the others, her hands still in her lap, as they had been all evening.

It was an attitude she might have remained in for the rest of the night had she not caught the sound of a car rumbling down Myrtle Street. She clearly recognized its distinctive clatter, turned toward the window, parted the curtains, and peered outside, her face suddenly bathed in light as the car wheeled into our driveway and came to a halt. I saw her eyes widen, her lips part silently as she watched a figure move down the driveway and up the stairs to our front door. One of her hands crawled into the other as she turned away from the window, listening first to the knock at the door, then Sarah's cheery greeting when she opened it. 'Well, good evening, Mr Reed.'

He came directly into the parlor, his hat in his hand, the old brown jacket draped over his shoulders, like a cape.

'Hello,' he said. 'I hope I'm not intruding.'

'No, not at all. Please, come in,' my father told him, though not with his usual enthusiasm. There was something rather stiff in the way he rose from his chair to shake Mr Reed's hand. 'I hope Mrs Reed is feeling better.'

Mr Reed nodded. 'Yes, she is,' he said.

'Please, sit down,' my father told him.

Mr Reed took a seat near the door, glancing about until his eyes fell upon Miss Channing. And though his lips lifted in a thin smile, his eyes seemed utterly mirthless and unsmiling. 'Hello, Miss Channing,' he said.

She nodded coolly. 'Mr Reed.'

My father glanced back and forth between them. 'Well, now,' he said loudly, clearly trying to draw Mr Reed's attention back to the group, 'we were all discussing the possibility of adding a course in Shakespeare to next year's curriculum.'

Mr Reed turned toward him but offered no reply.

'We were wondering who might best be able to teach such a course,' my father went on.

Mr Reed stared my father dead in the eye. 'I really don't know,' he said with what must have struck my father as a shocking sense of indifference, as if Chatham School had ceased to play any significant part in his life, but only continued to hang from it, numb, limp, useless, like an atrophied appendage waiting to be cut away.

It was a tone that clearly disturbed my father, and which he could not confront, so he merely drew in a quick, troubled breath and returned his attention to the others. 'Well, how about a round of port?' he asked them.

All heads nodded, and with that my father summoned Sarah to serve the port.

'We're so lucky to have Sarah,' my mother said after she'd finished serving and left the room. 'We had a wonderful Negro girl before her. Amelia was her name, and she was quite able.' She glanced at Miss Channing. 'As a matter of fact, Amelia would have been very interested in talking to you, Elizabeth.'

Miss Channing's fingers tightened around her glass. 'Why is that?' she asked evenly.

'Because she'd have wanted to hear all about your life in Africa,' my mother answered. She'd picked her knitting from a basket beside her chair and the long silver needles flashed in the lamplight as she flicked them right and left.

'Amelia was a follower of Marcus Garvey, you see,' my father said. 'She was quite taken with this idea of going back to Africa, living free, and all that.' He shrugged. 'It was all terribly unrealistic, of course, the whole business.' Drawing a pipe from the rack that rested on the table beside his chair, he began to fill its dark briar bowl with tobacco. 'But what can you do about such a romantic notion?'

It was a question he'd asked rhetorically, not expecting an answer, least of all a brutal one.

'You can crush it,' Mr Reed blurted out harshly, his eyes darting over to Miss Channing, then back to my father.

My father looked at him quizzically, his hand now suspended motionlessly above the bowl of his pipe, his eyes widening to take him in. 'Crush it, Mr Reed?' he asked.

'That's right,' Mr Reed said. 'You can tell her how foolish such an idea of freedom is. How foolish and preposterous it is to believe that you can ever escape anything or change anything, or live in a way that—'

He stopped, his eyes now turning toward Miss Channing, who only glared at him, her face taut and unmoving.

Then my father said, 'Well, that would be rather cruel, wouldn't it, Mr Reed?' His voice was surprisingly gentle and restrained as he continued, his eyes leveled upon Mr Reed's. 'Perhaps you could simply remind her – Amelia, I mean – that there is much in life beyond such extreme desires.'

Mr Reed shook his head, drawing his gaze from Miss Channing, and waved his hand. 'It doesn't matter anyway,' he said wearily.

There was an exchange of glances among the guests, then, as if to lower the heat within the room, Mrs Benton chirped, 'It's a lovely room you have here, Mrs Griswald. The curtains are ... lovely.'

With that, the conversation took a different and decidedly less volatile turn, although I can't remember what was said, only that neither Mr Reed nor Miss Channing said anything at all. Mrs Abercrombie left within a few minutes, then Mrs Benton, each of them nodding cordially as they bade my father and mother good night.

Mr Reed rose directly after that. He seemed weary beyond measure, as if his earlier outburst had weakened him profoundly. At the entrance to the parlor he turned back. 'Do you need a ride home, Miss Channing?' he asked, though with an unmistakable hopelessness, her answer already made clear to him by the ravaged look in her eyes.

'No,' she said, adding nothing else as he turned from her and moved silently out the door.

And so it was my father and I who drove Miss Channing home that night, gliding through the now-deserted village, then out along Plymouth Road to where we finally came to a halt at the very end of it, the headlights of my father's car briefly illuminating the front of Milford Cottage before dissolving into the impenetrable depths of Black Pond.

'Well, good night, Miss Channing,' he said to her quietly.

I expected Miss Channing to get out of the car, but she remained in place. 'Mr Griswald,' she said. 'I wonder if I might ask you something?'

My heart stopped, for I felt sure that she was about to tell him everything, reveal the whole course and nature of her relationship with Mr Reed, ask my father for that wise guidance I know he would have given if she had done so.

But she did nothing of the kind. Instead, she said, 'I was thinking of making something for the school. A piece of sculpture. Plaster masks of all the boys and the teachers, everyone at the school. I could arrange them on a column. It would be a record of everyone at Chatham School this year.'

'That would be a lot of work for you, wouldn't it, Miss Channing?' my father asked.

'Yes, it would. But for the next few weeks—' She stopped, as if trying to decide what to say. 'For the next few weeks,' she began again, 'I'd just like to keep myself busy.'

My father leaned forward slightly, peering at her closely, and I knew that whatever he had refused to see before that moment he now saw in all its fatal depth, Miss Channing's misery and distress so obvious that when Mr Parsons finally asked his question, *You knew, didn't you, Mr Griswald, that by the night of your party Miss Channing had reached a desperate point?*, he could not help but answer, *Yes*.

But that night at Milford Cottage he only said, 'Yes, very well, Miss Channing. I'm sure your sculpture will be something the school can be proud of.'

Miss Channing nodded, then got out of the car and swiftly made her way down the narrow walkway to her cottage.

My father watched her go with an unspoken sympathy for a plight he seemed to comprehend more deeply than I would have expected, and which later caused me to wonder if perhaps somewhere down a remote road or along the outer bank, some woman had once waited for him, one he wished to go to but never did, and in return for that refusal received this small unutterably painful addition to his understanding.

If such a woman ever lived, her call unanswered, he never spoke of it.

And as to Miss Channing, as he watched her make her way toward the cottage that night, 'God help her' was all he said.

TWENTY-ONE

I think it was the somberness of my father's words that awakened me early the next morning, sent me downstairs, hoping that I wasn't too late to catch up with Sarah as she set off for her weekly reading lesson.

She was already at the end of Myrtle Street when I called to her. She waited, smiling, as I came up to her.

'I thought I'd go with you this morning,' I told her.

This seemed to please her. 'That would be grand,' she said, then turned briskly and continued on down the street, the basket swinging between us as we made our way toward Milford Cottage.

We reached it a short time later, the morning air bright and warm, with more of summer in it now than spring. Miss Channing was sitting outside, on the steps of the cottage, her body so still she looked as if she'd been in the same position for a long time.

'Good morning,' she said as we came down the walkway, her tone less open and welcoming than I had ever heard it, her eyes squeezed together slightly, like someone wincing with an inward pain.

It was only a few minutes later, after she'd begun Sarah's lesson, that Miss Channing grew less distracted in her voice and manner. She began to smile occasionally, though less vibrantly than in the past, so that her overall mood remained strangely subdued.

The lesson ended at eleven, just as it usually did.

'Good, Sarah,' Miss Channing said as she rose from the table and began to gather up the books and writing pads. 'You're coming along splendidly. I'll see you again next Sunday.'

Sarah looked at me quizzically, then turned back to Miss Channing, clearly worried by the distress she saw in her, perhaps even afraid to leave her in such a troubled state. 'Would you like to take a stroll, Miss Channing?' she asked softly. 'There's a little parade or something in the village today.' She looked at me for assistance. 'What is it, Henry, that parade?'

'It's to celebrate the beginning of the Revolution,' I said. 'The shot heard 'round the world.'

Sarah kept her eyes on Miss Channing. 'We could all walk into town together,' she said. 'It's such a pretty day.'

For a moment Miss Channing seemed thrown into a quandary by Sarah's invitation. Finally, she said, though still with some reluctance, 'Well, yes, I suppose I could do that.'

We set off right away, the three of us walking at a leisurely pace down Plymouth Road. It was deep enough into spring for the first greenery to have appeared, budding trees and ferns and a few forest wildflowers, a rich pungency in the air around us. 'There was once a French king who was very fond of sweet smells,' Miss Channing said after a moment, 'and when he gave parties in the ballroom, he would have his servants pour different perfumes over live pigeons, then release them into the air.' She stopped and drew in a long breath. 'It must have been like this,' she told us, 'a tapestry of smells.'

She began to walk again, adding nothing more, but I

would always remember that this was the final story I would hear from her, the slender smile she offered at the end of it, the last that I would see upon her face.

At noon the streets of Chatham were already filled with people who'd come into the village for the day's festivities. We found a vacant spot on the hill in front of the town hall and stood, along with everyone else, waiting for the parade. Below us, on the crowded sidewalks, we could see the people moving back and forth, trying to find a clear view of the street. Miss Channing remained silent most of the time, nearly motionless as well, save that her eyes had a tendency to follow knots of children as they darted along the sidewalk or across the lawn.

We were still standing on the lawn of the town hall when the local fife and bugle corps marched by, followed by a ragged gang of villagers dressed in Revolutionary costumes, my father among them, doffing a tricornered hat. The town's new fire engine came next, festooned with flags and bunting, and after it, a small contingent of the Massachusetts State Police, riding horseback, a tall, slender man in the lead, with gray hair and a formal manner, his silver badge winking in the afternoon light, and whom I later recognized as Captain Lawrence Hamilton.

The crowd began to disperse soon afterward, children rushing here and there as their parents summoned them to their sides, groups of young people heading off toward Quilty's for ice cream and soda, couples strolling idly toward the outskirts of town, no doubt headed for the beach, where a clambake had been scheduled for later in the day.

'Well, I guess that's it for the parade,' I said absently, looking to the right, toward Miss Channing.

She didn't answer me, or even turn her eyes in my direction. Instead, she continued to peer across the street. I glanced toward where she was staring, and saw Mrs Reed standing on the opposite corner, with Mary in her arms.

For a moment Mrs Reed held her attention on the parade. Then, at a pace that seemed surreally slow, she turned to face us, her gaze suddenly leveled upon Miss Channing, cold, steady, hateful, yet strangely haunted too, features that seemed locked forever in a ghostly rage.

It must have been a look that Miss Channing could not bear, for she whirled around immediately, like someone wrenching herself from a murderous, invisible grip, and began to push forward through the crowd, leaving Sarah and me in her wake, watching, astonished, as she plunged away from us, darting left and right through the milling crowd until she finally disappeared into the throng.

'What's the matter with Miss Channing?' Sarah asked, both of us still staring off in the direction where she'd gone.

'I don't know,' I answered. But I did.

For a long time I believed that it was what Miss Channing saw that afternoon, Mrs Reed in all her wounded anguish, little Mary helpless in her arms, that determined the nature of the conversation I overheard the very next day.

It happened late in the afternoon, a blue haze already settling over the school courtyard, hovering in the trees and over the pebbled walkway. Miss Channing had just completed a portrait session with my father, for I remember seeing her in his office only moments before, my father at the window where she'd placed him, she a few feet away, peering toward him from around the side of her easel.

He'd offered to drive her home, as he later told me,

but she had declined, telling him that she wanted to begin work on the other project she had proposed, the column of faces that was to be her gift to Chatham School. After that she'd returned to her classroom, brought out a lump of clay, and begun to fashion a model of the sculpture she was soon to make.

She was still at it sometime later when I walked through the courtyard, glanced to the right, and saw her standing at her sculpting pedestal, her hands sunk deep in the pockets of her smock. She was looking toward the front of the room, but until I moved farther west, heading toward the rear door of the school, I couldn't make out what she was looking at, for the large tree that stood near the center of the courtyard blocked my view. And so it was not until I'd passed beyond it that I saw Mr Reed standing at the entrance to her room.

It was a scene that startled me, the two of them facing each other so silently and at such a physical distance that they looked like duelists in an evening shade. And so I stopped and drew back behind the tree, listening like a common eavesdropper as their voices came toward me from the open windows of Miss Channing's room.

'What do you want, Leland?'

'Something impossible.'

'You know what has to be done.'

'How do you want me to do it?'

'Without looking back.'

There was a pause, then I heard Mr Reed speak again.

'Because I love you, I can do it.'

'Then do.'

'Let me take you home now. We can—'

'No.'

'Why?'

'You know why, Leland.'

Another pause. Then he said it.

'Do you want her dead?'

I heard no answer, but only the sound of Miss Channing's footsteps as she headed toward the door, and after I that her voice again, anguished, pleading.

'Leland, please. Let me go.'

'But don't you see that—'

'Don't touch me.'

'Elizabeth, you can't—'

I heard the door of the room fly open, then saw Miss Channing rush quickly past where I stood beside the tree, and into the school, her black hair flying like a dark pennant in her wake. Watching her go, then glancing back into her room to see Mr Reed now slumped in a chair, his head in his hands, I felt the same soaring anger I'd glimpsed in Mrs Reed's face as she'd glared at Miss Channing the day before, but with Mrs Reed now the object at *my* rage, Miss Channing and Mr Reed the birds I wished to free from her bony, strangling grasp.

I was still seething nearly an hour later, Mr Reed's words echoing in my mind – *Do you want her dead?* – when Sarah found me on the front steps of the house on Myrtle Street.

'Your father sent me to get you,' she told me as she lowered herself onto the step just beneath me. 'He's at the school. He has something he wants you to do.'

'Tell him you couldn't find me,' I replied sullenly.

I felt her hand touch mine.

'What's the matter, Henry?'

I shook my head, unable to answer her.

For a moment she watched me silently, then she said, 'Why are you so unhappy, Henry?'

I gave her the only answer I had at the time. 'Because no one's free, Sarah. None of us.'

Her question sprang from an ancient source. 'What would happen if we were? Free, I mean.'

My answer signaled the dawning of a self-indulgent age. 'We'd be happy,' I said angrily. 'If we were free to do what we want, don't you think we'd be happy?'

She had no answer for me, of course. Nor should I have expected one, since she was young, as I was, the hard fact that our lives cannot accommodate the very passions they inspire still a lesson waiting to be learned.

Sarah got to her feet again. 'You'd better go to your father, Henry. He's expecting you.'

I didn't move. 'In a minute,' I told her.

'I'll go tell him that you're on your way,' Sarah said.

With that, she walked away, leaving me to sit alone, watching as she reached Myrtle Street, then swung left and headed for the school, my mind by then already returning to its lethal imaginings, thoughts so malicious and ruthless that several weeks later, as Mr Parsons and I made our way around that playing field, he could ask his question in a tone of stark certainty, *So it was murder, wasn't it, Henry?* and to my silence he could add nothing more than *How long have you known?*

TWENTY-TWO

I never answered Mr Parsons' question, but even as he asked it I recalled the very moment when I first thought of murder.

It was late on a Saturday afternoon, the first week of May. I was alone in the boathouse, Mr Reed having gone to Mayflower's for a bag of nails. The boat was nearing completion by then, its sleek sides gleaming with a new coat of varnish, the mast now fitted with ropes, its broad sail wrapped tightly and tied in place.

The lights were on inside the boathouse, but Mr Reed had covered its windows with burlap sacks, the whole room shrouded, so that it resembled something gloomy and in hiding rather than the bright departure point of the great adventure it had once seemed to me.

I was standing near the stove, gathering the last few nails from the bottom of a toolbox, when the door suddenly opened. I turned toward it, expecting to see Mr Reed, then felt my breath catch in my throat.

'You're Henry,' she said.

She stood in the doorway, a bright noon light behind her, facing me, one hand on the door, the other at her side, the sun behind her turning the red tint of her hair into a fiery aurora.

'Mildred Griswald's son,' she added.

Leveled upon me as they were, her green eyes shone out

of the spectral light, wide and unblinking, like fish eyes from a murky tank.

I nodded. 'Yes, ma'am.'

She stepped through the door, her gaze upon me with a piercing keenness, alert and wolfish. 'You're helping him,' she said. 'Helping him build the boat.'

'Yes, I am.'

Her eyes drifted from me over to the gleaming side of the boat. Then, in a quick, nearly savage movement, they shot back to me.

'Where is he?' she asked.

'Gone to buy nails.'

She came toward me, and I felt my body tense. For there was something in her manner, a sense of having been slowly devoured over many weeks, fed upon by thousands of tiny, gnawing doubts, that gave her a strangely cadaverous appearance, as if the bones were already beginning to appear beneath the pale, nearly translucent film that had become her skin.

'Your mother and I were friends when we were girls,' she said with a faint, oddly painful smile.

She continued to come forward, and seconds later, when she spoke to me again, I could feel her breath on my face. 'The boat's nearly finished.'

'Yes, it is,' I said hollowly.

She glanced about the room, her eyes moving randomly until, with a terrible suddenness, they fixed on the drawing I'd made of Miss Channing, which now hung over the desk in the far corner. Her face became instantly expressionless and void, as if an invisible acid were being poured over her features, melting her identity away.

'Does she come here?' she asked, her gaze still concentrated upon the drawing.

I shrugged. 'I don't know.'

She lifted her head and twisted it sharply to the left, her attention now focused on the cardboard box that rested on the desk, just below the portrait. Like someone lifted on a cushion of smoky air, she drifted toward it effortlessly, soundlessly, the world held in a motionless suspension until she reached it, dropped her head forward, and peered inside.

I knew what she was looking at. A map. A knife. A coil of gray rope. And in the corner, a small brown bottle, the letters printed boldly in black ink: ARSENIC.

She stared into the box for what seemed a long time, like someone recording everything she saw. Then she raised her head in what I will always remember as a slow, steady movement, as if drawing it from the dark, airless water in which it had been submerged, and turned to face me once again. 'Is it just me?' she asked.

'Just you?'

'Is it just me? Or is it Mary too?'

'I don't know what you mean, Mrs Reed.'

During all the years that have passed since that moment, I have seen my share of fear and uncertainty and sorrow, but I don't think I ever saw it in the same combination again, terror so delicately blended with pain, pain so inseparably mingled with confusion, that the final effect was of a shivering, anguished bafflement.

That was what I saw in Mrs Reed's face. It is what I still see when I remember her. It was clear and vivid, all her misery in her eyes. Anyone might have seen it. It could hardly have been more obvious. The only mystery is why her plight, so dark and terrible, did not move me in the least.

*

It was my mother that it moved.

It was late in the afternoon when I returned home that same day. Sarah was in the dining room, setting places for the evening meal, but she stopped when she saw me enter the house, and rushed into the foyer. I could tell that she was alarmed. 'Henry, I have to talk to you,' she said urgently. 'Mrs Reed came here today. To talk to your mother.'

As Mrs Reed had turned up at our door only a short time after she'd appeared in the boathouse, I had little doubt as to the purpose of her visit. Still, I kept that earlier encounter to myself, allowing Sarah to go on with her story as if I had no hint of where it might be headed.

'She looked odd, Henry,' Sarah said. 'Mrs Reed did. An odd look in her eye.' She shivered slightly. 'It gave me a ... a creepy feeling, the way she looked.'

'What did she want?'

'She asked to speak with your mother.'

'Did they speak?'

'Oh, yes, they spoke, all right. Your mother called for tea, and I brought it to them. Right in the parlor. With the door closed, of course.'

I could see my mother and Mrs Reed sitting beside the empty hearth of the parlor, our best china teacups in their hands, Mrs Reed tormented beyond measure, telling of her husband's betrayal, my mother growing more and more angry and alarmed as she listened to her story.

'I couldn't hear what they said,' Sarah added. 'But it looked serious.'

'Where are they now?'

'They went for a walk, the two of them.' Sarah gave me a piercing look. 'What's this all about, Henry?' she demanded.

'I don't know,' I lied, then turned away and mounted the stairs to my room.

I was still there an hour later when my father returned from his office at Chatham School. He called me downstairs and asked me directly where my mother was. I glanced toward where Sarah stood silently at the entrance of the dining room, waiting for my answer.

'She went out for a walk,' I said.

'A walk?' my father asked. 'At this hour? With whom?'

'With Mrs Reed,' I told him.

He could not conceal his troubled surprise at such a visit. 'Mrs Reed? Mrs Reed came here?'

'Yes. She came by this afternoon.'

'What did she want?'

'Just to see Mother, I guess.'

He nodded casually, determined to put the best possible light on such a meeting. 'Well, they were neighbors, you know,' he said. 'Your mother and Mrs Reed. They're probably talking about old times, that sort of thing.'

'I didn't know they were neighbors,' I said.

'Yes, they were,' my father said, obviously reluctant to provide any further details. 'Well, go on about your business, then, son,' he added, then turned and walked into the parlor.

I stood at the parlor door. 'When were they neighbors?' I asked.

He sat down, picked up the newspaper from the table beside his chair, and began turning the pages, still trying to avoid any further discussion of the matter. 'When they were young. Your mother lived next to the people Mrs Reed worked for after she was—' He stopped and looked at me suddenly. 'Mrs Reed was abandoned, Henry. When she was a young woman.'

'Abandoned?'

'Left at the altar, as they say.' My father's eyes now retreated behind the paper once again. 'And so your mother has a certain ... well, a certain sympathy, I suppose you'd call it. For Mrs Reed, I mean.' He drew in a long breath. 'For what she's gone through in her life.'

He said nothing more about Mrs Reed, so that I left the parlor shortly after, returned to my room upstairs, and stayed there until I heard the creak of the front gate, glanced out the window, and saw my mother striding up the walkway to the front stairs.

I had one of those premonitions children often have, moments when they sense that things are about to fly apart. Perhaps it was the firm, heavy-footed way my mother took the stairs, or the hard slap of the screen door as it closed behind her.

In any event, I went downstairs to find her in the parlor with my father. He'd lowered the paper and gotten to his feet, facing her from what looked like a defensive position beside the mantel.

'A woman knows, Arthur,' I heard my mother say.

'That's preposterous, Mildred, and you know it.'

'You won't face it, that's the problem.'

'There has to be some sort of—'

'A woman knows,' my mother cried. 'A woman doesn't need proof.'

'Yes, but I do, Mildred,' my father told her. 'I can't just bring two respected teachers into my office and—'

'Respected?' My mother spat out the word. 'Why should they be respected?'

'That's enough,' my father said.

My mother sank briefly into a fuming silence. Then, in a calm, deadly voice she said, 'If you won't do something about this, Arthur, then I'll have no respect for you either.'

My father's voice filled with dismay. 'How can you say such a thing to me?'

'Because I mean it,' my mother said. 'I married you because I respected you, Arthur. You seemed like a good man to me. Honest. Steady. But if you don't do something about this situation between Mr Reed and that woman – well, then, the way I see it, you're not the man I married.'

What I have always remembered most from that dreadful moment is that as my mother listed those things that had drawn her to my father, she never once mentioned love.

For a few smoldering seconds they faced each other without speaking. Then my father walked to his chair and slumped down into it. 'It doesn't matter anyway, Mildred,' he said softly, his eyes now drifting toward the window. 'Miss Channing is leaving Chatham School. She will not return next year.' He picked up the newspaper from the floor beside his chair but did not open it. 'She resigned this afternoon. Whatever it is that Mrs Reed thinks must be going on between Miss Channing and ... well ... you can tell her that it has come to an end.'

My mother stood rigidly in place. 'You men always feel the same way. That when it's over, a woman can just forget that it ever happened.'

Wearily, my father shook his head. 'I didn't say that, Mildred, and you know it.'

What my mother said next amazed me. 'Have you ever betrayed me, Arthur?'

My father looked at her with an astonishment exactly like my own. 'What?' he blurted out. 'My God, Mildred, what's gotten into you? How could you ask me such a question?'

'Answer it, Arthur.'

He stared at her, curiously silent, before he finally took a breath and gave his answer. 'No, Mildred,' he said evenly. 'I have never betrayed you.'

I looked at my mother, her eyes upon my father with a lethal gaze, and it struck me that she did not believe him, or at least that she would never be sure that he'd told her the truth.

For a moment they simply faced each other silently. Then my mother walked past him, edging her way through the parlor door as she headed for the kitchen. 'Dinner in an hour' was all she said.

The dinner we sat through an hour later was extremely tense. My father and mother spoke only of trivial things – my father's plan to include a couple of new courses in the curriculum, my mother's to have a larger summer garden at the back of the house. When it was over, my mother walked into the parlor, where she stayed, knitting by the unlighted hearth, until she went up to her bed. My father went back to the school, where he worked in his office until nearly nine, returning home only after my mother had already gone upstairs.

I was sitting in my customary spot in the swing on the front porch when I saw him coming down the street, his gait very slow, his head lowered slightly, the posture he always assumed when he was deep in thought.

He nodded to me as he came up the stairs.

'Nice evening, isn't it, Henry?'

I expected him to go directly into the house, as he usually did. But instead, he came over to the swing and sat down beside me. At first I didn't know what to do in regard to the exchange I'd heard between him and my mother a few hours before, but after a time my curiosity got the better of me, so I decided to bring it up.

Still, I didn't want to approach things too directly, so I said, 'When I was coming downstairs this afternoon, I thought I heard you say that Miss Channing was leaving Chatham School.'

He did not appear surprised that I'd overheard him, nor particularly alarmed by it, so that I felt the faint hope that, perhaps for the first time, he'd begun to see me not as a little boy from whom life must be concealed behind a wall of secrecy and silence, but as someone on the brink of adulthood to whom, however painfully, its truths must be revealed.

'Yes, she's leaving, Henry.'

'Where's she going?'

'I don't know.' He glanced toward me, then away again. 'But I wouldn't worry about Miss Channing. She'll do quite well, I'm sure. She's a very able teacher. Very able. I'm sure she'll find another post somewhere else.'

The subject seemed closed. Then, abruptly, my father turned to me. 'Henry, you must keep quiet about whatever you've heard at home,' he said. 'About Miss Channing and Mr Reed, I mean.'

I could tell that he was trying to find the words for some other, deeper thought. 'Life is inadequate, Henry,' he said finally, his eyes upon me very solemnly. 'Sometimes the most we can give, or get, is trust.' With that he leaned forward, patted my leg, rose, and went inside. Nor did he ever make any further attempt to explain what he'd said to me. But over the years, as he grew older and I grew older, I came to understand what he'd meant that night, that hunger is our destiny, faith what we use to soothe its dreadful pang.

I know now that my father had tried to reach out to me that night, show the path ahead, but I remember that as I watched him trudge wearily through the door, he seemed smaller to me than he ever had. I felt a malevolent wave of contempt for everything he stood for. It was swift and boiling, and in its wake I felt an absolute determination never to be like my father, never so pathetic, nor so beaten down.

Now, when I think of that moment in my life, of what I felt, and later did, the inevitable strikes me as nothing more than that which has just happened unexpectedly.

PART V

TWENTY-THREE

Some years ago I happened upon a line in Tacitus. It came near the end of the section of *Germania* that described the utter subjugation of the barbaric German tribes at the hands of the more tightly regimented Roman legions, a campaign that had stripped the Germans of the last vestiges of their savagery, all their primitive rites and rituals taken from them, their dances, songs, and stories. 'They have made a wilderness,' Tacitus wrote, 'and call it peace.'

In the brief period that remained before it closed for the summer, a similarly bare and withered peace appeared to descend upon Chatham School, turning it into a passionless world, as it seemed to me at the time, very nearly a void, all its former vibrancy, the tingling sense of intrigue and desire, now buried beneath a layer of stark propriety.

During this time Miss Channing no longer arrived and departed with Mr Reed, but walked back and forth from Milford Cottage alone. In the morning I would often see her moving up our street, her pace slow, meditative, so that she appeared to be in continual conversation with herself. At school she remained in her room, eating her lunch there, or sitting by the cabinet, reading, between classes. There were no more strolls into the village with Mr Reed, no more meetings with him by the coastal bluff. And when the day was over, she would head back toward Black Pond, moving through the evening shade with the same thoughtful air with which she'd arrived at school that same morning.

Her classes took on a similar mood of withdrawal. She became more formal than she had before, her demeanor more controlled, as if she now felt it necessary to conceal every aspect of her life, both past and present, from the many prying eyes she'd sensed around her for so long.

During these final three weeks it was the column of faces that occupied most of her time. She covered a table with a dark green tarpaulin, and one by one the teachers and students of Chatham School came to her room and lay down upon it to have plaster masks made of their faces. Once I saw Mrs Benton lying there, her eyes closed, her body tense and rigid, Miss Channing poised above her, staring down, a single finger daubed with moist clay drawing a line across her throat.

My turn came during the middle of May.

'Hello, Miss Channing,' I said as I stepped into her classroom.

It was after six in the evening, the air outside growing dark, a soft breeze rustling gently through the late spring leaves of the old oak that stood in the courtyard.

She was wearing a long blue dress, but she'd thrown on one of the gray smocks she used to protect her clothing. Her hair was pulled back and tied with what appeared to be a piece of ordinary twine.

'Hello, Henry,' she said in that aloof and oddly brittle tone she'd fallen into by that time. 'What do you want?'

'I've come to get a cast made of my face,' I told her. 'For the column.'

She nodded toward the table. 'Lie down,' she said.

I walked to the table, pulled myself onto it, and lay on my back, my eyes turned toward the ceiling.

'I'm sorry I've come so late,' I said.

She stepped up to the table, dipped her fingers in the wet clay, then began to apply it smoothly, first across my forehead, then along the sides of my face. 'Close your eyes,' she said.

I did as she told me, breathing softly as she coated my eyelids, her touch very tender, almost airy.

'This is the way they make a death mask, isn't it?' I asked.

'Yes,' she said. 'It is.' She continued to work, covering my face with a cold, thin layer of clay.

Once she'd finished applying the clay, I lay on the table while it dried, listening as she moved about the room. I could hear the soft tread of her feet as she walked from the tables to the cabinet, putting things away, and I recalled how she'd drifted across the summer grass toward my father on that now-distant afternoon, the look in his eyes as he'd caught sight of her bare feet.

After a time she returned to me, removed the cast, then wiped away the residue from my face with a moist towel.

'It's done,' she said as she dropped the towel into a basket by the table. 'You can go.'

I pulled myself to a sitting position, then got to my feet. By then Miss Channing was several feet away, where many other masks lay faceup on a wide table, eyes closed, lips pressed tightly together, cadaverously gray.

'Well, good night, Miss Channing,' I said when I reached the door.

'Good night, Henry,' she answered, her eyes now fixed on the mask she'd just made of my face as she wrapped it in a length of white cloth.

I remained at the door, wanting to reach her somehow, remove her from the pall she seemed imprisoned in, tell her what she should do, how she must follow her father's lead, live the life he'd prepared her for. I could almost see her rushing through the dark marina, a red cape flowing behind her, Mr Reed waiting in the boat, lifting her into it, the hunger of their embrace, that thirsty kiss.

'Is there something else, Henry?' she asked, now staring at me intently, her fingers still wet and glistening, bits of moist clay in her hair. She appeared strikingly similar to the way I'd later see her, rising from the water, her hair soaked and stringy, hung with debris from the depths of Black Pond, her question asked in the same bloodless tone, *Is she dead?* My answer delivered as passionlessly as my life would be lived from then on, *Yes.*

Miss Channing finished the column only a few days later, and it was erected on the eighteenth of May in a ceremony my father arranged for the occasion. The ceremony took place on the front lawn of the school, and in the photograph taken that morning, and later included in my father's archive of the Chatham School Affair, Miss Channing stands to the right of the sculpture, her arms clasped to her sides, my father to its left, one hand tucked beneath his coat, Napoleonic fashion. All the teachers and students of the Chatham School are gathered around them, along with Sarah, who stands just off to the side, dressed up for the occasion, smiling brightly, her long black hair tucked inside a straw hat with a wide ribbon trailing off the back.

Miss Channing didn't speak to the assembly that morning, but my father did. He thanked her for her work, not only on the sculpture, but as a teacher who, he said, had done a 'remarkable job all round'. At the end of the speech he announced that Miss Channing would not be returning to Chatham School the following year, and that she would be 'deeply, deeply missed'.

Mr Reed was the only teacher who did not attend the ceremony that morning. Nor did I expect him to. For during the preceding two weeks he'd grown increasingly remote, arriving alone at school just before his first class and leaving alone directly after the last one. During the school day he no longer lingered in the hallway with students, nor took them into the courtyard for a recitation, despite the unseasonable warmth of those first days of summer. Instead, he conducted his classes in the usual manner, lecturing and reading, but with much of the spirit he'd once brought to it now drained away. From time to time, as he stood at the front of the room, he would let his gaze wander toward the window, where, across the courtyard, he could see Miss Channing with her own students before her. At those moments he appeared frozen in a grim and futile yearning, and seemed unable to draw his eyes away from her, until, at last, they would dart back to us, his head jerking slightly as they did so, like someone who'd been slapped.

Still, despite the furious melancholy that so clearly hovered around him, Mr Reed continued to work on his boat. It was finished by the third week in May, and the following Saturday he asked me to join him for the maiden voyage.

The boat had already been taken from the boathouse when I arrived at the marina that morning, the wooden rack that had once held it now empty, the tools and supplies that had been used in its construction put away. The top of the desk had been cleared as well, the cardboard box in which Mrs Reed had found such an assortment of disturbing things already taken to the house on Black Pond and placed in the attic where Captain Hamilton would later find it, the small brown bottle of arsenic still huddled in the corner, its cap tightly fitted, but the contents nearly gone.

Only my drawing of Miss Channing still remained in its former place, though it now hung slightly askew, its surface coated with a thin layer of dust. It would still be there two weeks later, when I showed it to Mr Parsons, his comment destined to linger in my mind forever after that. *She's what did it to him, Henry, she's what drove him mad.*

But on that foggy Saturday morning, so strange an eventuality seemed inconceivable, and the boathouse appeared merely like a structure that had weathered a violent but departed storm rather than one about to be blown apart by an approaching one.

'All right, let's try her out,' Mr Reed said as he led me out of the boathouse and down the wooden pier to where I could see the *Elizabeth* lolling softly in the undulating water, its tall mast weaving rhythmically left and right, a white baton in the surrounding fog.

Once we'd climbed into the boat, Mr Reed untied the rope that held it to its mooring, adjusted the sail so that we briefly drifted backward, then took the rudder and guided it out of the marina.

We followed what appeared to be a predetermined course, exactly like the one I'd seen drawn on Mr Reed's nautical map, along the western coast of Monomoy Island, past Hammond's Bend and Powder Hole, and finally around the tip of the island at Monomoy Point and into the open sea. Mr Reed kept his eyes forward for the most part, but from time to time he would peer about, like someone scouting dangers all around, so that for a single, exhilarating instant I felt once again a party to some desperate and wildly romantic conspiracy, this early morning voyage, begun before the harbor master had arrived at work, with the marina deserted and the coastline shrouded in mist, serving as our practice run. 'A man could vanish into a fog like this,' he said at one point. 'Disappear. Disappear.'

It was nearly ten o'clock when we sailed back into Chatham harbor. The early morning fog had now burned off entirely; the air around us was crystal clear. Mr Reed guided the boat into its place in the marina, then looped the rope to the wooden pylon, mooring it in the same dock where we'd found it earlier that same morning.

But rather than being uplifted by the maiden voyage of a boat he'd been working on for three years, Mr Reed remained solemn and downcast. I moved along beside him, down the long wooden pier and into the boathouse, wondering what I might do to lift his spirits, draw him out of the dreadful despair that had fallen over him, renew the vitality and soaring discontent I'd so admired before, perhaps even point the way to some victory that might still be his.

Mr Reed drew himself up on the desk in the corner of the boathouse, resting his cane against it, his hands folded one over the other. For a few minutes he talked about the Galápagos Islands, the ones off the coast of South America that Darwin had written of in *The Voyage of the Beagle*. 'Everything must have looked new to him,' he told me. 'Everything in life brand new.' He shook his head with a strange mirthlessness. 'Imagine that,' he said. 'A whole new world.'

Watching him from my place a few feet away, I felt coldly

stricken, like a boy at a deathwatch, helplessly observing the slow disintegration of someone he'd admired.

As for Mr Reed, he seemed hardly aware that I was in the room at all. At times his mind appeared to drift directionlessly from one subject to the next, his eyes sometimes fixed in a motionless frieze, sometimes roaming from place to place about the room, as if in flight from the one object he would not let them light upon, the portrait of Miss Channing that still hung on the far wall, her face forever captured in what must have come to strike him as a cruelly beckoning gaze.

During all that afternoon he spoke only once about the boat, the long labor of the last few years, his eyes locked on the empty rack that had once held its lofty frame. 'Well, she was seaworthy, at least,' he said. Then he grasped his cane, edged himself off the desk, and walked to one of the windows that looked out into the harbor. It was still covered with a strip of burlap, and for a moment Mr Reed simply stared at the rough, impenetrable cloth. Then, with a sudden, violent jerk he yanked it down, a sheet of dust and a shaft of hard incandescent light pouring over him, and into which, for a single, surreal instant, he seemed to disappear.

TWENTY-FOUR

I often felt as if I had disappeared as well, vanished into the same dusky light that had briefly engulfed Mr Reed.

For with the boat now finished, I saw him only occasionally, either in his classroom or at a distance, a figure who seemed perpetually in flight, walking rapidly down a far corridor or turning the corner of Myrtle Street, silent, harried, like someone running beneath the lash of invisible whips.

As for Miss Channing, I rarely saw her anywhere but in her room, so I felt once again like one student among many, with nothing to distinguish me or set me apart from the rest, watching silently, just as they did, while she gave her final lessons with a formality that struck me as very nearly rigid, all the ease and spontaneity that had marked her former relationship with us completely cast aside, leaving her distant and preoccupied, her focus turned inward with a deadly gravity.

Left more or less to myself, I became increasingly agitated as the end of the school year approached. I fidgeted nervously through Miss Channing's classes, my attention drifting toward the window, not with the lack of interest that sometimes afflicted the other boys, but in an attitude of barely controlled hostility and contempt, as if she were a lover who had led me on and then betrayed me, and whom I now despised.

I felt bereft and abandoned, deserted by my closest allies. And so I poured all my energy into my drawing, watching helplessly as those darker elements that had earlier marked it now took on a demonic blackness, the village forever hung in gothic shadows, the sea disappearing into a grim invading horde of thunderclouds. The angles and perspectives changed as well, tilting Chatham on a cruel axis, its crooked streets plunging in jagged lines toward a central maelstrom, houses careening left or right, a world of colliding shapes. Stranger still, I drew my distortions as if they were not really distortions at all, but our village seen rightly, caught in the actual warp and wrench of the world, a grotesque deformity its true face.

During this time I had only Sarah to remind me of everything that had once seemed so exciting, the piercing intensity I'd felt the day we'd all stood on the snowy hilltop together and gazed down at Black Pond, how open life had seemed at that moment, how thrillingly romantic. All of that now appeared smothered and inert. So much so that I even began to avoid Sarah, closing my bedroom door at the sound of her approach, as if she were nothing more than a bitter reminder of some lost ideal, a charred locket that had once hung from a lover's neck.

Sarah no doubt sensed the way I felt, but she refused to withdraw from me despite it. Instead, she often came to where I lay in my room, knocked at the door, and demanded that I join her for a walk along the beach or accompany her on a shopping trip to the village.

On the final Thursday of that school year, she found me sitting at the edge of the playing field. It was late in the afternoon. The teachers had already gone home to prepare the final examinations of the coming week, and some of the boys had decided to play a game of touch football before going to their rooms for a night of study.

'What are you doing here, Henry?' she asked as she strode up and lowered herself onto the ground beside me.

I shrugged silently, pretending that my attention was on the boys as they continued at the game, their movements dictated by its unbending rules, no hitting, scratching, kicking, rules that must have, in the end, given them comfort, the limits laid out so clearly, but which I saw as yet another example of their strapped and adventureless lives.

'You hate it, don't you, Henry?' Sarah demanded. 'You hate Chatham School.'

The game dissolved. I looked at her evenly, the truth bursting from me. 'Yes, I do.'

Sarah nodded, and to my surprise read my thoughts with perfect accuracy. 'Don't run away, Henry. You'll be leaving for college soon. After that, you won't have to ...'

I turned away from her and nodded toward the boys. 'What if I end up like them?'

She settled her gaze on the playing field, watching and listening as the boys darted about and called to one another. From the look in her eyes I could tell that she did not think them so bad, the boys of Chatham School, nor even the lives they would later make. For she was already mature enough to sense that the wilder life I so yearned for might finally come to little, the road less traveled end in nothing more than the dull familiarity of having traveled it.

But I lacked that same maturity, and so Sarah's rebel spirit now seemed as dead as Mr Reed's and Miss Channing's, the whole world mired in a vile dispiritedness and cowardice. 'When you get right down to it, you're just like them, Sarah,' I told her sneeringly, nodding toward the boys, my words meant to strike deep, leave her soul bleeding on the ground. 'You're a girl. That's the only difference.'

I might have said more, struck at her with an even greater arrogance and cruelty, but a loud crash suddenly stopped me. It was hard and metallic, and it had come from the lighthouse. Glancing toward it, I saw Miss Channing rush out its open door, a red scarf whipping behind her as she made her way across the lawn.

Sarah's eyes widened. 'Miss Channing,' she whispered.

Miss Channing reached the street, wheeled to the right, and headed down it, her stride long and rapid until she came to the coastal road. For a moment she stopped, briefly dropped her head into her hands, then lifted it again and whirled around, glaring toward the lighthouse for an instant before she turned away and rushed down the road toward town.

It was then that we looked back toward the lighthouse. Mr Reed stood in its still-open door, his head drooping forward as he leaned, exhausted, upon his cane.

'Why don't they just run away together?' I blurted out with a vehemence so deep the words seemed directed less to them than to me. 'Why are people such cowards?'

Sarah watched me softly, gently, the harsh words I'd just said to her already put aside. 'They're not cowards, Henry,' she told me firmly.

'Then why don't they just go ahead and do what they want to do and forget everything else?'

She did not answer me. And when I recall that moment now, I realize that she could not possibly have answered. For we have never discovered why, given the brevity of life and the depth of our need and the force of our passions, we do not pursue our own individual happiness with an annihilating zeal, throwing all else to the wind. We know only that we don't, and that all our goodness, our only claim to glory, resides in this inexplicable devotion to things other than ourselves.

I turned back toward the lighthouse. Its open door was now empty, for Mr Reed had mounted the stairs to its top by then. I could see him standing there, staring out over the village, his hands gripped to the iron rail, posed exactly as I would no doubt have painted him, a crippled silhouette against a bloodred sky.

'She's killing him,' I said, my mind now so fierce and darkly raging that I all but trembled as I said it. 'They're killing each other. Why don't they just get in his boat and sail away from all this?'

Sarah looked at me intently. I could tell that she hardly had the courage for her next question, but felt that she had to ask it anyway. 'Is that what you were doing, Henry?' she asked. 'Building a boat for them to run away in?'

I thought of all I'd seen and heard over the last few weeks, the hours of labor I'd devoted to helping Mr Reed build his boat, the unspoken purpose I'd come to feel in the building of it. I looked at her boldly, proud of what I'd done, regretful only that so much work had come to nothing. 'Yes,' I told her. 'That's what I was building it for. So that they could run away.'

Sarah's eyes widened in dismay. 'But, Henry, what about—' She stopped, and for a moment we faced each other silently. Then, with no further word, she rose and walked away, taking her place, as it seemed to me, among that numb and passionless legion forever commanded by my father.

*

For the next few hours, lying sullenly in my bed upstairs, I felt nothing but my own inner seething. The most ordinary sounds came to me as an unbearable clamor, the heaviness of my mother's footsteps like the thud of horses' hooves, my father's voice a mindless croaking. The house itself seemed arrayed against me, my own room closing in upon me like a vise, the air inside it so thick and acrid that I felt myself locked in a furiously smoldering chamber.

It was nearly nine when I finally rushed down the stairs and out into the night. My mother had gone to a neighbor's house, so she didn't see me leave. As for my father, I could see the lights of his office at Chatham School as I slunk down Myrtle Street, and knew that he was at work there, curled like a huge black bear over the large desk beside the window, his quill pen jerking left and right as he signed 'important documents'.

I didn't know where I was going as I continued toward the bluff, only that it vaguely felt like I was running away, doing exactly what Sarah had warned me not to do, fleeing Chatham School on a wave of impulse, casting everything aside, throwing my future to the wind.

I knew that I was not really doing that, of course, but I kept moving anyway, down through the streets of the village I so despised, past its darkened shops, and further still, out along the road that ran between the marshes and the sea, to where Plymouth Road suddenly appeared, a powdery lane of oyster shells, eerily pale as a bank of clouds parted and a shaft of moonlight fell upon it, abruptly rendering it as gothic and overwrought as I would no doubt have drawn it, its route stretching toward me like a ghostly hand.

In my mind I saw Miss Channing as she'd rushed from

the lighthouse hours before, the red scarf trailing after her, Mr Reed left behind, his head bowed, his hand clutching his cane. They had never appeared more tragically romantic to me than at that moment, more deserving to be together, to find the sort of happiness that only people like themselves, so fierce and passionately driven, can find, or even deserve to find.

I turned onto Plymouth Road with little specific intention in mind, recalling the many times I'd strolled down it with Sarah to find Miss Channing sitting on the steps of Milford Cottage or standing beside the pond. I remembered the snowy day in November when we'd all walked to the top of a nearby hill, how happy everyone had been that day, how open all our lives had briefly appeared, how utterly and permanently closed they now did.

I reached Milford Cottage with no prior determination to go there. Had I found the lights off, I would have turned away. Had a car been parked in the drive, I would have retreated back into the darkness and returned to Myrtle Street. But the lights were on, and no car blocked my path. Perhaps even more important, it began to rain. Not softly, but with a deafening burst of thunder, so that I knew it would be over quickly, that I would need the shelter of Milford Cottage only just long enough for the storm to pass, and then be on my way.

When she opened the door, I saw a face unlike any I had ever seen, her eyes so pale they seemed nearly colorless, two black dots on a field of white, dark crescents beneath them, her hair thrown back and tangled as if she had been shaken violently, then hurled against a wall. Never had anyone looked more cursed by love than Miss Channing did at that dreadful instant.

'Henry,' she said, squinting slightly, trying to bring me

into focus, her voice a broken whisper. 'What are you doing here?'

'I was just out walking,' I explained, speaking rapidly, already stepping back into the night, aware that I had come upon her in a grave moment. 'Then it started to rain and so ...'

She drew back into the cottage, opening the door more widely as she did so. 'Come in,' she told me.

Candles were burning everywhere inside the cottage, but there was also a fire in the hearth, a stack of letters on the mantel, some of them, as I could see, already burning in the flames. The air inside was thick and overheated, a steam already gathering in the corners of the windows.

'I was just getting rid of a few things,' Miss Channing told me, her voice tense, almost breathless, beads of sweat gathered on her forehead and along the edge of her upper lip, her long fingers toying distractedly at the collar of her blouse. 'Before I leave,' she added. Her eyes shot toward the window, the rain that could be seen battering against it. 'Things I don't want,' she said as she glanced back to me.

I didn't know what to say, so I said only, 'What can I do to help?'

Her gaze was directed toward me with a terrible anguish, all her feeling spilling out. 'I can't go on,' she said, her eyes now glistening in the candlelight.

I stepped toward her. 'Anything, Miss Channing,' I said. 'I just want to help.'

She shook her head. 'There's nothing you can do, Henry,' she told me.

I looked at her imploringly. 'There must be something,' I insisted.

I saw a strange steeliness come into her face, a sense of

flesh turning into stone, as if, in that single instant, she had determined that she would survive whatever it was that love had done to her. With a quick backward step she drew away from me and walked into the adjoining bedroom. For a moment she stood beside the bookshelf near her bed, staring down at it with a cold, inflexible glare. Then she plucked a necklace from its top shelf, her fingers clutching it like pale talons as she returned to me.

'Get rid of this,' she said.

'But, Miss Channing ...'

She grabbed my hand, placed the necklace in its open palm, and closed my fingers around it. 'That's all I want you to do, Henry,' she said.

The rain had stopped when I left Milford Cottage a few minutes later, Miss Channing standing in the door, framed by the interior light. She was still there when I rounded the near bend and, with that turn, swept out of her view.

I walked on in darkness, moving slowly over the wet ground, thinking of what I'd glimpsed in Miss Channing's face, shaken by what I'd seen, the awful ruin of the passions she'd once shared with Mr Reed, unable to imagine anything that might return her to its earlier joy save for the one that had always presented itself, the two of them in Mr Reed's boat, a high wind sweeping through its white sails, propelling them around Monomoy Point and into the surging, boundless sea.

For a time I was locked in pure fantasy, as if I were with them, sweeping southward, a Caribbean wind whipping the tropical waters off the coast of Cuba, Miss Channing's face radiantly tanned, her black hair flying free in warm sea breezes, Mr Reed at the helm, miraculously cured of his limp, the scar erased forever from his face, the winters of New England, with all their frozen vows, unable to reach them now or call them back to anything.

It was the headlights of an approaching car that brought my attention back to Plymouth Road. They came forward slowly, almost stalkingly, like two yellow eyes, covering me in so bright a shaft of blinding light that it was only after the car had come to a halt beside me that I saw Mr Reed behind the wheel, his eyes hidden beneath the shadows of his hat.

'Get in,' he said.

I got in and he pulled away, continuing down Plymouth Road, but turning to the left at the fork, moving toward his house on the other side of the pond rather than Milford Cottage.

'What are you doing out here, Henry?'

'Just walking.'

He kept his eyes trained on the road, his fingers wrapped tightly around the wheel. 'Were you with Miss Channing?'

'Yes,' I told him.

'Why?'

'I was out walking and it started to rain. I went there to get out of the rain.'

The car continued forward, two shafts of yellow light dimly illuminating the glistening road ahead.

'What did she tell you?' Mr Reed asked.

'Tell me?'

His eyes swept over to me. 'About this afternoon. At the lighthouse.'

I shook my head. 'Nothing,' I answered.

For a moment he seemed not to believe me. We sped on for a few seconds, his attention held on the road ahead. Then I saw his shoulders fall slightly, as if a great weight had suddenly been pressed down upon them. He lifted his foot from the accelerator and pressed down on the brake, bringing the car to a skidding halt. In the distance I could see the lights of his house glowing softly out of the darkness. 'Sometimes I wish that she were dead,' he whispered. Then he turned to me, his face nearly as gray and lifeless as the masks of Miss Channing's column. 'You'd better get home now, Henry' was all he said.

I did as he told me, then watched as he pulled away, the taillights of his car glaring back toward me like small mad eyes.

Mr Reed did not come to school the next day, but Miss Channing did, her mood very somber, the agitation of the night before now held within the iron grip of her relentless self-control.

It was the Friday before final examinations, and we all knew that since she was leaving Chatham School, it would be the last class we would ever have with her. Other departing teachers, those who had retired or found better posts, even the few whose abilities my father had found unacceptable and sent packing, had always taken a moment to say good-bye to us, usually with a few casual words about how much they had enjoyed being with us and hoped we'd stay in touch. I suppose that as the class neared its final minutes that day, we expected Miss Channing to do something similar, perhaps give a vague indication of what she intended to do after leaving Chatham School.

But Miss Channing didn't do any of that. Instead, she raced through a review of the major things she'd taught us, her manner brittle, giving only the most clipped answers to our questions, ending it all with a single, lifeless comment.

'It's time to go,' she said only a few seconds before the final bell. Then she strode down the aisle and stationed herself at the entrance to her classroom.

The bell sounded, and as we all rose and filed out of the room, Miss Channing nodded to each of us as we went past, her final word only a quick, barely audible, 'Good-bye.'

'We don't have to say good-bye now,' I told her when I reached the door. 'I'll be coming over with Sarah on Sunday.'

She nodded briskly. 'All right,' she said, then swiftly turned her attention to the boy behind me. 'Good-bye, William,' she said as he stepped forward and took her hand.

For the rest of the day Miss Channing spent her time cleaning out the small converted shed that had served as her room and studio for the preceding nine months. She put away her materials, stacked the sculpting pedestals, folded up the dropcloth she'd placed over the tables on which she'd fashioned the masks for the column on the front lawn.

By four in the afternoon she'd nearly finished most of the work and was now concentrating upon the final details of the cleanup. Mrs Benton saw her washing the windows with the frantic wiping motions she later described to Mr Parsons and Captain Hamilton. Toward evening, the air in the courtyard now a pale blue, Mrs Abercrombie saw the lights go out in her classroom, then Miss Channing step out of it, closing the door behind her. For a moment she peered back inside it, Mrs Abercrombie said, then she turned and walked away. A few seconds later Mr Taylor, a local banker who lived in the one great house on Myrtle Street, saw her standing beside the column on the front lawn of Chatham School, her fingers lightly touching one of its faces. And finally, just before nightfall, with a line of storm clouds advancing along the far horizon, my father came out of the front door of the school, glanced idly to the left, and saw her standing on the bluff, the tall white lighthouse to her back, her long black hair tossing wildly in the wind as she stared out over the darkening sea.

During the next day, Saturday, May 28, 1927, no one saw Miss Channing at all. The local postman said the cottage was deserted when he delivered her mail at eleven o'clock, and a hunter by the name of Marcus Lowe, caught in the same sort of sudden thunderstorm that had swept over the Cape two nights before, later said that he'd stood for nearly half an hour on the small porch of Milford Cottage and heard no stirring inside it. Nor had any of its lamps been lighted, he added, despite the gloom that had by then settled along the outer reaches of Black Pond.

TWENTY-FIVE

It's quite possible that from the time Miss Channing left Chatham School on that last Friday before final exams, no one at all saw her until the following Sunday morning, when Sarah arrived for her final reading lesson.

The storm of the previous evening had passed, leaving the air glistening and almost sultry as we walked down Plymouth Road that morning. Sarah appeared hardly to have remembered the sharp words I'd said to her as we'd sat at the edge of the playing field two days before. Once she even took my arm, holding it lightly as we continued down the road, her whole manner cheerful and confident, the timid girl of a year before completely left behind.

'I'll miss Miss Channing,' she told me. 'But I'm not going to stop studying.'

She had mastered the basics of reading and writing by then, and from time to time during the past few weeks I'd seen her sitting in the kitchen, an open book in her lap, her beautiful eyes fiercely concentrated on the page, getting some of the words, clearly stumped by others, but in general making exactly the sort of progress I would have expected in one so dedicated and ambitious and eager to escape the life she might otherwise have been trapped in.

She released my arm and looked at me determinedly. 'I'm not going to ever give up, Henry,' she said.

She'd dressed herself quite formally that morning, no

doubt in a gesture of respect toward Miss Channing. She wore a white blouse and a dark red skirt, and her hair fell loosely over her shoulders and down her back in a long, dark wave. She'd made something special as well, not merely cookies or a pie, but a shawl, dark blue with a gold fringe, the colors of Chatham School.

'Do you think Miss Channing will like it?' she asked eagerly as she drew it from the basket.

I shrugged. 'I don't know,' I answered, recalling how distant and unhappy Miss Channing had seemed in her final class on Friday, the way she'd only nodded to us as we'd left her room. But even that distance seemed better than the torment I'd seen two nights before, the look in her eyes as she'd placed the necklace in my hand, the cold finality of the words she'd said, *Get rid of this*.

But I hadn't gotten rid of it, so that by the time Sarah and I reached the fork in Plymouth Road, I could feel it like a small snake wriggling in my trouser pocket, demanding to be set free.

I stopped suddenly, knowing what I would do.

'What's the matter, Henry?' Sarah asked.

I felt my hand slide into my pocket, the glass necklace curl around my fingers. 'I have to go over to Mr Reed's for a minute,' I told her.

'Mr Reed's? Why?'

'I have to give him something. I'll come to Miss Channing's after that.'

Sarah nodded, then turned and headed on down the road, taking the fork that led to Milford Cottage while I took the one that led to Mr Reed's.

I arrived at his house a few minutes later. His car was sitting in the driveway, but the yard was deserted, and I heard no sounds coming from the house.

Then I saw her, Mrs Reed walking toward me from the old gray shed that stood in the distance, her body lumbering heavily across the weedy ground, so deep in thought she did not look up until she'd nearly reached the front steps of the house.

'Good morning, Mrs Reed,' I said.

She stopped abruptly, startled, her hand rising to shield her eyes from the bright morning sun, gazing at me with a strange wariness, as if I were a shadow she'd suddenly glimpsed in the forest or something she'd caught lurking behind a door.

'I'm Henry Griswald,' I reminded her. 'The boy you—'

'I know who you are,' she said, her chin lifting with a sudden jerk, as if in anticipation of a blow. 'You helped him with the boat.'

I could hear the accusation in her voice, but decided to ignore it. 'Is Mr Reed home?'

The question appeared to throw her into distress. 'No,' she answered in a voice now suddenly more agitated. 'He's out somewhere, walking.' Her eyes shot toward the pond, the little white cottage that rested on its far bank. 'I don't know where he is.'

'Do you know when he'll be back?'

'No, I don't,' she answered, her manner increasingly tense, brittle, a single reddish eyebrow arching abruptly, then lowering slowly, like a dying breath. 'Why are you here?' she asked, peering at me with a grave distress, as if I were diving toward her from a great height, a black bird in fatal descent. 'What did you come here for?'

'I just wanted to see Mr Reed.'

Another thought appeared to strike her, her mind now twisting in a new direction.

'Is he running away?' she demanded, her eyes upon me

with a savage spite, her voice very thin, a cutting wire drawn taut. 'Leaving me and Mary?' She tilted her head to the left, toward the pond. 'Running away with *her*?'

I shrugged. 'I ... don't ...'

Something seemed to ignite in her mind. 'He wouldn't be the first, you know. The first one to leave me.'

I said nothing.

She was watching me apprehensively, as if I were not a boy at all, but someone sent to do her harm, my fingers wrapped not around a frail glass necklace, but a length of gray rope, the steel grip of a knife.

'I just wanted to see Mr Reed,' I told her. 'I'll come back some other time.'

She stared at me angrily. 'You tell him I'll not have it again,' she said loudly, distractedly, as if she were speaking to someone in the distance. 'He said he would be home.'

'I'm sure he'll be back in a few minutes,' I said.

She remained silent, locked in what now seemed an impenetrable distraction, her eyes drifting, unhinged, so that they seemed unable to focus on anything more definite than the old apron her fingers now began to squeeze and jerk.

Looking at her at that moment, I could not imagine that she would ever embrace Mr Reed again, draw him into her bed, or even go walking with him through the woods on a snowy afternoon. How could he possibly live the rest of his life with her, eating a milky chowder while she stared at him from the other side of the table, babbling about the price of lard, but thinking only of betrayal?

Suddenly, the alternative to such a fate presented itself more forcefully than it ever had, and I saw Miss Channing rushing from the lighthouse, Mr Reed at her side, the two of them making their way down the coastal road, through the village streets, until they reached the *Elizabeth*, its broad sails magnificently unfurled, the trade winds waiting like white stallions to carry them away.

It was then, in a moment of supreme revelation, that the answer came to me. Someone else had to do it. Someone else had to set them free. Miss Channing and Mr Reed were helplessly imprisoned in the dungeon of Chatham School, my father its grim warden, Mrs Reed the guardian of the gate. It was up to me to be the real hero of their romance, turn the iron key, pull back the heavy door.

And so I leveled my eyes upon Mrs Reed and said, 'Let them go, Mrs Reed. They want to be free.'

Her eyes froze, everything in her face tightening, her features now a twisted rope. 'What did you say?'

'They want to be free,' I repeated, now both astonished and emboldened by my own daring.

She stared at me stonily. 'Free?'

I glanced toward the pond. In the distance I could see the willow behind Milford Cottage, the pier that stretched out over the water. I thought of the moment when Miss Channing had pressed a trembling hand against Mr Reed's cheek, the look in his eyes as he'd felt her touch.

It was a vision that urged me onward with a ruthless zeal. 'Yes,' I said coldly. 'To be free. That's what they want. Miss Channing and Mr Reed.'

For a moment she stared at me silently, her eyes now strangely dull, her features flat and blunted, as if they'd been beaten down by a heavy rod. Then her body stiffened, like someone jerked up by a noose, and she whirled around and bolted away from me, calling out as she did so, *Mary, come inside*, her voice pealing through the surrounding woods as she swept up the stairs and disappeared into the house, a little girl darting around its far corner only seconds later, climbing up the wooden stairs, laughing brightly as she vanished into its unlighted depths.

Miss Channing and Sarah were inside Milford Cottage when I arrived there a few minutes later, standing very erectly in their midst, still in awe of the great thing I felt sure I had just accomplished.

Sarah had obviously waited for my arrival before giving Miss Channing her present. 'This is for you,' she said, smiling delightedly, as she brought the shawl from her basket.

'Thank you,' Miss Channing said, taking it from her gently, as if it were an infant. 'It's beautiful, Sarah.'

We were all standing in the front room of the cottage. Many of Miss Channing's belongings were now packed into the same leather traveling cases I'd brought there nearly a year before, along with a few boxes in which she'd placed a small number of things she'd acquired since then. In my mind I saw myself loading them onto Mr Reed's boat, then standing at the edge of the pier, waving farewell as they drifted out of the moonlit marina, never to be seen again at Chatham School.

'I have something for you too,' Miss Channing said to Sarah. She walked into her bedroom, then came out with the African bracelet in her hand, its brightly colored beads glinting in the light. 'For all your work,' she said as she handed it to Sarah.

Sarah's eyes widened. 'Oh, thank you, Miss Channing,' she said as she put it on.

Miss Channing nodded crisply. 'Well, we should start our lesson now,' she said.

They took their seats at the table by the window, Sarah arranging her books while Miss Channing read over the writing she'd assigned the Sunday before.

I left them to their work, strolled to the edge of the pond. In the distance I could see Mr Reed's house half concealed within a grove of trees, his car sitting motionless in the driveway.

I was still at the water's edge an hour later, when I saw Sarah and Miss Channing come walking toward me, Sarah chatting away, as she often did at the end of a lesson.

'Where is it you will be going now?' she asked Miss Channing as they strolled up to me.

Miss Channing's answer came more quickly than I'd expected, since I hadn't heard anyone in my household mention her intentions.

'Boston, perhaps,' she said. 'At least for a while.'

Sarah smiled excitedly. 'Now, that's a fine city,' she said. 'And what do you plan to be doing once you're settled in?'

Miss Channing shrugged. 'I don't know.' It was a subject that appeared to trouble her. To avoid it, she said to me, 'Henry, I have some books from the school library. Would you mind taking them back for me?'

'Of course, Miss Channing.'

She turned and headed toward the cottage, walking so briskly that I had to quicken my pace in order to keep up with her. Once inside, she retrieved a box of books from her bedroom. 'Henry, I'd like to apologize for the state I was in when you came to the cottage the other night,' she said as she handed it to me.

'There's nothing to apologize for, Miss Channing,' I told her, smiling inwardly at how much she might soon have to thank me for, the fact that I'd taken the fatal step, done what neither she nor Mr Reed had been able to do, struck at the heavy chain that bound them to Chatham.

After that we walked out of the cottage to stand together

near the willow. It was nearly noon by then, quiet, windless, the long tentacles of the tree falling motionlessly toward the moist ground. To the right I could see Sarah moving toward the old wooden pier. At the end of it she hesitated for a time, as if unsure of its stability, then strolled to its edge, a slender, erect figure in her finest dress.

'I hope you'll look after Sarah,' Miss Channing said, watching her from our place beside the willow. 'Encourage her to keep at her studies.'

'I don't think she'll need much encouragement,' I said, glancing out across the pond toward Mr Reed's house, where I suddenly saw Mrs Reed as she rushed down the front steps, dragging Mary roughly behind her. At the bottom of the stairs she paused a moment, her head rotating left and right, like someone looking for answers in the air. Then she wheeled to the left and headed toward the shed, moving swiftly now, Mary trotting along beside her.

For a time they disappeared behind a wall of foliage. Then Mrs Reed emerged again, marching stiffly toward the car. She'd begun to pull away when I glanced at Miss Channing and saw that she was staring across the pond, observing the same scene.

'She's crazy,' I said. 'Mrs Reed.'

Miss Channing's eyes shot over to me. She started to speak, then stopped herself. I could see something gathering in her mind. I suppose I expected her to add some comment about Mrs Reed, but she said nothing of the kind. 'Be like your father, Henry,' she said. 'Be a good man, like your father.'

I stared at her, shocked by the high regard she'd just expressed for my father, and searching desperately for some way to lower her regard for him. But I found that I could discover nothing that, in saying it, would not lower

Miss Channing's regard for me as well. Because of that, we were still standing silently at the water's edge when we suddenly heard a car approaching from Plymouth Road, its engine grinding fiercely, the sound rising steadily as it neared us, becoming at last a shuddering roar.

I turned to the right and saw it thunder past us in a thick cloud of white dust, a wall of black hurling down the weedy embankment, its ancient chassis slamming left and right as it plunged at what seemed inhuman speed toward the rickety wooden pier.

For a single, appalling instant, I felt utterly frozen in place, watching like a death mask fixed to a lifeless column until Miss Channing's scream set the world in motion again, and I saw Sarah wheel around, the car then jerk to the right, as if to avoid her, but too late, so that it struck her with full force, her body tumbling over the left side of the hood and into the water, the car plowing past her, then lifting off the end of the pier like a great black bird, heavy and wingless as it plummeted into the depths of Black Pond, then sank with a terrible swiftness, its rear tires still spinning madly, throwing silver arcs of water into the summer air.

We rushed forward at the same time, Miss Channing crashing into the water, where she sank down and gathered Sarah's broken body into her arms. I ran to the edge of the pier and dove into the still wildly surging water.

When I surfaced again only a minute or so later, drenched and shaken, my mind caught in a dreadful horror of what I had just seen, I found Miss Channing slumped at the edge of the pond, Sarah cradled in her arms.

'It's Mrs Reed,' I told her as I trudged out of the water.

She looked at me in shock and grief. 'Is she dead?'

My answer came already frozen in that passionlessness that would mark me from then on. 'Yes.'

TWENTY-SIX

I've never been able to remember exactly what happened after I came out of the water. I know that I ran over to where Miss Channing now sat, drenched and shivering, on the bank, with Sarah's head resting in her lap. I remember that Sarah's eyes were open as I approached her, blank and staring, but that I saw them close slowly, then open again, so that I felt a tremendous wave of hope that she might be all right.

At some point after that I took off down Plymouth Road, soaking wet, with my hair in my eyes, and flagged down the first passing car. There was an old man behind the wheel, a local cranberry farmer as I later found out, and he watched in disbelief as I sputtered about there having been an accident on Black Pond, that he had to get a doctor, the police, that he had to please, please hurry. I remember how he sprang into action suddenly, his movements quick and agile, as if made young by a desperate purpose. 'Be right back, son,' he promised as he sped away, the old gray car thundering toward Chatham.

After that I rushed back to Milford Cottage. Miss Channing was still where she'd been when I left her, Sarah cradled in her arms, alive, though unconscious, her eyes closed, her breath rattling softly, a single arrowhead of white bone protruding from the broken skin of her left elbow, but otherwise unmarked.

We sat in an almost unbroken silence with nothing but the lapping of the pond and an occasional rustle of wind through the trees to remind us that it was real, that it had actually happened, that Sarah had been struck down, and that beneath the surface of Black Pond, Mrs Reed lay curled over the steering wheel of the car.

Dr Craddock was the first to arrive. His sleek new sedan barreled down Plymouth Road, then noisily skidded to a halt in front of Milford Cottage. He leaped from the car, then bolted toward us, a black leather bag dangling from his hand.

'What happened?' he asked as he knelt down, grabbed Sarah's arm, and began to feel for her pulse.

'A car,' I blurted out. 'She was hit by a car.'

He released Sarah's arm, swiftly opened his bag, and pulled out a stethoscope. 'What car?' he asked.

I saw Miss Channing's eyes drift toward the pond as she waited for my answer.

'It's in the water,' I said. 'The car's in the water. It went off the pier.'

Dr Craddock gave me a quick glance as he pressed the tympanum against Sarah's chest. 'And this young woman was driving it?'

'No,' I told him. 'There's someone in the car.'

I saw the first glimmer of that astonished horror that was soon to overtake our village settle like a gray mist upon his face.

'It's a woman,' I added, unable to say her name, already trying to erase her from my memory. 'She's dead.'

'Are you sure?'

'Yes.'

He returned the stethoscope to the bag, then brought

out a hypodermic needle and a vial of clear liquid. 'How about you, are you all right?' he asked me.

'Yes.'

He looked at Miss Channing. 'And you?' he asked as he pierced the vial with the needle, then pressed its silver point into Sarah's arm.

'I'm all right,' Miss Channing said, her features now hung in that deep, strangely impenetrable grief that would forever rest upon her face.

'The woman in the car,' Dr Craddock said. 'Who is she?'

'Abigail Reed,' Miss Channing answered. Then she looked down at Sarah and drew back a strand of glossy wet hair. 'And this is Sarah Doyle,' she said.

Sarah had already been taken away when Captain Lawrence P. Hamilton of the Massachusetts State Police arrived at Milford Cottage. He was a tall man, with gray hair and a lean figure, his physical manner curiously graceful, but with an obvious severity clinging to him, born, perhaps, of the dark things he had seen.

Miss Channing and I were standing beside the cottage when he arrived, the once-deserted lawn now dotted with other people, the village constable, the coroner, two of Chatham's four selectmen, the tiny engine of local official-dom already beginning to crank up.

Captain Hamilton was not a part of that local establish-ment, as every aspect of his bearing demonstrated. There was something about him that suggested a breadth both of authority and of experience that lay well beyond the confines of Chatham village, or even of Cape Cod. It was in the assuredness of his stride as he walked toward us, the command within his voice when he spoke, the way he seemed to know the answers even before he posed the questions.

'You're Henry Griswald?' he asked me.

'Yes.'

He looked at Miss Channing. 'You live here at the cottage, Miss Channing?'

She nodded mutely and gathered her arms around herself as if against a sudden chill.

'I have most of the details,' Captain Hamilton said. 'About the accident, I mean.' His eyes shifted toward the pond. A tractor had been backed to its edge, and I could see a man walking out into the water, dressed in a bathing suit, a heavy chain in his right hand.

'We're going to pull the car out now,' Captain Hamilton told us.

The man in the water curled over and disappeared beneath the surface of the pond, his feet throwing up small explosions of white foam.

'There's a husband, I understand,' Captain Hamilton said. 'Leland Reed?'

Odd though it seems to me now, I had not thought of Mr Reed at all before that moment, nor of the other person Captain Hamilton mentioned almost in the same breath.

'And there's a little girl, I'm told. A daughter. Have you seen her?'

'No.'

'Could she have been in the car?'

I shook my head. 'No.'

'Well, nobody seems to be at home over there,' Captain Hamilton said, nodding out across the pond. 'Do you have any idea where Mr Reed and the little girl might be?'

I remembered the last thing I'd seen at Mr Reed's house,

Mrs Reed bolting across the lawn, Mary trotting at her side, both of them headed for the old gray shed.

'I think I know where she is,' I said.

Captain Hamilton appeared surprised to hear it. 'You do?'

'In the shed,' I answered.

'What shed?'

'There's a shed about a hundred and fifty yards or so from the house.'

Captain Hamilton watched me closely. 'Would you mind showing it to me, Henry?'

I nodded. 'All right,' I said, though the very thought of returning to Mr Reed's house sent a dreadful chill through me.

Captain Hamilton glanced at Miss Channing, then touched the brim of his hat. 'We'll be talking again,' he said as he took my arm and led me away.

Moments later, as he would testify the following August, Captain Hamilton and I made our way along the edges of Black Pond. The old shed stood in a grove of trees, its door tightly closed, locked from the outside with a large, rusty eyebolt.

Only a few feet away we heard a sound coming from inside. It was low and indistinct, a soft whimper, like a kitten or a puppy.

'Step back, son,' Captain Hamilton said when we reached the door.

I did as he told me, waiting a short distance away from the shed as he opened the door and peered in. 'Don't be afraid,' I heard him say as he disappeared inside it. Seconds later he stepped back out into the light, now with Mary in his arms, her clothes drenched with her own sweat, her long blond hair hanging in a tangle over her shoulders, her blue eyes staring fearfully at Captain Hamilton, asking her single question in a soft, uncomprehending voice – *Where's my mama gone?* – and which she would hear answered forever after in a cruel school-yard song:

> Into Black Pond
> Is where she's gone
> Drowned by a demon lover

Mr Reed's car had already been dragged from the pond when Captain Hamilton and I got back to Milford Cottage. Mrs Reed's body had been taken from it by then, transported to Henson's Funeral Parlor, as I later learned, where it was placed on a metal table and covered with a single sheet.

Miss Channing and I were standing near the cottage when my father arrived. He looked very nearly dazed as he moved toward us.

'Dear God, is it true, Henry?' he asked, staring at me.

I nodded.

He looked at Miss Channing, and in that instant I saw a terrible dread sweep into his face, a sense that there were yet darker things to be learned from Black Pond. Without a word he stepped forward, took her arm, and escorted her inside the cottage, where they remained for some minutes, talking privately, my father standing by the fireplace, Miss Channing in a chair, looking up at him.

They had come back outside again by the time Captain Hamilton strode up to the cottage. He nodded to my father in a way that made it obvious that they already knew each other.

'Your son's a brave boy, Mr Griswald,' Captain Hamilton said. 'He tried his best to save her.'

I felt my eyes close slowly, saw Mrs Reed staring at me through a film of green water.

'The car looks fine,' Captain Hamilton added, now talking to all of us. 'No problem with the brakes or the steering column. No reason for an ... accident. Henry, when the car went by, could you see Mrs Reed behind the wheel?'

I shook my head. 'I didn't notice anything but the car.'

Captain Hamilton started to ask another question, but my father intervened.

'Why would that matter, Captain?' he asked. 'Whether Henry saw Mrs Reed or not?'

'Because if there was nothing wrong with the car, then we begin to wonder if there was something wrong with the person driving it.' He shrugged. 'I mean something like a seizure or a heart attack, some reason for Mrs Reed to lose control the way she did.'

For a moment, no one spoke. Then Captain Hamilton turned his attention to Miss Channing. 'This young woman, Sarah Doyle. Did Mrs Reed know her?'

Miss Channing shook her head. 'I don't think so.'

Captain Hamilton appeared to turn this over in his mind, come to some conclusion about it before going on to his next thought. 'And what about you, Miss Channing? Did Mrs Reed know you?'

'Only slightly.'

'Had she ever visited you here at the cottage?'

'No.'

The captain's eyes drifted toward the road, remained there briefly, then returned to Miss Channing. 'Well, if Mrs Reed didn't know you, why would she have been coming this way?' he asked her. 'It's a dead end, you see. So if she didn't have any business with you, Miss Channing, then why would she have been headed this way at all?'

Miss Channing replied with the only answer available to her. 'I don't know, Captain Hamilton,' she said.

With that, my father suddenly stepped away, tugging me along with him. 'I have to get my son home now,' he explained. 'He needs a change of clothes.'

Captain Hamilton made no attempt to stop us, and within a few seconds we were in my father's car. It was the middle of the afternoon by then, the air impossibly bright and clear. As we backed away, I saw Captain Hamilton tip his hat to Miss Channing, then step away from her and head out toward the pier, where, at the very end of it, I could see Mr Parsons facing out over the water, clothed in his dark suit, his homburg set firmly on his head.

TWENTY-SEVEN

Once we got back home, my father told me to change quickly and come downstairs. Sarah had been taken to Dr Craddock's clinic, he said, and all of us were to come to her bedside as soon as possible. I did as I was told, pulling off clothes that had once been soaked through but were now only damp, then rushed back downstairs to find my father waiting edgily on the front porch, my mother already in the car.

'I knew something bad was coming,' she said as I climbed into the backseat of the car. 'A woman knows.'

Dr Craddock's clinic was situated in a large house on the eastern end of Chatham. It had once been the home of a prosperous sea captain, but now functioned as what amounted to a small hospital, complete with private rooms on the second floor.

He met us at the door, dressed in a long white coat, a stethoscope dangling from his neck.

'How is she?' my father asked immediately.

'She's still unconscious,' Dr Craddock replied. 'I think you should prepare for the worst.'

'Do you mean she may die?'

Dr Craddock nodded. 'She's in shock. That's always very dangerous.' He motioned us into the building, then up the stairs to where we found Sarah in her bed, her eyes still closed, but now motionless behind the lids, her breathing short and erratic.

'Oh, Lord,' my mother whispered as she stepped over to the bed. 'Poor Sarah.'

Looking at her, it was hard to imagine that she was in such peril. Her face was unmarked and lovely, like a sleeping beauty, her long black hair neatly combed, as I found out later, by Dr Craddock himself. A gesture that has always struck me as infinitely kind.

My father moved to touch her cheek, then drew back his hand and turned toward Dr Craddock. 'When will you know if she's ... if she's going to be all right?'

'I don't know,' Craddock answered. 'If there's no brain injury, then it's possible she could—' He stopped, clearly unwilling to offer unfounded hope. 'I'll know more in the next few hours.'

'Please let me know if there are any changes, or if there's anything I can do,' my father said.

Dr Craddock nodded. 'How long has she been with you?'

'Nearly two years,' my father answered. He looked down at her tenderly. 'Such a lovely child. Bright. Ambitious. She was learning to read.'

Watching her from where I stood directly beside the bed, it was hard to imagine that only a few hours before she'd been so fully alive, so proud of the progress she'd made in her lessons with Miss Channing, drawing the African bracelet onto her wrist as if it were an emblem of her newfound mastery. Nothing had ever made life seem so tentative to me, so purely physical, and therefore utterly powerless to secure itself against the terrible assaults of accident or illness or even the invisible deadliness of time. It was just a little point of light, this life we harbored, just a tiny beam of consciousness, frail beyond measure, brief and unsustainable, the greatest lives like the smallest ones, delicately held together by the merest thread of breath.

We returned home that afternoon in an icy silence, my mother in the front seat of the car, fuming darkly, my father with his eyes leveled on the road, no doubt trying to fix this latest catastrophe within his scheme of things, give it the meaning it deserved, perhaps even some imagined grace.

As for me, I found that I could not bear to think of what had happened on Black Pond, either to Sarah or to Mrs Reed, could not bear to hold such devastation in my mind, envision Sarah's shattered bones or the last hellish gasps of Mrs Reed.

And so I concentrated only on Miss Channing, imagining her alone in her cottage or out wandering in the nearby woods. It seemed entirely unfitting that she should be left to herself under such circumstances. And so, as we neared Myrtle Street, I said, 'What about Miss Channing? Do you think we should ...'

'Miss Channing?' my mother blurted out, twisting around to face me.

'Yes.'

'What about her?'

'Well, she may be all alone. I was thinking that we might bring her ...'

'Here?' my mother demanded sharply. 'Bring her here? To our home?'

I glanced at my father, clearly hoping for some assistance, but he continued to keep his eyes on the road, his mouth closed, unwilling to confront the roaring flame of my mother's rage.

'That woman will never set foot in our house again,' my mother declared. 'Is that clear, Henry?'

I nodded weakly and said nothing else.

The atmosphere in the house on Myrtle Street had grown so sullen by nightfall that I was happy to leave it. My father dropped me off in front of Dr Craddock's clinic, saying only that someone would relieve me at midnight.

The doctor met me at the door. He said that Sarah's condition hadn't changed, that she appeared reasonably comfortable. 'There's a nurse at the end of the corridor,' he added. 'Call her if you notice Sarah experiencing any distress.'

'I will,' I told him, then watched as he moved down the stairs, got into his car and drove away.

Sarah lay in the same position as before, on her back, a sheet drawn up to her waist, her shattered arm in a plaster cast. In the light from the lamp beside her bed, her face took on a bloodless sheen, all its ruby glow now drained into a ghostly pallor.

I watched her a moment longer, touched her temple with my fingertips, then settled into the chair beside the window to wait with her through the night. I'd brought a book with me, some thick seafaring tale culled from the limited collection available from the school library. I would concentrate on it exclusively, I'd told myself as I'd quickly pulled it from the shelf, let it fill my mind to the brim, allow no other thoughts inside it.

But I'd gotten through only twenty pages or so when I saw someone emerge out of the dimly lighted hallway, tall and slender, her dark hair hung like a wreath around her face.

'Hello, Henry,' Miss Channing said.

I got to my feet, unable to speak, her presence like a splash of icy water thrown into my face, waking me up to what I'd done.

'How is she?'

I let the book drop onto my chair. 'She hasn't changed much since the ... since ...'

She came forward slowly and stood by the bed, peering down. She was wearing a plain white dress, the shawl Sarah had knitted for her draped over her shoulders. She watched Sarah silently for a time, then let her eyes drift over to where I continued to stand beside my empty chair. 'Tell your father that I'd like to sit with Sarah tomorrow,' she said.

'Yes, Miss Channing.'

'For as long as she needs me.'

'I'll tell him.'

She pressed her hand against the side of Sarah's face, then turned and walked past me, disappearing from the room as quickly as she'd entered it.

I know that for the rest of that long night she remained alone in her cottage, no doubt staring at the old wooden pier as she sat in her chair by the window, the unlighted hearth only a few feet away, the ashes of Mr Reed's letters still resting in a gray heap where, three days later, Mr Parsons would find them when he came to question her about what he called 'certain things' he'd heard at Chatham School.

As for me, I remained at Sarah's bedside, trying to lose myself in the book, but unable to shut out the sound of her breathing, the fact that as the hours passed, it grew steadily more faint. From time to time a soft murmur came from her, but I never saw any sign of the 'distress' Dr Craddock had warned me about. If anything, she appeared utterly at peace, so that I often found myself looking up from my book, imagining her unconsciousness, wondering if, locked so deeply within the chamber of herself, she could feel things unfelt by the rest of us, the slosh of her blood through the valves of her heart, the infinitesimal firings of her brain, perhaps even the movement of those tiny muscles Miss Channing had once spoken of, and which any true artist must come to understand.

And so I didn't know until nearly midnight when Dr Craddock came into the room, walked over to her bed, took hold of her wrist, held it briefly, then released it, shaking his head as he did so, that whatever small sensations Sarah might have felt from the depths of that final privacy, she now could feel no more.

My father had already been told that Sarah had died when he came for me. As he trudged toward me from down the hallway he looked as if he were slogging through a thick, nearly impenetrable air. He drew in a long breath as he gathered me into his arms. 'So sad, Henry,' he whispered, 'so sad.'

We went directly home, drifting slowly through the center of the village, its shops closed, the streets deserted, no one stirring at all save for the few fishermen I saw as we swept past the marina. Glancing out over its dark waters, I could see Mr Reed's boat lolling peacefully. The *Elizabeth's* high white mast weaved left and right, and for a moment, I remembered it all again, he and Miss Channing sitting together on the steps of Chatham School or on the bench beside the bluff, the cane like a line drawn between them. By spring, as I recalled, they'd begun to stroll through the village together, companionably, shoulder to shoulder, their love growing steadily by then. No, not growing, as I thought suddenly, but tightening around them like a noose, around Mrs Reed and Sarah, too, and even little Mary, so that love no longer seemed a high, romantic thing to me at all, no longer a fit subject for our poems and for songs, nor even to be something we should seek.

And so I never sought it after that.

'We'll have to make an announcement in school tomorrow morning,' my father told my mother as he came into the parlor. 'The boys have to be told. And Captain Hamilton wants to question a few people tomorrow afternoon.'

My mother, working fiercely at her knitting, so much death burning in her mind, did not seem in the least surprised by such a development. 'No doubt there'll be plenty of questions,' she said without looking up.

'Who do they want to question?' I asked my father.

'Me, of course,' he answered, now trying to pretend that it was merely some kind of police routine, a formality. 'Some of the teachers.'

'They'll want to talk to me as well,' my mother said, her eyes glowing hotly, clearly looking forward to the prospect.

'Why would they want to talk to you, Mildred?' my father asked.

'Because of what Mrs Reed told me,' she answered, her eyes fixed on her knitting. 'About that woman and Mr Reed.'

For the first time, I saw my father bristle. 'You're not to be spreading tales, Mildred,' he told her.

My mother's head shot up, her eyes narrowing fiercely. 'Tales?' she said. 'I'm not talking about tales, Arthur. I'm talking about what Mrs Reed told me right here in this room, things she asked me to keep quiet about, and so I did ... until now.'

'And what are these "things", may I ask?'

'She thought that there were bad things afoot,' my mother replied. 'In the boathouse. Down at the marina. She thought there was a plot against her.'

Aghast, my father looked at her. 'You can't be serious.'

My mother stood her ground. 'She thought he might murder her. Mr Reed, I mean. She was terrified of that.'

'But Mrs Reed wasn't murdered, Mildred,' my father replied. 'It was an accident.'

The needles stopped. My mother leaned forward, glaring at him. 'She saw a knife, Arthur. A rope too. And they'd already mapped out where they were running to.' Her eyes narrowed menacingly. 'And poison too.'

I felt my breath abruptly stop. 'Poison?'

My mother nodded. 'A bottle of arsenic. That's what she saw. Right there with the knife and the rope.'

I could hardly believe my ears. 'That was for the rats,' I told her. 'In the boathouse. I helped Mr Reed spread it myself.'

She appeared not to have heard me, or to have ignored what she heard. She eased herself back, the needles whipping frantically again. 'Oh, there're going to be questions all right,' she said. 'Lots of questions, that's for sure.'

I suppose it was at that moment that the further consequences of what had happened on Black Pond that afternoon first occurred to me. It would not end with Mrs Reed dead behind the wheel or Sarah dead in her bed at Dr Craddock's clinic. Their deaths were but the beginning of more destruction still.

TWENTY-EIGHT

Throughout that long night I floated in green water, saw Mrs Reed's head plunge toward me from out of the murky depths, her features pressed frantically against the glass, eyes wide and staring.

By morning I was exhausted, and I felt as if I could barely stand with the other boys when they assembled on the front lawn of Chatham School and listened as my father told them all he thought they needed to know about the previous day's events, the fact that 'a tragic accident' had occurred on Black Pond, that Mrs Reed's car had 'gone out of control', and that both she and Sarah Doyle were now dead.

As to the state of Mr Reed and Miss Channing, my father told them nothing whatsoever, save that they remained in their respective homes, Mr Reed tending to his daughter, Miss Channing continuing to prepare for her departure from Chatham. He did not know if either of them would return to Chatham School before it closed for the summer, and asked the boys to 'keep them in their thoughts'.

For most of the rest of that long day I stayed in my room, almost in an attitude of concealment, not wanting to meet my mother's gaze as she stormed about the house, nor talk to any of the boys of Chatham School, since it was only natural that they'd ply me with questions about what had happened on Black Pond. Most of all, however, I wanted to avoid any chance meeting with Captain Hamilton, the way I felt when he looked at me, as if I were a small animal scurrying across a strip of desert waste, he the great bird diving toward me at tremendous speed and from an impossible height, looking only for the truth.

And so I was in my room when I heard a knock at the front door, cautiously peered downstairs and saw Mr Parsons, his hat in his hand, facing my mother in the foyer. 'Is Mr Griswald here?' he asked.

'No. He's at the funeral parlor,' my mother told him. 'Making arrangements for Sarah.'

Mr Parsons nodded. 'Well, would you tell him to call me when he returns?'

My mother said she would, but added nothing else.

Mr Parsons smiled politely and turned to leave. I thought my mother was going to let him go, that she had decided to hold her tongue. But abruptly, the door still open, Mr Parsons halfway through it, she said, 'Such a terrible thing, what happened to Sarah ... and, of course ... Mrs Reed.'

Mr Parsons nodded. 'Yes, terrible,' he said, though with little emphasis, heading out the door, other matters clearly on his mind.

'She came to see me, you know,' my mother added. 'Mrs Reed did.'

Mr Parsons stopped and turned to face her. 'When was that, Mrs Griswald?' he asked.

'Only a short time ago,' my mother answered. She paused a moment, then added with a grim significance, 'She seemed quite troubled.'

'About what?'

'Family matters. Troubles in the family.'

Mr Parsons eased himself back into the foyer. 'Would you be willing to talk about that conversation, Mrs Griswald?' he asked.

I saw my mother nod, then lead him into the parlor and close the door.

My father returned home an hour or so later. Mr Parsons had left by then, but my mother made no attempt to conceal his visit, nor what she had told him during it. From the top of the stairs, crouched there like a court spy, I listened to her tell my father exactly what had transpired.

'I wasn't making accusations,' my mother said. 'Just speaking the plain truth, that's all.'

'What truth is that, Mildred?'

'Just what Mrs Reed said.'

'About Mr Reed?'

'Him and that woman.'

'You mentioned Miss Channing? You mentioned her to Mr Parsons?'

'Yes.'

'Why?'

'Because Mrs Reed said she saw her picture in the boathouse. She knew it was her that Mr Reed was involved with.'

'What did you tell him?'

'That she suspected something. Between the two of them. That it frightened her.'

'Frightened her?'

'That she was afraid of them, the two of them. What they might do. Run off together. Or worse.'

'Or worse?'

'What she found in the boathouse. The knife she saw, and the ...'

'You told Mr Parsons that?'

'I told him what Mrs Reed said. That's all.'

I waited for something more, but there was only silence. From my place at the top of the stairs I saw my father walk out the door, my mother behind him, then both of them in the car, pulling out of the driveway, no doubt headed for the funeral parlor where Sarah now lay in a room decked with flowers sent by the teachers of Chatham School.

When they returned home sometime later, the air grown dark by then, the same silence enveloped them. They sat silently in the parlor, and silently through dinner. Nor did they ever speak to each other with any real tenderness again.

I spent the rest of the next day in my room, lying on my bed. Downstairs, I could hear my mother doing the chores that had once been Sarah's. I suppose from time to time I drifted into sleep, but if so, I don't remember it.

By noon the summer heat had begun to make the room unbearable, and so I walked out onto the porch and sat down in the swing, drifting slowly back and forth, recalling Sarah in random pieces of memory, words and glances flying through my mind like bits of torn paper in a whirling wind. At some point my mother brought me a sandwich and a glass of water, but the sandwich was never eaten, nor the water drunk.

Later I decided to take a short walk, perhaps to the beach, where I hoped to get some relief from the terrible scenes playing in my mind. I made my way down Myrtle Street, the bluff widening before me. To my left I could see the now-deserted grounds of Chatham School, Miss

Channing's column of faces still standing in the bright summer light, and to my right, the lighthouse, a dazzling white tower, motionless and eternal, as if in mute contradiction to the human chaos sprawled around it.

I made it to the bluff but did not go down. So a few minutes later I was still sitting on the same bench that had once accommodated Miss Channing and Mr Reed, when I saw Mr Parsons' car mount the hill, then glide to the left and come to a stop directly before me.

'Hello, Henry,' Mr Parsons said as he got out.

I nodded.

He walked to the bench and sat down beside me. 'I wonder if we might have a talk,' he said.

I said nothing, but rather than press the issue, Mr Parsons sat quietly for a moment, then said, 'Let's go for a little walk, Henry.'

We both rose and headed down Myrtle Street, past Chatham School, and, still strolling at a leisurely pace, made our way out toward the playing field and then around it.

'I've talked to quite a few people at Chatham School,' Mr Parsons said.

I stared straight ahead, gave him no response.

'Your name has been mentioned quite a few times, Henry. Everybody seems to think that you were pretty close to both of them. Miss Channing and Mr Reed, I mean.'

I nodded, but offered nothing more.

'They say that you spent a lot of time with Mr Reed. In a boathouse he's got down at the harbor. That you helped him build a boat, that's what they say.' He stopped and turned toward me. 'The thing is, Henry, we've begun to wonder how all this happened. I mean, we've begun to wonder what Mrs Reed was intending when she drove over to Milford Cottage last Sunday.'

I said nothing.

Mr Parsons began to walk again, gently tugging me along with him. 'Now, you're a brave young man,' he said. 'Nobody can question that. You did your best to save Mrs Reed. But now you've got another duty. We know that Mrs Reed was pretty sure that her husband was involved with another woman. And we know that that other woman was Elizabeth Channing.'

I felt my eyes close slowly as we walked along, as if by such a motion I could erase everything that had happened on Black Pond.

'We think she was after Miss Channing that day,' Mr Parsons said. 'That it wasn't an accident, what happened on Black Pond.'

I kept silent.

'We think Mrs Reed mistook Sarah Doyle for Elizabeth Channing, and so killed her instead.'

We walked a few seconds more, then Mr Parsons once again stopped, his eyes bearing into me. 'So it was murder, wasn't it, Henry? It was murder Mrs Reed intended when she aimed that car at Sarah Doyle.'

He saw the answer in my eyes.

'How long have you known?'

I shrugged.

'Look, Henry, everybody's proud of you, of how you went into the water and all. But like I said before, you have another duty now. To tell the truth, the whole truth ... I'll bet you know the rest of it.'

'And nothing but the truth,' I said, my voice barely above a whisper.

'That's right,' Mr Parsons said. He placed his hand on

my shoulder. 'Let's go down to the boathouse, son, and talk a little more.'

I gave him a private tour of the boathouse, watching as his eyes continually returned to my drawing of Miss Channing. 'She's what did it to him,' he said with a certainty that astonished me. 'She's what drove him mad.' Then he walked to the back window. In the distance we could see the *Elizabeth* bobbing gently in the quiet water. 'Somebody has to pay for all this, Henry,' he said without looking back toward me. 'There're just too many deaths to let it go.'

We left the boathouse together shortly after that, walked to his car, and drove back up the coastal road to the house on Myrtle Street. Before pulling away, he made a final remark. 'What we can't figure out is what finally set her off,' he said almost absently, a mere point of curiosity. 'Mrs Reed, that is. I mean, she'd known about her husband and Miss Channing for quite some time. We just wonder what happened on that particular day that sent her over the edge like that, made her go after Miss Channing the way she did, kill that poor girl instead.'

He never posed it as a question, and so I never answered him, but only stepped away from the car and watched as it pulled away, my silence drawing around me like a cloak of stone.

TWENTY-NINE

It was not until many years later that I learned exactly what had happened the next day. I knew only that Mr Parsons and Captain Hamilton arrived at our house early that morning, that my father ushered them quickly into the parlor, then departed with them a few minutes later, sitting grimly in the backseat of Captain Hamilton's patrol car as it backed out of our driveway. He returned in the same car a few minutes later, this time with a little girl in a light blue dress in his arms, her long blond hair tumbled about her face, and whom I immediately recognized as Mary Reed.

'They want us to keep Mary for a while,' he explained to me. Then he sent me off on a picnic with her, my mother having packed a basket for the occasion, the same one Sarah had used to bring cakes and cookies to Miss Channing. 'Take her to the beach and try to keep her mind off things, Henry,' he told me. 'She's going to be pretty scared for a while.'

And so, before leaving that morning, I ran up to my room and got an old kite I hadn't flown in years. At the beach I taught Mary Reed how to string it, then to run against the wind so that it would be taken up. For a long time we watched it soar beneath the blue, and I will always remember the small, thin smiles that sometimes rose precariously to her lips, then vanished without a trace, her face darkening suddenly, so that I knew the darkness came from deep within.

'It was because they suspected that Mr Reed might have been plotting to kill his wife, that's why they took Mary,' my father told me many years later when I was a grown man, and he an old one, the two of us sitting in the tiny, cluttered room he used as his private chamber. 'To make sure she was safe, that's what Mr Parsons told me when he drove me over to Mr Reed's house that morning.'

What my father witnessed on Black Pond a few minutes later stayed with him forever, the anguish in Mr Reed's face so pure, so unalloyed by any other feeling, that it seemed, he told me, 'like something elemental'.

At first Mr Reed had appeared puzzled to find so many men at his door, my father told me. Not only himself, Mr Parsons, and Captain Hamilton, but two uniformed officers of the Massachusetts State Police as well.

It was Mr Parsons who spoke first. 'We'd like to talk to you for a moment, Mr Reed.'

Mr Reed nodded, then walked outside, closing the door behind him.

'We've been looking into a few things,' Mr Parsons said. He glanced inside the house and saw Mary's face pressed against the screen of an otherwise open window. 'Let's go into the yard,' he said, taking Mr Reed by the elbow and guiding him down the stairs and out into the yard, where he stood by the pond, encircled by the other men.

'Mr Reed,' Mr Parsons began. 'We've become concerned about the welfare of your daughter.'

It was then, my father said, that Mr Reed appeared to understand that something serious was upon him, though he may well not have grasped exactly what it was. 'Concerned about Mary?' he asked. 'Why are you concerned about Mary?'

'We've heard some suggestions,' Mr Parsons told him. 'Having to do with your relationship with Mrs Reed.'

'What suggestions?'

'There's no need to go into them at this time,' Mr Parsons said. 'But they have caused the commonwealth to feel some concern about your daughter.'

'What kind of concern?'

'For her safety.'

'She's perfectly safe,' Mr Reed said firmly.

Mr Parsons shook his head, then drew a piece of paper from his jacket pocket and handed it to Mr Reed. 'There's been enough death. We can't take the chance on there being any more.'

Mr Reed stared at Mr Parsons, still vaguely puzzled. 'What are you talking about?' he asked. He glanced at the paper. 'What is this?'

'We're going to take custody of your daughter,' Mr Parsons told him. 'Mr Griswald has agreed to look after her until certain things can be cleared up.'

Mr Reed thrust the paper toward Mr Parsons. 'You're not going to take Mary,' he said. 'You're not going to do that.'

Mr Parsons' voice hardened. 'I'm afraid we are, Mr Reed.'

Mr Reed began to back away, the men gathering around him as he did so. 'No,' he said, 'you can't do that.'

Captain Hamilton stepped forward. 'Mr Reed, your daughter doesn't need to see us use force, does she?'

Mr Reed glanced toward the porch, where Mary now stood, a little girl in a pale blue dress, staring down at him. 'Please, don't do this,' he said in a desperate whisper, his attention now riveted on Mr Parsons. 'Not now. Not with her mother just—' He gazed imploringly at my father. 'Please, Mr Griswald, can't you—'

'It's only until we can clear things up,' Mr Parsons said, interrupting him. 'But for now we have to be sure that your daughter is safe.'

Suddenly, Mr Reed shook his head and began to push his way out of the circle. The men closed in upon him, and as he thrashed about, he lost his grip on his cane, crumpled to the ground and lay sprawled before them, laboring to get up, but unable to do so. It was then, my father said, that a cry broke from him, one that seemed to offer up the last frail measure of his will.

'He looked like a different man when he got to his feet,' my father told me. 'Like everything had been drained out of him. He didn't say anything. He just looked over to the porch, where Mary was, and waved for her to come to him. At first she wouldn't. She was so scared, of course. All those men she didn't know. The way they'd surrounded her father.' He shook his head. 'You can imagine how she felt, Henry.'

But at last the child came. Mr Reed met her, lifted her into his arms, kissed her softly, then handed her to my father, his words oddly final as he did so: *She'll be better off this way.* He reached out and touched her hair; he never said good-bye.

Only an hour or so after those harrowing events, Mary walked to the beach with me, the two of us flying my old red striped kite until the first line of thunderclouds appeared on the horizon, its jagged bolts of lightning still far away, so that we'd gotten home well in advance of the rain.

By nightfall the rain had subsided, but a few hours later

it began again. It was still falling when Dr Craddock's car came to a halt in front of our house. The doctor was wearing a long raincoat and a gray hat which he drew from his head as he mounted the stairs to where my father sat in a wicker chair a few feet away, I in the swing nearby.

'I've come about the little girl,' he said. 'Mary Reed.'

My father got to his feet, puzzled. 'Mary Reed? What about her?'

Dr Craddock hesitated a moment, and I could tell that something of vast importance lay in the balance for him. 'I'm sure you know that my wife and I ... that we've ... that we have no children.'

My father nodded.

'Well, I wanted to let you know that we would be very interested in taking Mary in,' Dr Craddock said. 'My wife would be a good mother for her, I'm sure. And I believe that I would be a good father.'

'Mary has a father,' my father answered with an unexpected sternness, as if he were talking to one who wished to steal a child.

Dr Craddock stared at him, surprised. 'You've not heard?' he asked.

'Heard what?'

I remember rising slowly and drifting across the porch toward my father as Dr Craddock told him that Mr Reed's boat had been found adrift in the bay, with nothing but his old wooden cane inside it, save for a note written on a piece of sail and tacked to the mast. *Please see to it that Mary is treated well, and tell her that I do this out of love.*

I think that over the years Mary Reed was well-treated, that, overall, despite the many problems that later arose, the howling phantoms that consumed her, the bleak silences into which she sometimes fell, that despite all that, Dr Craddock and his wife continued to love her and strive to help her. At first it looked as though they had succeeded, that Mary had come to think of them as her parents, put her own dreadful legacy behind her. By the time she entered the local school, she'd come to be called by her middle name, which was Alice, as well as that of her adoptive parents, which was Craddock.

It was a deliverance my father had hoped for, and perhaps even believed to be possible. 'In time, she'll heal,' I heard him say as Dr Craddock took her small white hand and led her down the stairs and out into the rain.

But she never did.

Mr Reed's death left only Miss Channing upon whom the law could now seek retribution, and so, after a few more days of investigation, and at Mr Parsons' direction, the grand jury charged her in a two-count indictment, the first count being the most serious, conspiracy to murder Abigail Reed, but the second also quite grave at that time, adultery.

It was my father who delivered the news of the indictment to Miss Channing, allowed to do so by Captain Hamilton, whose duty it otherwise would have been.

'Get in the car, Henry,' my father said the morning we made our final drive to Milford Cottage. 'If she becomes ... well ... difficult ... I might need your help.'

But Miss Channing did not become difficult that morning. Instead, she stood quite still, listening as my father told her that the two indictments had been handed down, that she would have to stand trial, then went on to recommend a local attorney who was willing to defend her.

'I don't want a lawyer, Mr Griswald,' Miss Channing said.

'But these are serious charges, Miss Channing,' my father said somberly. 'There are witnesses against you. People who should be questioned as to whatever it is they're claiming to have seen or heard.' I could feel the pain his next words caused him. 'My wife will be one of those witnesses,' he told her. 'Henry too.'

I'd expected her eyes to shoot toward me at that moment, freeze me in a hideous glare, but she did not shift her attention from my father's face. 'Even so' was all she said.

We left a few minutes later, and I didn't say a single word to Miss Channing that morning, but only gazed at her stonily, my demeanor already forming into the hard shell it would assume on the day I testified against her, answering every question with the truth, the whole truth, and nothing but the truth, knowing all the while that there was one question Mr Parsons would never ask me, nor even remotely suspect that I had the answer to: *What really happened on Black Pond that day?*

THIRTY

Miss Channing came to trial that August. During that interval I never saw her, nor knew of anyone who did. My father was now more or less banned from any further contact with her by my mother's abject fury.

As to the charges against her, the evidence was never very great. But bit by bit it was presented to the jury, tales of odd sightings and snatches of conversation, a portrait hung in a boathouse, an old primer curiously inscribed, a nautical map with what Mr Parsons called an 'escape route' already drawn, a boat named *Elizabeth*, a pile of letters hastily burned in an otherwise empty hearth, a knife, a piece of rope, a bottle of arsenic.

Against all that, as well as Chatham's ferocious need to 'make someone pay', Miss Channing stood alone. She listened as the witnesses were called, people who had seen and heard things distantly, as well as the more compelling testimony that I gave, shortly followed by my mother.

Through it all she sat at the defense table in so deep a stillness, I half expected her not to rise when the time finally came and the bailiff called her to the stand.

But she did rise, resolutely, her gaze trained on the witness box until she reached it and sat, waiting as Mr Parsons approached her from across the room, the eyes of the jurors drifting from her face to her white, unmoving fingers, peering at them intently, as if looking for blood-stains on her hands.

I will always remember that my father watched Miss Channing's testimony with a tenderness so genuine that I later came to believe that understanding and forgiveness were the deepest passions that he knew.

My mother's expression was more severe, of course, less merciful thoughts no doubt playing in her mind – memories of people she had known, a husband's career now in the balance, a school teetering on the brink of ruin. Her eyes were leveled with an unmistakable contempt upon the woman she held responsible for all that.

As for me, I found that I glanced away from Miss Channing as she rose and walked toward the witness box, unable to bear the way she looked, so set upon and isolated that she resembled a figure out of ancient drama, Antigone or Medea, a woman headed for a sacrificial doom, and in relation to whom I felt like a shadow crouched behind a tapestry, the secret agent of her fall.

She wore a long black dress that day, ruffled at the throat and at the ends of the sleeves. But more than her dress, more than the way she'd pulled back her hair and bound it tightly with a slender black ribbon, I noticed how little she resembled the young woman I'd seen get off a Boston bus nearly a year before, how darkly seasoned, as if she'd spent the last few weeks reviewing the very events about which she'd now, at her own insistence, been called to speak.

I know now that even at that moment, and in the wake of such awesome devastation, some part of me still lingered in the throes of the high romantic purpose that had seized me on Black Pond, driven me to the reckless and destructive act I was still laboring to conceal. And yet, despite all the pain and death that had ensued, I still wanted Miss Channing to speak boldly of love and the right to love, use the same brave and uncompromising words her father had used in his book. I wanted her to rise and take the people of Chatham on like Hypatia had taken on the mobs of Alexandria, standing in her chariot, lashing at them with a long black whip. I wanted her to be as ruthless and determined with Mr Parsons and all he represented as I had been toward Mrs Reed, to justify, at least for a brief but towering moment, the dreadful thing that I'd done to her, and through her, to Sarah Doyle. For it seemed the only thing that might yet be salvaged from the wreckage of Black Pond, a fierce, shimmering moment when a woman stood her ground, defied the crowd, sounded the truth with a blazing trumpet. All else, it seemed to me, was death and ruin.

But Miss Channing did not do what I wanted her to do on the stand that day. Instead, she meekly followed along as Mr Parsons began to question her about the early stages of her 'relationship' with Mr Reed, convinced, as he was, that everything that had later transpired on Black Pond had begun in the quiet drives she and Mr Reed had taken back and forth from Milford Cottage to their classes at Chatham School, their leisurely strolls into the village, the idle hours they'd spent together, seated on a bench on the coastal bluff, all of which had flowed like an evil stream toward what he insisted on calling the 'murders' on Black Pond.

Through it all, Miss Channing sat rigidly in place, her hands in her lap, as prim and proper as any maiden, her voice clear and steady, while she did the opposite of what I'd hoped, lied and lied and lied, shocking me with the depths of her lies, claiming that her relationship with Mr

Reed had never gone beyond 'the limits of acceptable contact'.

At those words, I saw myself again at Milford Cottage on a cold January day, her fingers trembling as she pressed them against Mr Reed's cheek, then, weeks later, in the cottage, the rain battering against the window, the anguish in her face when she'd said, 'I can't go on.' That she could now deny the depths of her own passion appalled me and filled me with a cold contempt, made everything I'd done, the unspeakably cruel step I'd taken on her behalf, seem like little more than a foolish adolescent act that had gone fatally awry.

Watching her as she sat like a schoolmarm, politely responding to Mr Parsons' increasingly heated questions, I felt the full force of her betrayal. For I knew now how Mrs Reed must have felt, that I had given love and devotion, and in return received nothing but lies and deception.

And so I felt a kind of hatred rise in me, a sense that I'd been left to swing from the gallows of my own conscience, while Miss Channing now attempted to dismiss as mere fantasy that wild romantic love I'd so clearly seen and which it seemed her duty to defend, if not for me, then for Mr Reed, perhaps even her own father.

In such a mood, I began to root for Mr Parsons as he worked to expose Miss Channing, ripping at her story even as she labored to tell it, continually interrupting her with harsh, accusatory questions. *When you went driving with Mr Reed, you knew he was married, didn't you, Miss Channing? You knew he had a child?*

As she'd gone on to give her answers, I recalled the many times I'd seen her in Mr Reed's car, growing more animated as the days passed, happy when he dropped by her cottage on that snowy November day when we'd all eaten Sarah's fruitcake together, happy to sit with him on the bluff, stroll with him along the village streets, chat with him in her classroom at the end of day. If, during all that, the 'limits of acceptable contact' had never been breached, then I'd played my fatal card for nothing, worshipped at the altar of a love that had never truly existed, save in my own perfervid imagination.

And yet, as Miss Channing continued, so self-contained and oddly persuasive, I began to wonder if indeed I *had* made it all up, seen things that weren't there, eyes full of yearning, trembling fingers, a romantic agony that was only in my head.

Because of that, I felt an immense relief sweep over me when Mr Parsons suddenly asked, 'Are you saying, Miss Channing, that you were *never* in love with Leland Reed?'

Her answer came without the slightest hesitation:

Witness: No. I am not saying that. I would never say that. I loved Leland Reed. I have never loved anyone else as I loved him.

In a voice that seemed to have been hurled from Sinai, Mr Parsons asked, 'But you knew that he was married, didn't you, Miss Channing? You knew he had a child?'

Witness: Yes, of course I knew he was married and had a child.

Mr Parsons: And each time Mr Reed left you – whether it was at your cottage or in some grove in the middle of a cemetery, or after you'd strolled along some secluded beach – he returned to the home across the pond that he shared with his wife and daughter, did he not?

Witness: Yes, he did.

Mr Parsons: And what did the existence of a wife and child mean to you, Miss Channing?

Her answer lifted me like a wild wind.

Witness: It didn't mean anything to me, Mr Parsons. When you love someone the way I loved Leland Reed, nothing matters but that love.

Heroic as her statement seemed to me, it was the opening Mr Parsons had no doubt dreamed of, and he seized it.

Mr Parsons: But they did exist, didn't they? Mrs Reed and little Mary?

Witness: Yes, they did.

Mr Parsons: And had Mr Reed told you that he and Mrs Reed had had terrible arguments during the past two weeks, and that his daughter had witnessed these arguments?

Witness: No, he had not.

Mr Parsons: Had he told you that Mrs Reed had become suspicious of his relationship with you?

Witness: No.

Mr Parsons: That she had even come to suspect that he was plotting her murder?

Witness: No, he didn't.

Mr Parsons: Well, isn't it true that Mr Reed wanted to be rid of his wife?

Sitting in the courtroom at that moment, I recalled the last time I'd heard Mr Reed speak of Mrs Reed, the two of us in his car together, a yellow shaft of light disappearing down the road ahead, his own house in the distance, his eyes upon its small square windows, the coldness of his words: *Sometimes I wish that she were dead.*

Because of that, Miss Channing's answer, coming on the heels of the proud figure she'd only recently begun to assume, utterly astonished me.

Witness: No, he did not want to be rid of his wife, Mr Parsons.

Mr Parsons: He never spoke ill of Mrs Reed?

Witness: No, he never did.

Mr Parsons: Nor conspired to murder her?

Witness: Of course not.

Mr Parsons: Well, many people have testified that Mr Reed was very upset during the last days of the school year. Do you deny that?

Witness: No, I don't.

Mr Parsons: And in that state he did peculiar things. He named his boat after you, Miss Channing, rather than his wife or daughter.

Witness: Yes.

Mr Parsons: He made some rather ominous purchases as well. He bought a rope and a knife. He bought poison. It would seem that at least during his last few weeks at Chatham School, Mr Reed surely wanted to rid himself of somebody, don't you think, Miss Channing?

It was a question Mr Parsons had asked rhetorically, for its effect upon the jury, knowing that he had no evidence whatever that any of these things had been purchased for the purpose of murdering Abigail Reed. Because of that, I'd expected Miss Channing to give him no more than a quick, dismissive denial. But that was not what she did.

Witness: Yes, he wanted to be rid of someone, Mr Parsons. But it was not Mrs Reed.

Mr Parsons: Well, if it wasn't Mrs Reed, then who did he want to be rid of, Miss Channing?

Witness: He wanted to be rid of me.

Mr Parsons: You? You're saying he wanted to be rid of you?

Witness: Yes, he did. He wanted me to leave him alone. To go away. He told me that in the strongest possible terms.

Mr Parsons: When did he tell you these things?

Witness: The last time I saw him. When we met in the lighthouse. That's when he told me he wanted to be rid of me. He said that he wished that I were dead.

When I left the courthouse that afternoon, the final seconds of Miss Channing's testimony were still playing in my mind:

Mr Parsons: Leland Reed said that to you, Miss Channing? He said that he wished that you were dead?

Witness: Yes.

Mr Parsons: And is it also your testimony, Miss Channing, that Mr Reed never actually loved you?

Witness: He may have loved me, Mr Parsons, but not enough.

Mr Parsons: Enough for what?

Witness: Enough to abandon other loves. The love he had for his wife and his daughter.

Mr Parsons: You are saying that Mr Reed had already rejected you and wished to be rid of you and return to his wife and daughter, that he had already come to that decision when Mrs Reed died?

Witness: He never really left them. There was never any decision to be made. They were the ones he truly cared about and wished to be with, Mr Parsons. It was never me.

In my mind I saw Mrs Reed rushing up the stairs as she had on that final day, calling to Mary, then back down them again sometime later, dragging her roughly toward the shed. After that it was a swirl of death, a car's thunderous assault, Sarah's body twisting in the air, Mrs Reed staring at me from infinite green depths, Mr Reed lowering his cane to the bottom of the boat, slipping silently into the engulfing waves. Had all of that come about over a single misunderstood remark? *Sometimes I wish that she were dead.* Had it really been Miss Channing whom Mr Reed, rocked by such vastly conflicting loves, had sometimes wanted dead? Had I gotten it all wrong, and in doing that, recklessly done an even greater wrong? I thought of the line I'd so admired in Mr Channing's book – *Life is best lived at the edge of folly* – and suddenly it seemed to me that of all the reckless, ill-considered lies I'd ever heard, this was the deepest, the gravest, the most designed to lead us to destruction.

THIRTY-ONE

At the end of Miss Channing's testimony, the prosecution rested its case. The jury began its deliberations. During the next two days, a hush fell over Chatham. The crowds no longer gathered on the front steps of the courthouse. Nor huddled in groups on street corners or on the lawn of the town hall.

In the house on Myrtle Street we waited in our own glum silence, my mother puttering absently in her garden, my father working unnecessarily extended hours at the school, I reading in my room, or going for long walks along the beach.

On the following Monday morning, at nine A.M., the jury returned to its place in the courtroom. The foreman handed the verdict to the bailiff, who in turn gave it to Judge Crenshaw. In a voice that was resolutely measured, he delivered the news that Elizabeth Rockbridge Channing had been found not guilty on the first count of the indictment, conspiracy to murder. I remember glancing at my father to see a look of profound relief sweep into his face, then a stillness gather on it as the verdict on the second count was read.

Court: On the charge of adultery, how do you find the defendant, Elizabeth Rockbridge Channing?

A smile of grim satisfaction fluttered onto my mother's lips as the foreman gave his answer: *Guilty*.

I glanced at the defense table where Miss Channing stood, facing the judge, her face emotionless, save that her eyes closed briefly and she released a soft, weary breath. Minutes later, as she was led down the stairs to the waiting car, the crowd pressing in around her, I saw her glance toward my father, nod silently. In return, he took off his hat with a kind of reverence, which, given the nature of her testimony, the portrait of herself as little more than a wanton temptress, struck me as the oddest thing he had ever done.

I don't think Miss Channing saw me at all, since I'd stationed myself farther from her, the crowd wrapped around me like a thick wool cloak. But I could see her plainly nonetheless, her face once again held in that profound sense of self-containment I'd first glimpsed months before, her eyes staring straight ahead, lips tightly closed, as if determined – perhaps like proud Hypatia – to hold back her cry.

She was sentenced to three years' imprisonment, the maximum allowed by Massachusetts law, and I remember that my father greeted the severity of her punishment with absolute amazement, my mother as if it had been handed down from heaven. 'It's finally over,' she said with obvious relief. She didn't mention the trial again during the rest of that week, but she did insist upon visiting Sarah's grave, as well as Mrs Reed's, carrying vases of fresh flowers for each of them. Mr Reed had been buried only a short distance from them, but I never saw my mother give his grave so much as a sideward glance.

It was not over, of course, despite my mother's declaration. At least not for my father. For there was still the matter of Chatham School to deal with.

During the next few weeks its fate hung in the balance. My father labored to restore its reputation, along with that part of his own good name that had been tarnished by the tragedy on Black Pond. A governing board was established to look into the school's affairs and consider its future prospects. One by one, over the few weeks that remained of that summer, benefactors dropped away and letters came from distant fathers to say that their sons would not be returning to Chatham School next fall.

At last, all hope for the school's survival was abandoned, and on a meeting in late September, it was officially closed, my father given two weeks' severance pay and left to find his way.

He found it in a teaching job at a public school in neighboring Harwichport, and during that long, rain-swept autumn, he rose early, pulled on his old gray duster, and trudged to the car from our new, much smaller house to the east of Chatham.

Others at Chatham School made similar accommodations to their abrupt unemployment. Mrs Benton took a job as a clerk at Warren's Sundries, Mrs Abercrombie as a secretary for Mr Lloyd, a prominent local banker. Other teachers did other things, of course, although most of them, in the end, drifted away from Chatham to take jobs in Boston or Fall River or other towns along the Cape.

The first snows did not arrive until the last of the village Christmas decorations had been pulled down and returned to their boxes in the basement of the town hall. By February, when the snows were deepest and the sky hung in a perpetual gloom of low-slung clouds, the building that had once housed Chatham School had been converted into a small dressmaking factory, its second floor stacked with bolts of cloth and boxes of thread and buttons, the sound of sewing machines humming continually from its lower rooms.

But in other ways, things went back to normal, and there seemed to be little thought of Miss Channing, with only quick glimpses of Mary Reed sitting between Dr and Mrs Craddock at Quilty's or building a snowman on her front lawn to remind me of her fate.

And so the years passed as they always do, faster than we can grasp where we have been or may be going to. New buildings replaced older ones. Streets were paved, new lights hung. And high above the sea, the great bluff crumbled in that slow, nearly undetectable way that our bodies crumble before time, and our dreams before reality, and the life we sought before the one we found.

Then, in December of the final year of Miss Channing's imprisonment, when I was home for the Christmas break of my freshman year in Princeton, a letter came, addressed to my father, in an envelope sent from Hardwick Women's Prison, and which he later slipped into the little brown folder that became his archive of the Chatham School Affair.

The letter read:

Dear Mr Griswald:

I write concerning one of my prisoners, Elizabeth Rockbridge Channing, and in order to inform you that she has fallen ill. Her file lists neither relatives nor friends who, under such circumstances, should be contacted. However, in conversations with Miss Channing, I have often heard mention of your name, of her time in, I take it, your employ, and I wonder if you could provide me with

the names and addresses of any relatives or other close
associates who should be informed of her condition.

Best regards,
Mortimer Bly
Warden, Hardwick Women's Prison

My father replied immediately, sending the name and
address of Miss Channing's uncle in British East Africa.
But he did more than that as well, did it with an open
heart and against the firmly stated wishes of my mother,
who seemed both shocked and appalled by the words he
said to her that same night over dinner: *I've decided to
look in on Miss Channing, and take Henry with me.*

Four days later, on a cold, rainy Saturday, my father
and I arrived at the prison in which Miss Channing had
been kept for the last three years. We were greeted by
Warden Bly, a small, owlish man, but whose courtly manner seemed almost aristocratic. He assured us that Miss
Channing was slated to be taken to the prison hospital as
soon as a bed was available, and thanked us for coming.
'I'm sure it will brighten her spirits,' he said.

After that, my father and I were directed into the heart
of the prison, walking down a long corridor, the bars rising on either side, our ears attuned to the low murmur of
the women who lived behind them, dressed in gray frocks,
smelly and unkempt, their bare feet padding softly across
the concrete floor as they shuffled forward to stare at us,
their faces pressed against the bars, their eyes following
us with what seemed an absolute and irreparable broken-
ness.

'She's at the back, all by herself,' the guard said, the

keys on the metal ring jangling as he pulled it from his belt. 'She ain't one for mixing.'

We continued to walk alongside him, our senses helplessly drawn toward the cells that flowed past us on either side, the dank odor that emanated from them, the faces that peered at us from behind the steel bars, women in their wreckage.

Finally, we reached the end of the corridor. There the guard turned to the left and stopped, his body briefly blocking our view into the cell. While we waited, he inserted the key, gave it a quick turn, and swung open the door. 'In here, gentlemen,' he said, waving broadly. 'Step lively.'

With that, he drew away, and my father and I saw her for the first time since the trial, so much smaller than I remembered her, a figure sitting on the narrow mattress of an iron bed, her long hair now cut short, but still blacker than the shadows that surrounded her, her pale eyes staring out from those same shadows like two small blue lights.

'Miss Channing,' I heard my father murmur.

Standing together, silent and aghast, we saw her rise and come toward us, her body shifting beneath the gray prison dress, her hand reaching out first to my father, then to me, cold when he took it, no warmer when I let it go.

'How good of you to come, Mr Griswald,' she said, her voice low and unexpectedly tender, her eyes still piercingly direct, yet oddly sunken now, as if pressed inward by the dungeon's leaden air. 'And you, Henry,' she said as she settled them upon me.

'I'm so sorry I never came before,' my father told her, expressing what I recognized as a true regret.

For an instant she glanced away, a gray light sweeping

over her face, revealing the purple swell of her lips, the weedy lines that had begun to gather at her eyes. 'I had no wish to trouble you,' she said as she turned back to us.

My father smiled delicately. 'You were never a trouble to me, Miss Channing,' he said.

She nodded softly, then said, 'And how are things at Chatham School?'

My father shot me a pointed look. 'Just fine,' he said quickly. 'Quite back to normal, as you can imagine. We think we may beat New Bedford come next spring. Several of the new boys are very good at the game.'

I watched her silently as my father went on, noting the ragged cut of her hair, oily and unwashed, a nest of damp black straw, remembering how she'd looked at Chatham School and laboring to make myself believe that there was some part of her fate that she deserved.

For the next few minutes they continued to talk together, and at no time did my father let slip the true state of our affairs, or of what had happened to Chatham School. Instead, he spoke of things that had long passed, a school that had once existed, a marriage for a time not frozen in a block of ice, villagers who never whispered of his poor judgment from places safe behind his back.

Finally, we heard a watchman call out to us, and rose to leave her.

'It was good seeing you, Miss Channing,' I said as lightly as I could.

'You too, Henry,' she replied.

My father draped his arm over my shoulder. 'Henry won a scholarship to Princeton, you know. All he does is study now.'

She looked at me as if nothing had changed since our first meeting. 'Be a good man, Henry,' she told me.

'I will try, Miss Channing,' I said. Though I knew that it was already too late for so high a word as goodness ever to distinguish me.

She nodded, then turned to my father. 'I so regret, Mr Griswald, that you and the school were ever brought into my—'

My father lifted his hand to silence her. 'You did nothing wrong, Miss Channing. I have never doubted that.'

'Still, I regret that—'

In an act whose unexpected courage has never left my mind, my father suddenly stepped forward and gathered her gently into his arms. 'My dear, dear child,' he said.

Standing beside them, I saw Miss Channing draw him closer and closer, holding him very tightly, and for what seemed a long time, until, at last, she let him go.

'Thank you, Mr Griswald,' she said as she released him and stepped away.

'We will come again,' my father told her. 'I promise you that.'

'Thank you,' Miss Channing said.

We stepped out of her cell, my father quickly moving away from it and back down the corridor, while I remained, my eyes fixed upon her as she retreated to the rear of her cell, to the place where we had found her. For a time she stared at her hands, then her eyes lifted and she saw me lingering in the corridor. 'Go, Henry,' she said. 'Please.'

I wanted to do exactly that, even felt the impulse to rush down the corridor as my father had, unable to bear a moment longer the tragedy before me. But I found that for the briefest instant I couldn't draw my eyes away from her, and as she turned away, I saw her once again as she'd first appeared, so beautiful as she'd stared out at the landscape of Cape Cod, pronounced it a world of stricken martyrs. It was then I felt something break in me, a little wall that had held through all my nightmarish dreams of Sarah and Mrs Reed, of women floating in dark water. I thought of the rash and terrible thing I'd done and knew that I would never be able to trust myself again. And so the only answer seemed never to get close to anyone, to hold books as my sole companions, accept a bloodless, unimpassioned life, revere the law's steadfast clarity against the lethal chaos of the heart.

I was silent for a long time after that, silent as I turned from her cell, silent as I walked down the corridor to where my father waited, hollow-eyed, before the iron door, silent as we drove back to Chatham, a clear night sky above us.

'What is it, Henry?' my father asked finally as we crossed the bridge from the mainland, the old car rumbling over the wooden trellis.

I shook my head. 'You can never take anything back,' I said, feeling for the first time the full call of confession, wanting to let it go, to tell him what had really happened on Black Pond.

He looked at me worriedly, his eyes filled with a father's care. 'What do you mean, Henry?'

I shrugged, closing myself off again, retreating, as Miss Channing had, into the shadowy darkness of my own cell.

'Nothing,' I told him.

And I never told him more.

I'm sure that my father fully intended to visit Miss Channing again, despite the objections my mother had already voiced. But he still had the remainder of the school year to contend with, and so it was not until summer that he began to mention making such a visit.

I had returned home from college by then, taken a summer job as a clerk in a law office in Chatham, its cordial atmosphere a pleasant respite from the mood at home, the way my mother and father forever bickered over small matters, while leaving the great one that had long ago divided them buried deep inside.

And so I was once again in Chatham when another letter arrived suddenly from Hardwick Prison, addressed to my father, just as the first one had been, but this time bearing graver news.

My father read it in the small room he'd turned into a cluttered study, sitting in one of the great chairs that had once been in the parlor of our house on Myrtle Street and which seemed to fill up the entire room.

'Here, Henry,' he said, lifting it toward me after he'd read it.

I took the letter from him and read it while standing beside his chair. It had been written by Warden Bly, and it informed us in language that was decidedly matter-of-fact that following a short recovery, Miss Channing had fallen ill again, that she had finally been transferred to the prison clinic, then to a local hospital, where, two days after her admittance, she had died. Her body was currently being housed in the local morgue, Warden Bly said, and he wished instructions as to what should be done with it.

I will always remember how curiously exhausted my father looked after reading this letter, how his hands sank down into his lap, his shoulders slumped. 'Poor child,' he murmured, then rose and went to his room, where he remained alone throughout that long afternoon.

The next day he telegraphed Miss Channing's uncle,

informing him of his niece's death and requesting instructions as to the disposition of her body. Two days later, Edward Channing replied with a telegram requesting my father to make whatever arrangements he deemed necessary, and to forward him 'a bill for all expenses incurred in the burial of my unfortunate niece'.

Miss Channing was buried in the little cemetery on Brewster Road four days later. Her plain wooden coffin was drawn by four uniformed guards from a prison hearse and carried on their shoulders to her grave.

'Would you be wanting us to hang about?' one asked my father, no doubt noticing that no one else had come to, as he put it, 'see her off'.

'No,' my father answered. 'You didn't know her. But thank you for asking.'

With that, the guards left, the prison wagon sputtering along the far edge of the cemetery, past the grove with its cement pond, then disappearing down Brewster Road.

My father opened the old black Bible he'd brought with him, and while I stood silently at his side, read a few verses from the Song of Songs, *Lo, the winter is past, the rain is over and gone.*

'We'll need to send her things back to her uncle,' he said when he'd finished and we'd begun to make our way out of the cemetery.

My father had gotten permission to store Miss Channing's things at Milford Cottage, fully expecting that she would one day return to Chatham to reclaim them. When we walked into its front room, we found most everything still in place, the table by the window, the red cushions on the chairs.

Everything else had been packed away. We found three boxes stacked neatly in Miss Channing's bedroom, along with the two leather valises she'd brought with her from Africa. Only the black dress she'd worn on the day she'd taken the stand hung inside the large wooden armoire. My father took it out, opened one of the boxes, and placed it inside. Then he turned and looked at me, his face suddenly very grave. 'Someone should know the truth, Henry,' he said. 'If I died suddenly, no one would.'

I said nothing, but only stood before him, a grim apprehensiveness settling upon me.

'The truth about Miss Channing,' he added. 'About what really happened.'

I felt my heart stop. 'On Black Pond?' I asked, trying to keep the dread out of my voice.

He shook his head. 'No. Before that. In the lighthouse.' He lowered himself onto the bed, paused a moment, then looked up. 'You remember when I came here the day of the ... accident?'

I nodded.

'And Miss Channing and I went into the cottage alone to have a private talk?'

'Yes,' I said, remembering how he'd stood by the mantel, Miss Channing in a chair, her eyes lifted toward him.

'That's when she told me, Henry,' my father said. 'The truth.'

Then he told me what she'd said.

She had not wanted to go to the lighthouse that afternoon, Miss Channing told my father, had not wanted to meet Mr Reed, be alone with him again. For it seemed to her that each time they were together, something unraveled inside of him. Still, he'd asked her to meet him one last time, asked her in letter after letter during that last month, until she'd finally agreed to do it.

He was standing against the far wall of the lighthouse when she entered it, his back pressed into its softly rounded curve, the old brown jacket draped over his shoulders, his black hair tossed and unruly.

'Elizabeth,' he whispered. 'I've missed you.'

She closed the metal door behind her but did not move toward him. 'I've missed you too, Leland,' she said, though careful to keep a distance in her voice.

He smiled delicately, in that way she'd noticed the first time she'd seen him, a frail, uneasy smile. 'It feels strange to be alone with you again.'

She remembered the few times they'd been alone in the way he meant, with his arms around her, his breath on her neck, the warmth of his skin next to hers.

'You haven't forgotten, have you?' he asked.

She shook her head. 'No,' she admitted.

He drew himself from the wall, staring at her silently. The chamber's single light glowed faintly from behind a cage of wire mesh, throwing a gray crosshatch of shadows over his face. 'How has it been for you, Elizabeth? Being away from me?'

She looked at him sadly, mournfully, knowing that she would never allow herself to be taken into his arms again. 'We have to go on, Leland,' she said.

'Go on to what?' he asked. 'To nothing?' He seemed on the verge of sweeping toward her.

'I can't stay long,' she told him quickly, then glanced out the small square window of the door, the playing field beyond it, the boys of Chatham School scurrying about in a game of touch football.

'Is it so hard to be with me now?' he asked, an edginess in his voice.

She shook her head wearily, now regretting that she'd

come at all. 'Leland, there's no point in this. The only answer is for me to leave.'

'And what will I do then, Elizabeth?'

'What you did before.'

His eyes darkened, as if she had insulted him. 'No. Never. I can never go back to the life I used to live.' He began to pace back and forth, his cane tapping sharply on the cement floor. 'I can never do that, Elizabeth.' He stopped, his eyes now glaring at her. 'Do you want to just throw me away? Is that what you want?'

She felt a sudden surge of anger toward herself, the fact that she had ever let him love her as he did, or loved him in return, ever pretended that they lived in a world where no one else lived, where no other hearts could be broken.

'We can go away, Elizabeth,' he said. 'We can do what I always planned for us to do.'

The very suggestion returned her to her own childhood, to a father with grand notions of freedom he never followed out of love for her, how bereft she would have felt, how worthless and unloved, had he been taken from her by any force less irresistible than death. 'You know I won't do that,' she said. 'Or let you do it.'

He stepped toward her, opening his arms. 'Elizabeth, please.'

She lifted her hand, warning him away. 'I have to go, Leland.'

'No, don't. Not yet.'

She looked at him imploringly. 'Leland, please. Let me leave, still loving you.'

He stepped forward again, closing the space between them, staring at her needfully, but now with a terrible cruelty in his eyes. 'Sometimes I wish I'd never met you,' he told her. 'Sometimes I wish that you were dead.'

She shook her head. 'Stop it.'

He closed in upon her, his hands reaching for her shoulders.

She turned and grabbed the handle of the door, but he suddenly swept up behind her and jerked her around to face him, his hands grasping at her waist.

'Stop it,' she repeated. 'Let me go.'

His grip tightened around her, drawing her into a violent embrace.

'Stop it. Leland ... Leland ...'

He thrust up and pushed her hard against the door, then spun her roughly to the right, away from the door, and pressed her against the wall, so that she could feel it, hard and gritty, at her back.

'I can't let you go,' he said, his eyes now shining wildly in the gray light.

She pressed her hands flat against his shoulders. 'Stop it!' she cried, now thrusting, right and left, desperately trying to get free.

But each time she moved, he pressed in upon her more violently, until she stopped suddenly, drew in a deep breath, leveled her eyes upon him, her body now completely still, her voice an icy sliver when she spoke. 'Are you going to rape me, Leland? Is that what you've become?'

He rocked backward, stricken by her words.

'I'm sorry,' he whispered, releasing her, stepping away, his eyes now fixed upon her with a shattered, unbelieving gaze. 'Elizabeth, I only—' He stopped and looked at her brokenly, saying nothing more as she turned and fled toward the door, her red scarf flowing behind her like a blood-soaked cloth.

*

My father watched me silently for a moment, then rose and walked to the window, his hands behind his back as he stared out into the yard.

I kept my place by the door, my eyes fixed on the two leather valises beside the bed as I tried to keep the rhythm of my breath quiet and steady, so that it would not reveal the upheaval in my mind. 'So it was all a lie,' I said at last. 'What Miss Channing said in court. About never going beyond the 'acceptable limits'. They *were* lovers.'

'Yes, they were, Henry,' my father said. 'But at the trial Miss Channing didn't want Mary to ever know that.'

I saw the *Elizabeth* sailing in an open sea, a ghost ship now, drifting eerily through a dense, engulfing fog.

My father walked over to me and placed his hand on my shoulder. 'Miss Channing had a good heart, Henry,' he said, then added pointedly, as if it were the central truth of life, 'Never forget, that it's the heart that matters.'

We left Milford Cottage a few minutes later, took Miss Channing's belongings to the post office, then returned home. My mother was preparing dinner, and so my father and I retired to his office. He sat down in his chair, took out his pipe. I sat opposite him, still thinking about what Miss Channing had told him, how much she must have trusted him to have done so, my eyes studying the portrait she'd painted of him, not as the staid schoolmaster I'd so despised at the time, but as a man who had something restless and unquenchable in him, something that stared out toward the thin blue lake that shimmered seductively in the distance. It was then I realized that Miss Channing had painted my father not as himself alone, but in some sense as herself as well, perhaps as all of us, stranded as we are, equally tormented by conflicting loves, trying, as best we can, to find a place between passion and boredom, ecstasy and despair, the life we can but dream of and the one we cannot bear.

'I'm glad I told you what I did this afternoon,' he said. 'You deserved to know the truth. Especially since you were there on Black Pond that day.' He shook his head. 'The sad thing is that it was all over between Miss Channing and Mr Reed. She was going away. And in the end, he would have taken up his life again.' He seemed captured by the mystery of things, how dark and unforgiving the web can sometimes be. 'Nothing would have happened if Mrs Reed hadn't died in Black Pond that day.'

'No,' I said. 'Nothing.'

He leaned back in his chair. 'So that's the whole story, Henry,' he said, bringing the pipe toward his lips. 'There's nothing more to know about the Chatham School Affair.'

I didn't answer him. But I knew that he was wrong.

THIRTY-TWO

Many years have passed since then, and all the others have departed now, taking with them, one by one, small pieces of the Chatham School Affair, my mother and father, Mr Parsons and Captain Hamilton, the last of the teachers who taught at Chatham School that year, even the boys who went there, all dead now, or living far away, probably in decrepitude, near death, with their final year at Chatham School no more than a faint remembrance of a curious and unhappy time.

Through all these many years, only Alice Craddock has remained to remind me of what happened on Black Pond, first as a little girl with melancholy eyes, then as a teenager, sullen and withdrawn, later as a woman of late middle age, grown monstrously fat and slovenly by then, friendless, alone, the village madwoman, chased by little boys, and finally as an old woman, rocking on her porch, with nothing but Dr Craddock's steadily dwindling fortune to sustain her.

I know that sometimes I would simply shake my head as she went by, dressed so strangely, as she often was, her toenails painted green, her mind so often lost in a sea of weird imaginings. Once, standing beside Mrs Benton on the village square, I saw her attention drawn to Alice as she drifted vacantly down the opposite street, wrapped in a ragged shawl, feet in rubber thongs. 'Now, there's a batty one,' Mrs Benton said, then added in a tone so casual it shocked me with its flippancy. 'Probably end up like her mother.'

But as the years had proven, Alice had not 'ended up' like Mrs Reed, so that after I'd done my work for Clement Boggs, gotten the zoning variance he needed to sell the land around Black Pond, it finally became my duty to deliver the money he'd received for it to the old house where Alice still lived, wandering aimlessly through its many dusty rooms, a candle sometimes in her hand, so people said, despite the fact that all the lights were on.

At first I'd declined to do it, not wanting to face Alice up close, see what time had wrought, along with suicide and murder. But Clement, determined that his gift remain anonymous, had refused the task himself, and so it had fallen to me to do it for him. 'It's only right that it should be you who tells her about the money, Henry,' he said. 'After all, you knew her father, and it was you at the pond when her mother died.'

It was an argument I had no defense against. And so, late on a clear December night, I drove to the house on the bay, the very one that had once housed Dr Craddock's clinic, and in which Sarah Doyle had died so many years before.

It was quite cold, but she was sitting on the large side porch when I arrived, wrapped in a thick blanket, her huge frame rocking softly in a high-backed chair.

She turned when she heard my footsteps on the stairs, squinting into the darkness, yet with a strange, expectant air, as if she had been waiting for some important guest.

'Hello, Alice,' I said as I came up the stairs, moving slowly, closing the space between us. 'You remember me, don't you?'

She watched me silently, her eyes moving up and down.

'I'm Henry,' I told her. 'Henry Griswald.'

She stared at me, uncomprehending.

'I knew you when you were Mary Reed,' I said. 'Back when you lived on Black Pond.'

Her face brightened instantly. 'With Mama,' she said.

'Yes.'

She smiled suddenly, a little girl's smile, then stood, lumbered heavily to a wide bench that rested, facing the sea, at the far end of the porch. She sat down and patted the space beside her, offering another slender smile. 'You can sit here,' she said.

I did as she told me, lowering myself unsteadily onto the bench, my eyes averted from her briefly before I forced myself to look at her again.

'I have something for you,' I told her, drawing the envelope from the pocket of my overcoat. 'It's a gift. From a friend. A check. I'm going to deposit it in your account tomorrow. Mr Jamison, at the bank, he'll handle it for you.'

She glanced at the envelope but did not take it from my hand. 'Okay,' she said, then returned her gaze to the sea. 'Boats go by,' she said. 'Sailboats.'

I nodded. 'Yes, they do.'

I saw her as a little girl again, heard her laughter as she'd darted up the stairs, answering her mother's call, *Mary, come inside*, then later, on the beach, her eyes so still as she'd watched the red striped kite dip and weave in the empty sky.

'We flew a kite once,' I told her. 'Do you remember that?'

She did not look at me, nor give an answer.

I looked away, out toward the nightbound sea, and

suddenly it shattered, all of it around me, the great shell I had lived in all my life. I felt the air warm up around me, a green water spread out before me, my body plunging into it from off the wooden pier, the world instantly transformed into a dense, suffocating green as I surged forward, first toward the rear end of the car, then along its side, my eyes open, searching, everything held in a deathly stillness as I peered inside, staring frantically into what seemed an impenetrable wall of green. Then I saw her face swim out of the murky darkness, her red hair waving behind her, her eyes open, staring at me helplessly, her mouth agape, a wave of blood pouring from it as she gasped for breath. I grabbed the handle of the door, started to jerk it open, free her from a watery grave, then heard a voice pierce the depths, cold and cruel, as if the dark mouth of Black Pond were whispering in my ear: *Sometimes I wish that she were dead*. I felt my fingers wrap more tightly around the metal handle, Mrs Reed now staring at me desperately, her face pressed against the glass, her green eyes blinking through the swirl of blood that had gathered around her head, her mouth moving wordlessly, unable to cry or scream, her eyes growing large, bulging, gaping at me with a strange incomprehension as I faced her through the glass, my hand on the handle, poised to pull open the door, but pressing against it instead, holding it in place. For a moment she saw it in my face, knew exactly what was happening. Her lips parted with her last words, *Please, no*. Then a wave of bloody water came from her mouth, and I saw her hands lift with an immense heaviness, her fingers claw almost gently at the glass as the seconds fell upon her like heavy weights, and her eyes dimmed, and the last bubbles rose, and her body began to drift backward, rising slowly as the weight of life deserted her, so that the last thing I saw was

THOMAS H. COOK

her body as it made a slow roll, then began to descend
again, curling finally over the jutting wheel, her eyes lifted
upward in the final moment, searching for the surface of
the pond, its distant glimmer of bright summer air.

I closed my eyes and felt winter gather around me once
again, the faintly sweet odor of Alice Craddock's blanket
wafting over me. I could feel my fingers trembling as I
returned the envelope to my jacket pocket, listening first
to my father's voice as it rang over the boys of Chatham
School, *Evil on itself doth back recoil*, then to the last
stanza of a song I'd heard repeated all my life and whose
every word had served to prove him wrong:

> For the fear and slaughter
> In the dark green water
> Miss Channing pays alone.

I started to rise, now wanting only to rush away, back to
my house, my books, retreat once again behind the shield
of my isolation, but I felt Alice's soft, fleshy hand grab my
coat, draw me back down onto the place beside her.

'You can stay with me awhile,' she said in a voice that
sounded like a child's command.

I eased myself back down upon the bench. 'All right,' I
said. 'I'll stay awhile.'

She smiled softly, unwrapped her blanket, and draped
it over both of us.

We sat very still for a long time, then I felt her fingers
reach for my hand and close around it. 'Pretty night,' she
said.

I nodded, waited a moment, then, because I couldn't
stop them, let the words fall from my lips. 'I'm sorry,
Mary,' I told her.

326

Her fingers tightened around mine. 'Oh, that's all right,' she said almost lightly, a child's forgiveness for some small slight, but her gaze lifting toward the sky, a curious gravity gathering in them, so that for a moment she seemed to take on the greater burden, a whole world of broken bodies, mangled hearts, her eyes searching through the vastness for some reason that would explain their ruin, past stars and worlds of stars, the boundless depths, the last dim light, where still there was no answer to her *Why?*

I put my arm around her shoulders, and drew her close against my side. It seemed so little, all I had. 'You're right,' I told her. 'It is a pretty night.'